The
Emerald
Key

The Emerald Key

CHRISTOPHER DINSDALE

DUNDURN
TORONTO

Editor: Sylvia McConnell
Design: Jesse Hooper
Printer: Webcom

Library and Archives Canada Cataloguing in Publication

Dinsdale, Christopher, 1965-
    The emerald key / Christopher Dinsdale.

Issued also in electronic formats.
ISBN 978-1-4597-0534-0

    I. Title.

PS8607.I58E44 2012   jC813'.6   C2012-901550-4

1   2   3   4   5   16   15   14   13   12

 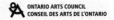

We acknowledge the support of the **Canada Council for the Arts** and the **Ontario Arts Council** for our publishing program. We also acknowledge the financial support of the **Government of Canada** through the **Canada Book Fund** and **Livres Canada Books**, and the **Government of Ontario** through the **Ontario Book Publishing Tax Credit** and the **Ontario Media Development Corporation**.

Care has been taken to trace the ownership of copyright material used in this book. The author and the publisher welcome any information enabling them to rectify any references or credits in subsequent editions.

J. Kirk Howard, President

Printed and bound in Canada.

Visit us at
Dundurn.com | Definingcanada.ca | @dundurnpress | Facebook.com/dundurnpress

Dundurn	Gazelle Book Services Limited	Dundurn
3 Church Street, Suite 500	White Cross Mills	2250 Military Road
Toronto, Ontario, Canada	High Town, Lancaster, England	Tonawanda, NY
M5E 1M2	LA1 4XS	U.S.A. 14150

For my brothers,
Brian, Robson, and Russell

You will make out intricacies, so delicate and so subtle, so full of knots and links, with colours so fresh and vivid, that you might say that all this were the work of an angel, and not of a man.

Twelfth-century writer Gerald of Wales, upon seeing an unidentified book from Ireland's Golden Era in Kildare, Ireland

Prologue

The Village of Athy, Ireland, 782 A.D.

Tonight would be the end of his universe. For three long years Father Francis had planned for this moment, and for the first time, doubts darkened his thoughts as to whether his audacious plan would actually succeed. Could he cheat the death and destruction that had voraciously consumed his beloved homeland? He was the last of an extinct breed, the only one remaining to fight an unstoppable darkness. Tonight, Father Francis was willing to risk everything for the children who were yet to be born.

As if on cue, through the swirling mist beyond, he could see the unmistakable flickering of a distant torch. The monks at Carlow were sending their one and only warning. The signal confirmed his worst fears; tonight would indeed be the end. He ran down the spiral steps of the tower. Each breath he huffed suddenly seemed precious, as if the air itself was a gift from God. When he reached the bottom of the staircase, he stopped hard in his tracks. The straw bed was empty. The sheets were in disarray on the floor. Where was the young lad who was to sound the alarm? The warning bell still lay next to his bed. At the window, the only way in or out of the round stone tower, a ladder extended down to the ground. The lad must have seen the warning signal and, in a panic, run off.

Picking up the bell, the priest climbed out the window as quickly as his aging joints would allow and clambered down the ladder to the wet ground below. What was he to do now? The warning must be given, yet he also had to complete his vital task or all would be lost. He ran toward the main gates, his footsteps echoing through the now empty chambers of his university. All of the books, artwork, and furniture had been removed, leaving only the lifeless, hollow shell of what once had been a cultural centre of higher education.

As he burst out of the main gates, Father Francis nearly bowled over a young girl with flaming red hair.

"Gracious, child, be careful!"

She looked up at him with large hazel eyes, brushing her hair out of her face.

"I'm sorry, Father. Have you seen my kitten? I'm afraid a fox might have stolen her away while I was sleeping."

"Kiera Galway," he cried, gripping her by the shoulders as he realized a way out of his dilemma, "the Lord Himself has sent you to me!"

"Excuse me, Father?"

"I am putting you in charge of a most important task. We will soon be under Viking attack. Ring this bell, first in the monastery and then throughout the village. You must alert everyone to run for safety before it is too late."

"The warning bell," Kiera whispered in alarm as she grasped it.

"After you have rung the bell, meet me at Fitzgerald's stable behind the tannery. Do you understand?"

Kiera nodded, wide-eyed.

"Then go. And may God be with you!"

Kiera ran off to the monastery as fast as her young legs could carry her, ringing the bell loudly above her head. Father Francis hurried away in the opposite direction. After passing the blacksmith shop, he dodged through a dark alley behind the tannery, coming to a halt in front of a large stable. As he pulled the door open, he could hear the town awakening to the ringing of the bell as it continued to clang along the streets. Shouting echoed in the air. Lights flickered. Farm animals stirred restlessly.

Father Francis knew a fleet of huge dragon-headed sailing ships would soon appear on the river. Unlike other visitors, these raiders had no interest in trade with the local population or the higher learning offered by the abbey. They came to this land simply to pillage, kidnap, and destroy. All of the other vital monasteries and universities in Ireland had already been ransacked and looted of their cherished art and golden relics. He frowned as he recalled the many stories of tortured priests, teachers, and students, as they were plied for information as to the location of any hidden treasure among the buildings. Almost all of the books that had been painstakingly written out by hand by dedicated monks were unceremoniously thrown onto massive bonfires. Village men who resisted the assault were lined up and killed while their children were corralled and herded to the boats, destined for a life of slavery. At first, the Vikings were satisfied with raiding only the coastal cities, but soon their hunger for Irish treasure grew, and they pushed their ships further and further inland along the rivers and waterways.

Athy Abbey was one of the most isolated monasteries in Ireland. Father Francis knew that this remote location had bought his parish precious time to design a way to keep his abbey's treasures out of the hands of the Viking raiders. He could only hope that his plan would be enough to keep the priceless treasure safe.

Father Francis lit a torch and entered the empty stable. He reached for a hidden handle in the floor. A large wooden hatch opened under the hay. Descending from the hatch was a shaft and a set of steep stairs that led deep underground. A large stone rested on the hay beside the hatch.

"Father?"

"Kiera, is that you? Come here quickly."

She stepped into the stable, the bell still in her hand. "What's going to happen, Father?"

"The Vikings are going to destroy our beautiful village, Kiera," he answered bluntly.

"But why, Father?" she asked, her voice wavering. "Why do they do this to us? Why can't they be our friends?"

The old priest sighed. "They are not interested in becoming our friends. They are pirates, killers, barbarians. Call them what you like. They have come to our land to pillage our wealth."

"Can't we stop them?"

"I wish we could. They are magnificent fighters, if nothing else. They are strong, fearless, and relentless. We have never seen anything like them before. No defence has stopped them, and if we do try to defend ourselves, they will kill everyone in the village, including the children. There's no point in resisting, Kiera. All we can hope to do is somehow survive their assault."

Kiera looked out the door nervously. "So what should I do?"

He gazed solemnly at her. "You run away. You try and stay alive so that you can grow up and tell your own children what our beautiful land was like before darkness fell upon us."

"Are you running away too, Father?"

"No, I'm not. Would you like to see why?"

She nodded.

He mustered a smile. "Seems right a child will be the last witness to our country's soul."

Taking his torch in one hand and Kiera's hand in the other, he descended through the trap door and into the gloom below. Once he reached the bottom of the stairway, he put the torch to a V-shaped trough hanging from the ceiling. Low orange flames leapt and snaked quickly down the long corridor, illuminating the spectacular catacomb. Endless aisles of leather-bound books lined the walls. Gold and silver statues along with religious relics covered the dry floors. Beautiful bronze statues crowded the corners. Intricate tapestries that had been carefully sealed in waxy coatings were stacked to the ceiling. Father Francis paused at the marvelous sight.

"Please don't let our efforts be for naught," he whispered to the heavens.

"Father?"

He took her bell and placed it on a shelf full of books. "This is the heart, mind, and soul of our land, Kiera. The three hundred years of civilization that once adorned my university's libraries and walls are now buried in this magnificent chamber."

"But why is it buried down here?"

"The Vikings are here in search of this very treasure. They want to take our beautiful works of art, melt them down, and make creations to honour their own pagan gods. They want to take all of our books and burn them, for their ignorance of the written Latin language infuriates them. They want to destroy our culture so that they can settle and impose their own culture upon us. They want to tear the heart out of Ireland."

"So we must hide our treasure from them so that they can't get it?"

He ruffled her hair and managed a smile. "Good for you. But we're not going to let them have our treasure, are we? They can't destroy our soul if they don't know where it is."

She looked up at him imploringly. "I promise never to tell them, Father!"

"I believe you. You have done well to warn the village. Now everyone will be safe. Before we hide our treasure for a very long time, there is one thing I want to give you."

Kiera watched Father Francis as he stepped forward and removed a small pendant from a peg on the wall. He turned and placed it around the little girl's neck. She took the pendant between her fingers and held it up. It was a small Celtic stone cross, carved with beautiful swirls and geometric shapes.

"It is said that St. Patrick himself carved this cross. When he returned to Ireland, he realized that in order to convert the local pagans to Christianity, he would have to somehow blend the Irish culture and his faith into one. The key, he discovered, was in art. Your necklace is the combination of those two cultures; the Christian cross and the Celtic weave. And you, my little Kiera, are

Ireland's future. It is through children like you that our culture will live on."

"Thank you, Father Francis," she said, admiring the pendant.

"And now we must go. The Vikings will soon be upon us."

Pouring a liquid into the trough, he snuffed out the fire and the treasure vault went dark. By the light of his single torch, the priest and child climbed back up into the stable. Father Francis bent over and pushed the large flat stone over the opening to the catacomb. It rumbled into position and thudded securely into place, hiding any trace of the chamber below. He then closed the wooden hatch on top of it.

"Will you help me with the final task?" he asked.

Kiera nodded.

Together they took the torch and set the straw in each corner of the stable on fire, then hurried out the doorway. When they'd left the confines of the stable, Kiera stopped and gasped. The entire village was already engulfed in flames.

"The Vikings are here?" she screamed.

"No, Kiera, the villagers themselves lit the buildings on fire. We agreed to burn the town to the ground ourselves to stop the Vikings from finding our treasure. This way, it will remain hidden for a long time."

Kiera tore her eyes away from the flames and what was once the only home she knew. "What else can I do?" she asked, bravely.

"You can now get yourself to safety. Promise me you will run straight to your family. Do not stop for any reason."

She nodded fearfully. The stable was licking the morning twilight with long orange tongues of flame.

"Go, Kiera. Run!"

Kiera glanced back at the old priest one last time before she turned and disappeared behind the tannery. Father Francis hurried toward the river. With luck, he would make it back to the monastery in time to mount his horse and join the brothers of the abbey in nearby Kildare. As he made a dash for the abbey gates, a giant hand reached out from the darkness, grasped him hard by the throat, and lifted his feet straight off the ground.

A thunderous shout echoed throughout the village.

"They've destroyed their own village! My treasure is lost!"

Olaf Erikson, the mountainous leader of the Vikings, was furious. He stomped along the river's edge and pounded the bow of his ship with his fist.

"Olaf," shouted a returning warrior, "I found this brown-robe running for the monastery."

Olaf turned and set his icy-blue stare on Bjorn, the only warrior in his raiding party who came close to his own legendary strength. He was carrying the monk by the scruff of his robe. The priest's feet were dangling at least a foot off the ground. Olaf was impressed by Bjorn's shrewdness. The brown-robe would likely know the location of the treasure, but quite often these men of a single god were reluctant to talk, even under the threat of death.

"Well done, Bjorn. Throw him down here."

Father Francis was dropped unceremoniously onto the mud of the riverbank.

"Father," the Viking said in rough Celtic, "I have heard from a respected source that your abbey is home to a valuable treasure. I would very much like to see it. Could you tell me of its location?"

"I'm sorry," the priest gasped as he rubbed his burning throat. "I don't know what you are talking about. I am just a humble servant of God."

Olaf grunted and placed the cold sharpened point of his sword under the chin of the priest.

"I am not a very patient man, Father. I can see that you set your village on fire. I would like to know which of the burning buildings is the tannery stable."

"The tannery stable?"

The Viking chuckled. "After a little persuasion from my leather whip, a sapper in a nearby village told me there might be something of interest under the floor of the tannery stable."

Father Francis looked up blank-faced. Olaf could tell this man was not going to be of any help. In a rage, Olaf brought the sword high in the air and was about to bring it down on the priest's neck when Bjorn grabbed his wrist.

"The brown-robe might be more cooperative with the proper motivation."

Bjorn pointed to a young red-headed girl running up the side of the hill on the edge of town. Olaf smiled.

"Get me that girl as well as any other village children you can find. If the old man does not talk, we will sell them as slaves."

"The children have done nothing to deserve such a fate!" the priest pleaded.

"That is up to you then, isn't it? If you do not tell me the location of the treasure, their little feet will never touch the soil of Ireland again!"

Father Francis's heart sank as he heard a scream. He turned to see a Viking warrior grab Kiera roughly as she neared the top of the hill. He prayed for forgiveness, for he knew that no matter what the Viking said or did to her, the safety of the treasure was more important than either of their lives. The soul of an entire country could not be sacrificed for the well-being of a few. He thought of St. Patrick's cross hanging around her young neck as she was dragged down the hill. He prayed it would keep her safe.

"God be with you, little Kiera."

Chapter 1

Near Cork, Ireland, 1847

Jamie Galway had already stared into the face of death too many times in his young life, yet a shiver still ran down his spine as he passed a family lying together in the ditch. The dead mother's arms were wrapped stiffly around her children's bony shoulders. The deceased father's head was turned away, his face lined in heartbreak and pain. The mother and father, the son and daughter had all died with their mouths open, still stuffed with the tough inedible grass that lined the side of the dirt road; their last desperate attempt at staving off starvation.

Ryan, Jamie's older brother, stopped and threw back his hood. He knelt down in the grass beside the family. Taller and ganglier than his younger brother, Ryan gently reached out and closed the family's tormented eyes with his fingertips, crossed himself, and said a prayer for the dead. Jamie removed his hood as well, his short brown hair framing emerald green eyes, and joined his brother in prayer. The moment of sombre meditation ended as Ryan shook him by the shoulder.

"I need to leave, right now." Ryan's hazel eyes and freckled face were burning red with anger.

"Having hate in your heart won't do anyone any good."

Ryan wheeled around on his brother, his eyes wild with fury. He thrust a finger back at the dead family.

"Hate? No, not hate, little brother. Rage, disgust, and a sense of treachery, perhaps … but not hate. How can *you*, of all people, not feel the same? Look back upon that family! How can you not be angry as well? That's two dozen dead we've passed since we left the abbey! Just lyin' there! On the side of the road, like the dried up cores of tossed apples! But these aren't eaten apples we're talking about. These are God's children! Dead! Just like our parents, all dead for no good reason!"

Jamie didn't back down. "Of course, I feel upset for all those who have suffered. And you very well know that I miss mother and father as much as you, but the Brotherhood has warned us not to lose control of our emotions. These are trying times. We must rise above the pain that surrounds us and stay true to our sacred vows."

Jamie held up his left hand in order to allow the golden ring to glimmer against the grey sky. A simple yet beautiful Celtic weave was etched into the outer surface of the gold.

Ryan thrust his own golden ring towards Jamie. "Don't start quoting Cardinal Shulls to me. We are human, and the Brotherhood sometimes asks the impossible!"

"The Brotherhood needs us right now," Jamie reminded him. "They're trusting us to complete this journey without incident. We have to concentrate our thoughts on bringing *that* safely to Cork."

Jamie pointed to the satchel hanging off his brother's shoulder. Ryan glared at him, then turned on his heels and strode off angrily down the road. Jamie sighed and jogged to catch up. To his left, abandoned stone huts lined the grassy ridge of the road, and the emptiness of the once bustling countryside, a countryside that used to bring Jamie and his brother so much joy, was unnaturally silent. The still dampness of death hung heavily in the air, as nature soaked the spilled souls of the dead into its thick cloth of fog.

Around the next bend, the brothers passed a tiny farmhouse. Wrapped together in only a thin blanket, a family sat in the doorway, shivering in the afternoon mist. Their starvation was so great, they did not have the energy to look up, but instead stared trance-like at their feet through sunken, lifeless eyes. The brothers looked knowingly at each other and, without a word, reached into their pockets. Each holding a small loaf of bread, they approached the family.

"Please, take this food," offered Ryan. "I wish I could give you more, but it's all we have."

The parents were so surprised to see strangers acknowledging their plight that it took their confused minds a moment to recognize that food was indeed being offered. The blanket dropped to the ground. Jamie cringed when he saw their bodies. The skeletal ribs of the children showed that it was an effort for them to even breathe.

The father took the bread with a quivering hand.

"Thank you, Fathers," he whispered. "God bless you both."

A single tear from the starving mother was all the heart-wrenching thanks the boys needed.

Ryan nodded. "God be with you and your family."

As they moved on, Jamie frowned at the stark landscape that surrounded him. The once lush forests of

Ireland had long ago been harvested by the British to build their ever-growing navy. Farms had moved into the open land, but where there were once dozens of vibrant stone homes there now stood only piles of rubble. The homes had been destroyed one by one by the British landlords. The families, unable to pay their rent after another season of failed potato harvests, had been evicted from their shelters. Instead of producing food for the starving people of Ireland, the farmland had been converted into pasture for cattle and sheep, meat that would later be shipped off the island to English markets.

Many of the displaced peasants had removed bits of the rubble to build scalpeens, tiny illegal stone shelters that now dotted the Irish countryside. Those even worse off for shelter had no choice but to dig holes into the soft ditches that lined the road. The holes were then covered with sticks, turf or whatever else they could find to help protect themselves from the elements. Like a pair of feral kits, two tiny boys peered out from the shadows of a nearby hole. Without any food to give them, all Jamie could offer was a quiet blessing.

The fog finally began to lift, and the city of Cork materialized in the distance. The city's great harbour sparkled, its protected waters a gateway to the Atlantic Ocean for the large collection of ocean-going vessels anchored in its waters. Seeing their final destination ahead raised their spirits. Soon they would be together again with the Brotherhood, and the priceless package in their possession would be safe.

A pleading scream broke their brief moment of tranquility. Nearby, a tiny farmhouse had been surrounded by four English soldiers in crimson suits, each brandishing a rifle. An argument was taking place between the husband and the lead soldier as his frightened family huddled in the doorway. A second soldier took hold of the single ox tied to the side of the house and led it out onto the road.

The farmer begged the soldiers. "No! Please! We'll starve without her! How will we plough our field and earn enough for our keep?"

"You haven't paid your landlord in almost a year," replied a soldier, coldly. "He has agreed to take your ox in exchange for rent."

The wife fell to her knees in tears, clutching her face in her hands.

"Jamie, I was wrong," muttered Ryan as they walked closer. "I do hate them."

"Don't start," said Jamie. "You know we can't get involved. Look! I can see the cathedral spire from here!"

Ryan was about to answer when he saw the father reach for the ox. The soldier with captain's stripes on his sleeve shoved the farmer hard and the weakened man collapsed backwards, crashing into the stone wall of the farmhouse.

The mother left her children and ran to him, shouting. "Leave my husband alone!"

The back of the captain's hand caught the mother on the side of the cheek as she passed, sending her spiralling into the dirt.

The captain hovered over the crying couple. "And if you forget your rent again, we'll be taking your house next."

Something in Ryan snapped. Whether it was the memory of what had happened to their parents or simply a moment of enraged insanity, Ryan strode up to the small farmhouse before Jamie could stop him. Ryan approached the captain who had struck the woman.

"I saw this woman collapse. Is everything all right?" he asked.

"Must have had a dizzy spell, Father," chuckled the captain, eyeing the young, hooded priest. "Fainted right here in front of me."

"Funny how that happens, especially when something crashes into your face ... like this."

Ryan was deceptively strong for his thin frame. His balled fist crashed hard into the cheek of the captain. The soldier's head snapped back so quickly that he flew through the air and landed in a heap on the dirt road. The other soldiers hollered in rage at the attack and were on Ryan like a pack of hounds. Ryan elbowed the nearest one hard in the chin and kicked out at the other. Off balance, his boot only grazed the soldier's ribs and the remaining two redcoats threw him to the ground and began pummelling him.

"Ryan!"

Jamie couldn't believe this was happening! He rushed to his brother's aid.

Fists were smashing into Ryan's face and chest. Jamie leaped at the nearest soldier, tackling him hard and sending him sprawling along the ground. The uninjured soldier left Ryan writhing in pain and turned to face Jamie. Jamie was preparing to defend himself when his head suddenly exploded in a sea of stars. He crumpled to the ground beside his groaning brother. The captain had recovered enough to grab hold of his rifle and club Jamie's head with its wooden butt, knocking him out.

"Is this priest the one that attacked me?" he asked, pointing to Ryan while touching the growing welt on the side of his face.

"Yes, sir."

"Filthy friar. He should be shot here and now for breaching his own vows to God."

A soldier held up his rifle and aimed it at Ryan's heaving chest. "Just say the word, sir."

"You can't shoot a priest!" interjected a third. "You'll be damned for all time!"

The captain paused at the thought and took a moment to contemplate the situation.

"All right, we won't kill him."

The captain brought his rifle butt down on the back of Ryan's head, bringing his moans to a sudden stop. The two unconscious priests lay together, as still as corpses in front of the terrified family. The captain looked out to the shimmering harbour and watched a tall ship raising her sails.

"I do hate to waste a life. My friend is an officer on board the *Carpathia*. The ship is scheduled to leave this evening for Quebec. What do you say we do our part for God and teach these young priests a valuable lesson? Take the tall one down to the harbour and give him a one-way ticket to Canada."

"Isn't the *Carpathia* better known as the 'Floating Morgue', sir?"

He chuckled. "Yes, I do believe that is the one. That's why its fare across the ocean is so cheap … so few actually survive the crossing. It should give our good friar here a lot of practice giving the last rites to the passengers who die along the way."

While two of the soldiers picked Ryan up by the arms, the third looked into the satchel draped across his chest.

"No money in here, Captain. Just an old, dusty book. And it's all written in that nonsense Celtic. Must be a monastery book."

"I don't see any reason to deny him his studies. Perhaps he'll learn the lesson of turning the other cheek in matters that do not concern him. Now, hurry him down to the harbour. I don't want the priest to miss his departure."

"And what of the other lad?"

The captain took hold of the reins of the ox, then looked back to the terrified family huddling around their groaning mother.

"Make sure that you tell the lad everything that has happened," he shouted back to the family. "This young priest can help spread the word to any other clergy in Ireland who dare intervene in the affairs of the British Empire. His authority is limited to what happens within the church and Heaven above. Tell him Britannia rules supreme everywhere else!"

Chapter 2

Coming to, Jamie moaned as he reached for the back of his head. Something in his hair was warm and sticky. Touching it, then bringing his hand to his face and finally managing to open his eyes, he saw the clotted redness of his own blood. His strange surroundings slowly came into focus. Something cool and damp was pressed against his forehead.

"Stuart, I think he's coming around."

In the dim light he could make out the face of a woman. She was pressing a wet rag to his forehead. He was surprised to find himself lying on a straw mattress inside a hut. The woman was joined by a man and two children. The vague memory of a fight slowly materialized within the fog of his spinning thoughts.

"What happened?" Jamie asked the farmer, who was sporting a swollen welt above his eye.

"There was a fight and you were in the middle of it."

Jamie looked to the children. "Is your family all right?"

The farmer managed a smile. "Aye, for now anyway. I've got a bump the size of a Blarney Stone on my head. I'm more worried about you. You took an awful beating. I'm Stuart, and this is my wife, Shannon. Thank you for trying to help us with the soldiers, but I'm afraid, in the end, it didn't do anyone any good."

"They took your ox?" asked Jamie, trying to recall the scene.

"That they did," he said, squeezing his wife's hand. "Now we're as good as dead. With the potatoes again rotting in the ground before harvest and the loss of our ox, we'll never be able both to feed ourselves and to pay the landlord his due."

Jamie struggled to a sitting position. He glanced around the hut. "Where's Ryan?"

Stuart and Shannon looked at each other, unsure of what to say to the young man. Jamie caught the glance and his heart stopped.

"What is it? What happened to my brother?"

Stuart nodded towards the village. "The redcoats took him, they did. Said they were going to throw him on the first boat heading to Canada. They mentioned the name *Carpathia*."

"What!" Jamie tried to stand, but the room spun and his legs gave out. Stuart caught him and helped him sit back down on the bed.

"Easy, lad. Your head took quite a beating."

"Ryan's on a ship heading to Canada?" Jamie repeated.

Jamie tried to picture all of the implications. His thoughts fought through the fog of his injury.

"Perhaps I can catch the ship before it leaves port! I can still stop this!"

Stuart shook his head. "Son, you've been lying here all night. It's morning now. According to what the soldiers told us, his ship left Cork yesterday evening. By now, it's out on the high seas."

"You're badly hurt," added Shannon. "Although we don't have a great deal to offer you, you can stay with us for as long as you need, until you're feeling better."

Jamie again tried to stagger to his feet, and this time he managed to stay upright. He felt as if he was going to be sick and fought the urge to sit back down.

"Thank you for your kind offer," groaned Jamie, grimacing as he took hold of Stuart's shoulder for balance. "And I do need your assistance. Please, help me get to the cathedral in Cork."

Stuart frowned. "I can help take you into town if you like. Are you sure you are up to the task? It's still a good hour walk from here."

"Please, you have no idea the importance of my task. I need to get to the cathedral as soon as possible."

Stuart nodded to his wife.

"I'll drop off the lad. I should be back before sunset."

Shannon grabbed a walking stick that was leaning against the wall and passed it to Jamie.

"Use this in case you feel dizzy again."

Stuart steadied him on the other side.

"And lean on me as much as you like until you get your legs back."

As they headed for the door, Shannon ran ahead and grabbed a water skin. She passed it to Jamie.

"Drink as much water as you can. It will help clear your head."

"Bless you," whispered Jamie through the spinning pain, and the men left the humble abode.

"This is a disaster beyond imagination!"

Cardinal Shulls sat at the head of the table and eyed the other participants with a mixture of fury and alarm. The meeting had been convened deep within the secret catacombs that crisscrossed beneath the sanctuary of Cork Cathedral. The aging cardinal was surrounded by seven other grey-haired priests. Together, the eight men comprised the highest order of the Irish Brotherhood. First assembled by Father Francis of Athy over a thousand years before, the Brotherhood was the trusted guardian of ancient Irish knowledge.

Jamie sat at the far corner of the table. He could feel the thick tension in the air. He and his brother had recently been made privy to the knowledge that a fabulous sacred treasure lay buried somewhere deep in the Irish countryside. Jamie now knew that Ryan's brash attack on the British soldiers had threatened everything the Brotherhood had been sworn to protect.

"A disaster!" bellowed the bald, rotund man Jamie knew as Father Liam.

"The *Book of Galway* was in that satchel!" exclaimed Father Shamus, the thin friar next to the Cardinal, whose hollow, haunted gaze reminded him of the starving families Jamie had seen in his travels across the countryside.

The Cardinal leaned on the table and looked to Jamie. "Are you sure Ryan still had the book with him when he was taken away?"

Jamie shook his head. "I don't know for sure. According to the family that looked after me, the soldiers said that Ryan could keep the book for his travels before dragging him off to the harbour."

Father Liam stood up, enraged. "For almost a thousand years, the Brotherhood has kept that text safe! If we had kept it in Limerick, this would never have happened!"

"We had to bring it to Cork," the Cardinal reminded him. "We had good evidence that its location had been discovered by a treasure hunter. It was no longer safe in its old location."

"Then why the boys?" asked Father Liam, pointing a finger at Jamie. "Why put a crucial text in the hands of two hopelessly incompetent boys and expect them to cross the entire Irish countryside without incident?"

Struck by the accusation, Jamie bit his lip and avoided the priest's glare. "I'm sorry, Father Liam," offered Jamie. "You trusted us to bring the book safely to Cork and we failed. We have let the Brotherhood down in every possible way."

Father Shamus came to his defence. "Jamie, you yourself did nothing wrong. You and your brother have both been excellent students, and I'm proud of your dedication to the Brotherhood. The men at this table seem to have forgotten that the treasure hunter might have been aware of our identities; therefore, we needed a courier who would be above suspicion to bring the *Book of Galway* to Cork. We thought the family connection between yourselves and your direct ancestors, who wrote the text, would make the trip all the more meaningful for you, so we gave you and Ryan the task. It was unforeseen that Ryan would react the way he did when he saw the soldiers at the farm."

"Unforeseen?" muttered Father Liam. "Anyone who ever met the boy could sense the simmering anger bubbling behind his gaze."

"Remember Christ in the temple? Anger channelled in a proper way can also be a powerful ally and a source of strength," countered Cardinal Shulls. "These arguments, however, are irrelevant to our current dilemma. What we must decide right now is a way to get our text back."

"Why is the text so important?" asked Jamie, boldly. "I've never entirely understood."

The Cardinal smiled at the young man's curiosity.

"A thousand years ago, Father Francis of Athy designed an ingenious way of keeping his ancient treasure safe. He designed a map that was separated into four parts, and every part was required to decode the exact location of the treasure. The four parts were carefully hidden within the realm of the Irish church. Having four separated parts to the map ensured that the treasure would remain safe should one of the pieces fall into the wrong hands. Father Francis rightfully preferred to have the treasure remain lost for all time rather than fall into the hands of those who did not appreciate its intrinsic value to the people of Ireland. For a thousand years, no one has laid eyes on the treasure. It was decided long ago that no one would see the treasure again until Ireland is once again ruled by the Irish and the Irish alone. The *Book of Galway* is one of those crucial keys to the map."

"Then what should we do?" asked Jamie.

"There is only one solution," said Cardinal Shulls. "We must go to Canada and bring the text back to Ireland."

"Whom shall we send?" asked Father Shamus.

"I'll go," offered Jamie.

"I think you've caused quite enough chaos already," grumbled Father Liam.

Cardinal Shulls raised a hand. "Wait, Father Shamus. There may be some benefit to sending Jamie. This task must be carried out with the utmost secrecy. We all have important positions in the Church and are known to many in Ireland. For one of us to leave will only raise questions. Jamie, however, could leave the country without notice."

"You're asking us to put the future of the Brotherhood in the hands of a boy?" roared Father Liam.

"Keep in mind that Jamie is no ordinary boy. Like his brother, he is gifted, finishing at the top of his class in every subject area. And," continued Cardinal Shulls, "Jamie has another gift many of us lack. He speaks French, don't you, lad?"

Jamie nodded. "I spent two years at a monastery in Paris, France."

"Canada East is mainly French-speaking," muttered Father Shamus. "Being able to speak French might help him track down Ryan."

Cardinal Shulls turned to each member of the Brotherhood. "Then we need to take this to a vote. Raise your hand if you are in favour of sending Jamie out to retrieve the text."

One by one, each of the eight members of the Brotherhood raised their hand.

"Then it's unanimous. Brother Galway, I suggest you go and pack, for you have a ship to catch and a book to retrieve. May God be with you."

Chapter 3

Never in Jamie's wildest imagination had he ever thought of setting out across the Atlantic Ocean on a six-week voyage to another continent. His life, however, had been filled with unexpected turns from a very young age, and as he walked towards the long departure quays that jutted out into the sparkling crown of Cork Harbour like sharpened thorns, Jamie thought back to those early happy years.

He had grown up helping his father run a well-managed flour mill in the village of Clara, Westmeath. His father was a respected elder in the community, and he was very vocal in his objections to the ways of the British government. It angered him when officials looked the other way as the many British landlords ran thousands of desperate tenants off the properties that they had farmed for generations. The potato blight had robbed many of the small farmers' incomes and they could no longer pay the rent. Desperate, the tenants led the villagers of Clara in an uprising against the government. Several irate farmers broke into the Lord Westmeath's personal smokehouse and stole a full side of pork. Several families might have eaten well that week, but the lord complained of the break-in to the authorities. They in turn sent a detachment of soldiers to punish the community.

In the middle of the night, armed with rifles and torches, the redcoats descended upon the Galway flour mill. The Galway family would be punished, since Lord Westmeath assumed their objections had likely incited the vandalism. The loss of the mill would, in turn, punish the community for not turning in the criminals who had stolen Lord Westmeath's property.

Within minutes, the prominent family business was engulfed in flames. The small Galway home sat next to the mill. Jamie could still remember staggering up to the window and seeing his father running through the flames of the mill's doorway, armed with only a single bucket of water. Whatever his father's plan was to stop the flames, Jamie never did find out. When he didn't return from the flames, Jamie doubted his father ever contemplated that his wife might enter the burning building in an attempt to rescue him. Her screams of fear turned to screams of pain, and then no screams at all. Jamie remembered his older brother's arm wrapping around him. He looked up at Ryan, tears in his eyes, unsure of what to do.

Ryan, eleven at that time, stood, not staring into the flames but at the redcoats on horseback, laughing at the inferno and warning the villagers who had gathered around the burning mill not to further break the laws of the land or more punishment would be heaped upon their village.

Perhaps it was remembering the single bucket of water in his father's hands that made Jamie think of that fateful night. Now he was staring out at a sea that could fill up an endless line of buckets and likely never lower the level of its mighty basin. Jamie examined the long wooden hull of the *Independence* and its three huge masts that seemed to reach as high as a cathedral spire. This was the vessel that would take him across that mighty expanse of water to the land called Canada.

Jamie, dressed in common travelling clothes, entered the sea of people that filled the pier. The Brotherhood had decided it would be wise not to bring undue attention to Jamie's departure. Around him, young men waved handfuls of tickets in the air, shouting out to the bedraggled crowd offering cheap passage to Quebec, New York, or Philadelphia.

A young sailor came up beside him as he continued to gawk at the ship. He joined Jamie's gaze skyward.

"She's a beauty, eh?"

"She's bigger than I imagined."

"This is my ship. It's my first duty on board the *Independence*. Jim Darby is my name."

"I'm Jamie Galway. Pleased to meet you." They shook hands.

"Good to meet you, Jamie. I heard that she has a good captain who treats the crew and passengers fairly. After my last tour across the Atlantic, I wasn't sure if I'd ever want to sail again."

Jamie looked at him. "Why? What happened?"

"The ship I sailed was an old slave ship. Shipping companies used to make a fortune running slaves from West Africa to the southern United States until the Civil War changed the rules. Slave running to the colonies was then outlawed. So the companies switched their human cargo from slaves to starving peasants. Not much of a difference, really, if you ask me. Governments still paid the shipping companies good money to haul needed labour to the colonies. On my last ship, the captain treated them the same if not worse than if he were transporting a ship-load of slaves."

Jamie had to force his next question from his lips. "On which ship did you serve?"

"The *Carpathia*," Jim said, shaking his head. "The captain didn't seem to understand that those were human beings down in his hold. He would treat those poor Irish worse than livestock. He crammed far more in than was allowable and then he barely fed them the whole way there. If any died, and many did, they were unceremoniously tossed into the sea during the crossing so he wouldn't have to deal with the paperwork upon his arrival in Canada. Lord, I hated working under him."

Jamie felt sick. "Is the *Independence* faster than the *Carpathia*? My brother is on board the *Carpathia* and I was hoping that we might catch up to them before it docked in Canada."

"Sorry to hear that," the young sailor said as he hoisted his kit onto his shoulders. "The *Independence* is fast for its size, but she won't catch the *Carpathia*. We'll be loaded down not only with passengers but with a full load of cargo as well. I imagine we'll be at least a good week behind her."

The sailor hurried off to join the rest of the crew boarding the ship up the rear gangplank. Jamie looked down at his ticket. It was labelled "2nd class." The Cardinal had been able to arrange the money to keep him out of the crowded holds that were the cause of so much sickness and death during the crossing. Jamie felt guilty accepting the generous offer as the church coffers had all but dried up during the horrendous famine. But, as the Cardinal said, it wouldn't do Ryan or the Brotherhood any good if he was dead upon arrival in Canada.

Jamie joined the other passengers boarding on the forward gangplank and slowly made his way up to the deck and the awaiting officer. There was a family of five ahead of him, a mother and father, two boys and a little girl. They seemed as destitute as the family that had tended to him after the attack. Their tattered clothing hung loosely from their bones, their sunken eyes underlined with dark rings.

"Have you been to Canada before?" Jamie asked, trying to ease his own nervousness with conversation.

The husband gave a bitter laugh. "Never been on a ship before, let alone the shores of another land."

"My sister has a small farm in Canada West and she's invited us to live on it with her family," said the wife, teary-eyed. "There's nothing left for us here."

The husband extended his hand. "I'm Brendan O'Connor. This is my wife Erin and my three children, Neil, Colin, and Patricia."

They shook hands. "Jamie Galway."

"Are you planning a move to Canada as well?"

"No, I'll be soon coming back home."

"Back to Ireland?" he asked incredulously. "What is there left to return to? This island is a floating morgue."

The officer, eyeing the destitute family over a thick greying moustache, kept his distance from the three sniffling children. After a brief examination of the tickets, he pointed them in the direction of the hold.

"Fourth class. Take the stairs to the very bottom. Your berth will be labelled."

The family shuffled slowly towards the opening through the deck and then disappeared into the bowels of the ship. The officer turned towards Jamie.

"Ticket."

Jamie passed it to him.

"Ah, second class. Follow the deck around to the forward cabin and a purser will show you to your room."

Jamie did as he was told. He made his way toward the front of the ship, past two towering masts, and handed his ticket to a young purser who was waiting for him at the doorway.

"Welcome to the *Independence*, sir."

The porter led him down a narrow hallway to a finely crafted door with a brass handle. Jamie opened the door and had to step over a tall ledge to enter the room.

"Safety reasons," commented the purser, nodding to the ledge at base of the door. "Keeps the water out of your cabin should the weather get bad."

"Then let's hope for good weather, shall we?" said Jamie, who then offered the young lad a coin, which he gratefully accepted.

After lowering his single bunk away from its stored position on the wall, Jamie collapsed onto its mattress and stared up at the freshly painted ceiling.

"Hold on, Ryan. I'm only a week behind you."

Jonathon Wilkes was a very patient man. Waiting on the docks at Cork with a young boy standing by his side, he realized that he would not be closing in on one of the greatest treasures in Europe if he had not planned every step of the way with painstaking precision. Somewhere in this crowd was the missing piece of the puzzle that was required to find Ireland's fabled ancient treasure. After all of his work and effort, a few more hours of waiting in a restless crowd would not bother him in the least. In fact, he rather enjoyed it. It was all part of the exhilarating game of the hunt, and he was the one controlling all the pieces.

As Wilkes eyed the crowd, he let his mind drift back to his first big payday. It had taken him three years, eleven months, and fourteen days to wait out the Buddhist monks in Tibet before he finally struck the motherlode. The Dalai Lama, the spiritual leader of the monks, had left his palace compound with his entourage as if he were a ghost, in the dead of night and with remarkable silence. The only reason Wilkes had discovered his silent departure was through one of his ingenious tripwires, which he had stretched across several paths that he had suspected might lead to the treasure. It was the tinkling of a soft bell that had woken him from his light sleep. He quietly rolled out of his covers, grabbed his machete, his unlit torch, and his gun, and by the light of the quarter moon ran for the marked path.

It was difficult to follow the mountainous trail at night with only sparse moonlight to guide him, but he had memorized the terrain so well, he knew exactly where the monk he was following was taking him, deep into the steep Himalayan cliffs that surrounded Tibet's capital city of Lhasa. The path quickly became treacherous and narrow, but Wilkes could sense that the monk was just ahead, and he was not about to let up on the chase.

His life nearly ended as he rounded a protruding crag in the mountain and his foot came down on nothing but air. The path had vanished at the edge of a cliff. Wilkes had not sensed the sudden drop and he began to fall toward his death. His flailing arms swung wildly for anything to help stop his fall. A lip of stone smacked against his right palm. He grabbed hold. It was not enough to stop his momentum, but it was just enough to swing him across to his right. While dangling on one arm, he controlled his panic long enough to allow his body to make the half turn. His head and body crashed hard into the towering rock face next to the path. With his right hand remaining on the protrusion, his left groped desperately along the rock for any purchase. Miraculously, it found the rough root of a plant jutting out into the darkness. He grabbed hold and prayed that it would take his weight. For a moment, Wilkes hung with his feet hovering three thousand feet above an invisible jagged valley far below.

Wilkes quickly recomposed himself and assessed his situation. Even in the inky darkness, he knew that the path he had taken up the mountain must be somewhere just to his right. He swung out a foot and felt for it. Yes! His boot caught the edge of it, but it was too far away for his foot to get a proper grip. He had only one chance. Before his strength gave out completely, he heaved on the root, found a temporary toehold, and brought both hands to the rocky ledge that had saved his life. Tentatively sticking out his foot again, he could finally hoist his leg up onto the flat surface. With a final push, he swung himself back onto the path. His body collapsed onto solid ground and he thanked the heavens that he couldn't see what nightmare lay below him at the base of the cliff.

Suddenly, his side exploded in pain. A foot had lashed out from somewhere in the dark, crunching hard into his ribs. Wilkes ignored the stinging fire from his side as he rolled away from the edge. He sprang up into a crouch. He heard a blade being unsheathed somewhere in the darkness. Wilkes slowly reached down to his feet and grabbed a large handful of dirt. His attacker must be close and likely moving in for the kill at this very moment. With a wide arc from his arm, he released a cloud of dirt at what he guessed would be head height. A grunt of pain just to his left told him the dirt had found the wide open eyes of his attacker. He leaped to his feet and charged like a bull at the sound, shoulder down, catching his attacker in the side. Wilkes felt a searing pain in his back from the swing of a sword as he slammed the attacker hard into the side of the mountain. Then he heard a satisfying crunch as his full weight crushed the attacker into the jagged rocks.

Stinging hand chops suddenly exploded around his neck and head. Instead of blocking them, Wilkes ducked and swung a leg low, tripping the attacker, who fell to the ground, but Wilkes lost his balance as well and fell hard onto his injured back. He could hear his attacker get to his feet first and charge forward. Wilkes curled into a ball, feet up, ignoring the fiery pain from his back. He felt a sudden weight on the soles of his boots. He used momentum to roll backwards and with the attacker's weight still perched on his feet, kicked his legs out over his head. For a second, there was only silence as his attacker was launched high into the night air. A terrified scream fell away as the invisible man tumbled down the side of the dark cliff to his doom.

Curled on his side, it took a minute for Wilkes to catch his breath. He felt his back, and the warm stickiness of fresh blood told him he would have yet another scar decorating his tattered body. He ripped off a piece of his shirt, rolled it into a ball and placed it over the wound. He then used the strap of his satchel to keep it in place.

Working his way back along the dark face of the mountain, his hands suddenly disappeared into a hidden fissure. It was a perfect secret entranceway that led into the heart of the mountain itself. Turning sideways, he squeezed his tall frame into the fissure. Complete darkness enveloped him. He paused and listened. From somewhere deep inside the mountain, he could hear the rhythmic chanting of Buddhist monks. Surely they would not be worshipping in the dark, he surmised. Therefore they must be a long way off.

Wilkes decided to take a huge gamble. He checked his gun to make sure that it was cocked and loaded. Then he pulled out his torch and lit it. A long, narrow tunnel suddenly flared to life in the orange glow of his torch. His eyes were drawn to a beautiful oval-shaped shrine that had been carved into the stone wall of the tunnel. Sitting inside the shrine, surrounded by a stunning halo of iridescent stars, was a golden statue of Buddha. His welcoming smile and extended arms were highlighted by a ruby-encrusted toga that adorned his rotund belly. Wilkes instantly knew the statue alone was worth a small fortune. He could only imagine what treasures lay further down the tunnel. Wilkes was not stupid. A bird in hand was worth more than two in the bush. He opened the flap to his leather bag, removed the Buddha from its perch, and carefully lowered it in.

The three years, eleven months, and fifteen days of waiting it out in the Himalayas had finally paid off in spades.

His adventure in Tibet now seemed so long ago. Wilkes did return to that same cave years later, but not surprisingly, after searching the entire cavern, whatever had been in there had long before been removed. The missing Buddha and dead guard were all the evidence the monks had needed to prove their secret location had been blown.

Since then, Wilkes had been able to scrounge up some interesting Egyptian artifacts and steal a couple of small Mayan statues, but he could no longer afford the life of luxury he had grown accustomed to after the sale of the Buddha. He needed another big payoff, and soon.

After hitting the history books in the London library as he searched for a new treasure trail, he had come across an old story about Ireland that explained how, after the fall of Rome, the Irish had become the wealthiest and most educated country in Europe. Several legends proclaimed that a vast treasure had been hidden during Ireland's golden years, but its location remained a mystery to this day.

"Not a mystery to everyone," chuckled Wilkes. "Surely someone, somewhere must know where it is."

He then glanced at his copy of the London *Times*. The headline quoted the prime minister as saying only market forces could cure the continuing Irish famine.

"An unending famine in a land that holds treasure," muttered Wilkes. "This is what a man who has an interest in antiquities would call 'easy pickings.'"

Wilkes booked a ticket on the next ship leaving London for Dublin. Upon his arrival in Ireland, he had gone straight to Trinity College, where he set eyes on the Book of Kells, one of the only books known to have survived from the golden age of Ireland. He had never seen anything like it before in his life. Each letter was a work of art in itself, producing almost magical depictions of Irish nature from the ancient ink. The text itself read in an almost spellbinding beauty that seemed more the written word of an angel than that of a human being. His appreciation for what the Irish had accomplished after the fall of Rome rose considerably. He no longer had any doubts that a country capable of such a high level of culture could also produce magnificent treasure.

He knew from experience that a coin placed in the right starving hand might get him the information he needed to begin his search, and indeed it had. He learned from a penniless historian that there was a secret group of men called the Brotherhood, and rumours continued that they knew the location of a buried Irish treasure. The historian also mentioned that the Brotherhood seemed to have connections to the Irish Catholic Church. Prodded further about the treasure, the historian believed that the key to finding the treasure lay encoded in several keys kept safe by the Brotherhood, and one key was rumoured to be encoded in an old text located within the walls of the abbey in Limerick.

Wilkes quietly slipped a few more coins into the hands of those with intimate knowledge of the abbey in Limerick, which turned up only wild goose chases — until he made contact with the starving choirmaster. That old man informed him that the text he was searching for had been hidden in the abbey, but word was out that someone had been enquiring about it. It had been removed from its hiding place only the previous night, and it was on its way south. Where, he couldn't be sure.

Wilkes immediately travelled south and put on his payroll a dozen hungry altar boys, all of whom had access to Ireland's large abbeys and cathedrals. Their job was to try and listen in on private conversations. If they heard the word "Brotherhood" or witnessed any unscheduled meetings, they were to remember as many details as possible of those meetings and then report back to him. The size of their reward would depend on the quality of the information returned.

After waiting nearly two weeks, the big break had finally come that morning. Out of breath, an altar boy banged on his inn door. While working at Cork Cathedral that evening, he had followed a visiting priest deep into the catacombs and managed to get close enough to a secret meeting to hear the words "Brotherhood," "key," and "text." It seemed that a young priest had to travel quickly across the ocean to Canada and return with his brother or with a text that was important to the Brotherhood that he had taken with him. Pleased with the news, the young lad was rewarded with a few coins and then sworn to secrecy. Wilkes immediately started to pack his gear and told the boy to meet him on the pier later that morning.

The lad met Wilkes near the shipping line ticket offices and Wilkes offered to double the reward if the boy could identify the young man who had attended the meeting in the catacombs of Cork Cathedral.

"I'm pretty sure I can," the boy said, climbing up on a crate. "I got a good look at him as he left."

Hours passed. The sun was lowering in the sky and Wilkes was starting to have his doubts that they would find their young priest. The crowds were still huge and the light was dimming. Would he have to attack the problem from a different angle if the priest somehow slipped through his fingers? He was pondering the possibilities when the boy's hand started rapping him hard on the shoulder.

"There he is, sir!" he shouted, pointing. "That's him, I'm sure of it!"

Wilkes followed the finger to a tall young man dressed in travelling attire, talking to a sailor at the bow of the nearest ship.

"He's not dressed like a priest," countered Wilkes.

The lad remained confident. "Then he must have changed. I'm sure that's him."

"Good lad," he smiled. "You've earned this."

He handed the boy more money than he could have made in a month.

"Thank you, sir!" He grinned as he climbed down off the crates.

"And don't forget to keep listening. There may be more rewards for you yet."

Lifting his expensive leather suitcase off the ground, Jonathon Wilkes kept an eye on the young man who was now boarding a Western Star clipper. Wilkes approached the Western Star Shipping Lines ticket office and purchased a ticket. Making his way through the crowd,

Wilkes followed the young man up the gangplank and onto the deck of the *Independence*. The moustached officer asked for his ticket.

"First class, Mr. Wilkes. Welcome aboard the *Independence*. Please, follow me to your cabin."

For the next week, Jamie left his berth only to obtain the occasional meal. He tried to ignore the increasingly violent ocean swells by concentrating on the books about Canada East and Canada West, the two halves of the United Province of Canada. He pored over Canadian historical records and maps lent to him by the church, and which were now scattered across his modest desk and over the floor. With study, he hoped to prepare himself for whatever might lie ahead in this foreign land.

Jamie had difficulty comprehending the numbers that lay in front of him. Canada was simply huge. Several Irelands could fit into just Canada East alone. And not everyone spoke the same languages. The French were the first settlers in the new land and had colonized an area along the banks of a great river named the St. Lawrence. This French-speaking land was now known as Canada East. The British were the second to settle. They built up ports along the Atlantic coast as well as further inland, on the shores of an impossibly large lake named Ontario. The land north of Lake Ontario became Canada West while the south shore marked the border of the United States of America. Jamie knew that both his ship and the *Carpathia* were destined for Quebec City. Quebec City was in Canada East and Jamie was thankful for the

French lessons he'd received in France. With a little luck, he would quickly find his brother in this port town, and together they would return to Ireland.

Suddenly, a monstrous swell sent the nose of the ship heavenward. Before Jamie could react, his books slid off the table and crashed onto the floor. He held his balance until the ship veered sharply downwards. Losing his footing, he cartwheeled sideways and crashed hard into the wooden bulkhead. Dazed, Jamie could hear shouting from the deck above. He managed to open the door and stagger out of the cabin. The hallway resembled a river as water rippled around his ankles. Water this far in could only mean one thing — the ship was in trouble.

He made his way to the deck hatchway, holding on to the railing for balance. When he opened the hatch, rain lashed his body furiously. The officer with the thick moustache was leaning into the wind, trying to make his way towards the bow.

"Are we in trouble, sir?" yelled Jamie, over the howling wind.

The officer protected his eyes with his free hand. "Aye, that we are! We just took a giant rogue wave to the bow. There might be some damage below decks. Keep that door closed! We don't want any more water inside the hull!"

"Can I help?" asked Jamie.

The officer sized him up then nodded. "All right. We might need your young arms. Close the hatch and follow me, but whatever you do, don't let go of this rope!"

Jamie nodded, stepped out into the lashing gale, and closed the hatch behind him. The wind tore at them relentlessly, trying to throw the men into the frothing sea. Hanging on to the guide rope for dear life, they finally slipped and crawled their way to the bow and the forward hatch. The officer unlatched it and a gust nearly tore it off its hinges. Jamie quickly shut the hatch behind them and then followed the officer into the descending darkness. The steep stairs took them deep into the hull of the creaking, rolling ship. Baying livestock filled the first deck. Penned cows, goats, and chickens lined either side of the forward hull. Heavy crates of goods were lashed to the floor.

"Are the crates centred for balance?" Jamie asked as they made their way to the next ladder.

"Aye," agreed the officer, "and it's a good thing they're lashed down. If the cargo had shifted when that wave hit, you and I wouldn't be having this conversation right now."

They continued their descent. They arrived at the lowest deck, where the curve of the hull flattened into the bottom of the ship. The sight that greeted Jamie instantly appalled him. Hundreds of people were packed into the immense, dreary chamber. Cries of hunger were punctuated with moans of pain. Jamie noticed the iron rings still hanging from the walls from the ship's earlier slavery runs to Africa. He wondered if the trip could have been any worse for those slaves than the sorry sight meeting his eyes at this very moment. And if this was good, according to the sailor back in Cork, how much worse could it possibly be on board the *Carpathia*?

"Fourth class?" asked Jamie.

The officer glanced at the sea of humanity. "Aye, fourth class. Follow me. We need to get to the pumps."

They waded through the sickness, coughs, and human fluids that filled the belly of the hold until they reached a set of hand-held pump handles. There were two other sailors already working the seesaw-like mechanism. Water could be heard sloshing through the attached pipes. The officer grabbed the opposite handle and nodded at Jamie to take the nearest one.

Together they gripped the handles and grimly worked the pumps. As he worked, Jamie took in the human misery that surrounded him and couldn't help but think of Ryan, likely suffering in a hold worse than this, injured and alone. It was over an hour of arm-breaking work before the pumps finally gurgled. Air was finally starting to be sucked through the system, and the team finally relaxed to stretch out their weary arms.

"Well done, lads," said the officer. "Let's head topside for a spot of tea."

Officer Keates started to lead the men aft when the ship suddenly lurched hard to the side. Everyone was thrown off their feet. Children screamed as parents reached frantically for flailing arms. A large crack reverberated through the ship. Water began to spray out from a hull plank just above the pumps. As the ship slowly righted itself, the crew looked on in horror.

"My God," cried one of the sailors, "Officer Keates, if that plank goes, we're done for!"

"Quick, run to the captain and tell him what's happening. Get him to send down a repair crew immediately!"

"Aye, sir!" The sailor ran up the stairs.

"It may be too late by the time they make it down," lamented Officer Keates, as water sprayed through in torrents.

Jamie looked around the hold. He spied a stack of lumber under the stairs.

"Are those planks?" shouted Jamie.

"Aye, for making the fourth-class berths."

"And did I see an axe in the cargo hold above us?"

He looked to the young man. "Yes, in case of a fire."

"Go and grab the axe. I have an idea!"

The officer looked at the young man suspiciously, but Jamie Galway had an air of authority about him that seemed beyond his age. Without any other recourse until the repair crew arrived, Officer Keates ran for the stairwell. Ignoring the mounting panic of the passengers surrounding them, Jamie grabbed the last remaining sailor and together they pushed their way through to the stack of timber. He eyed the pile and grabbed a thick beam that seemed to be the right length.

"Grab some extra pieces of wood about the same size!" he commanded. The sailor, twice Jamie's age, didn't argue. Together, they heaved the wood back to the spraying sea water. It was getting worse. Jamie took his piece of lumber and wedged it against a rib in the flooring and then leaned it into the spray. With grim determination, he threw that aside, grabbed another longer piece from the sailor, tossed that aside too, then tried a third. Officer Keates returned with the fire axe. Jamie dropped the wood, took the axe, strode through the spray, and drove its blade into the heart of the buckling plank in the hull.

"Are you mad?" Officer Keates screamed as Jamie splintered out a chunk of wood from the plank. "You'll destroy the entire plank!"

"He'll sink us all!" shouted another.

Officer Keates grabbed the handle of the axe and yanked it away from Jamie. Jamie didn't seem to mind as he reached down and picked up the last piece of wood he had dropped and again wedged it down against the thick rib on the ship's floor. He then lowered the top of the timber until it rested against the spray gushing out over the top of the stricken plank. The freezing sea water thoroughly soaked Jamie as he backed into the spray, took hold of the top of the piece of wood, and heaved downwards.

"That won't do any good," yelled one of the fathers, now seeing what he was up to. "The water's coming in too fast!"

"Do you want your families to see the shores of Canada?" Jamie hollered over the roar of the sea and the cries of the frightened crowd. "Grab hold and help me!"

"Come on, men!" shouted Officer Keates, wading into the icy spray and grabbing an edge of the board. "Let's do what the lad says!"

Jamie wrapped both arms around the top of the timber. Officer Keates, followed by his men, grabbed on as well. They all heaved down on the makeshift beam, but the pressure of the ocean water coming in was simply too great.

"Pull down with all you have!" shouted Jamie. It made no difference. The ocean poured in relentlessly.

"Everyone!" Jamie pleaded to the gathered crowd. "Grab on to this beam and help us pull!"

At first, the frightened crowd remained frozen, but then, a boy no older than ten ran up beside Jamie and grabbed on. The boy's father waded up and joined him. Several of the mothers then stepped into the water and grabbed hold. Suddenly, with shouts of growing encouragement, dozens of hands grabbed on to the timber, so many that large sections of the wood could no longer be seen.

"All together now! Heave!" Jamie screamed.

The tremendous tug suddenly jolted the wood along the wet surface until its edge slipped neatly into Jamie's newly hacked V-shaped groove. There was a tremendous whoop from the passengers as the gushing sea water was reduced to a thin spray. Jamie was suddenly in the centre of a swirling hurricane of hugs, kisses, and congratulatory rufflings of his sopping hair from the ecstatic passengers and crew.

The repair crew finally arrived among the revellers. The chief admired Jamie's work of engineering before setting out to complete a more permanent repair to the ship's hull.

Officer Keates managed to pry Jamie away from the admiring crowd.

"Let's get you back up top and dried off," Keates shouted above the hoopla.

Together they weaved their way through the crowd. Several young women blew Jamie kisses as he passed.

"Now how did you come up with that idea?" asked the officer as they reached the first staircase.

"I just used Pythagoras's theorem," said Jamie, following him up. Ryan, he knew, would have been proud.

Officer Keates shot him a strange glance. "A Greek trick? Well, whatever you want to call it, lad, I'm just glad it worked. Well done! I'd say this calls for a drink."

As they neared the hatch, a voice shouted out from the crowd.

"Jamie! Jamie Galway!"

For a moment, Jamie's heart leaped in hope that it was his brother calling out to him. He scanned the mass of people until his eyes came to rest on the face of a familiar man. It was the husband of the family that had been ahead of him when he'd boarded the ship.

"Thank you for saving my family, Jamie," he said, making his way to the bottom of the stairs. "What you did over there was simply brilliant."

Officer Keates gave Jamie an elbow in the ribs. "It appears that you have now reached hero status among the passengers, Mr. Galway."

In the distance, Jamie could see the rest of the man's family waving to him from their tiny, filthy berth near the curve of the wooden bow. As he waved back and climbed the final steps, Jamie couldn't help but feel the children's haunted stares follow him to the heaven-like cleanliness that waited for him above.

Chapter 4

The storm slowly slid to the east and the stricken ship entered calmer waters, allowing a celebration dinner in the captain's quarters to take place later on that evening. Officer Keates enjoyed retelling the story of the way Jamie had used an ancient Greek formula to help save the ship from going down to Davy Jones's locker. Captain O'Malley, in full formal attire, nodded appreciatively at the young man and then raised his glass of wine in Jamie's honour.

"To Jamie Galway. Consider yourself an honourary member of my crew."

The rest of the officers joined in and raised their glasses. "Here! Here!"

"This meal is more than thanks enough," Jamie said, smiling, while shaking a drumstick in one hand. "I haven't had a meal this good in months."

Captain O'Malley smiled. "I'll be sure to send your compliments to the cook. Now, tell us why you're making the long crossing to Canada?"

The question made Jamie's appetite waver. He put the drumstick back on the plate. "I'm heading to Canada to search for my brother. Two weeks ago, he was beaten and knocked unconscious in a skirmish outside of Cork. He was then thrown onto the *Carpathia*, which set sail for Canada before I could rescue him. I'm hoping to catch up with him in Quebec City and bring him home."

The officers gave one another a knowing glance. Captain O'Malley cleared his throat.

"I'm sorry to hear that your brother is aboard the *Carpathia*. It's one of the ships that have given the rest of our transatlantic vessels a very bad name. I can promise you that we will do everything in our power to travel at best speed to Quebec City."

For the next four days, Jamie concentrated on his books in order to learn every little detail that might make the difference in finding his brother upon arrival in Canada. Jamie's only break in his studies came when a purser, compliments of the captain, brought a hot meal to his cabin three times a day.

Jamie couldn't help but think how Canada's political situation was actually quite similar to the one he had just left in Ireland. Great Britain was the controlling power in a country in which only a small portion of the population was actually English. Were the people living in Canada being treated as poorly by the British government as were the people of Ireland? Did Canadians also dream of one day ruling their own land?

His thoughts were interrupted by a knock at his door.

"Come in."

Officer Keates stepped through the doorway. His sombre expression immediately told Jamie something was wrong.

"I'm sorry to disturb you, Mr. Galway."

Jamie pushed away the maps and books. "What's wrong?"

"The *Independence* is once again in trouble."

Jamie stood up, alarmed. "Why? What has happened?"

"A severe outbreak of typhoid fever has occurred among the fourth-class passengers. It has spread rapidly, and it's affecting a significant number of our crew. Many are now too ill to work on deck."

"I'm not a doctor," replied Jamie. "I'm not sure how I can help."

"Actually, the captain was wondering if you could lend us a healthy hand in running the ship. He is willing to pay you time and a half for your efforts."

"You want me to be a sailor?" asked Jamie, incredulously. "But this is the first time I have ever set foot on a ship!"

Officer Keates smiled. "I understand, but you seem to be well-educated and a quick learner. Plus, the captain said that we will only be able to continue at half sails as there is no longer the required number of crew to properly man the rigging. It might add another three days to our crossing time. One more person on deck might be the difference in allowing us to continue at full sail."

Jamie didn't hesitate. He stood up and saluted Officer Keates.

"Seaman Galway reporting for duty, sir."

When Officer Keates found out that Jamie had an intricate knowledge of knot-making from his days of working in the family mill, a mischievous grin crinkled his weathered cheeks. He asked Jamie if he had a fear of heights. Soon after, Jamie was high up in the ocean breeze, climbing the masts and yardarms of the ship. He was taught how to trim and reef the sails at the captain's command. He also learned how to secure the sails by lashing them down with ropes if the winds became too strong.

Jamie would never admit it to his new friend Officer Keates, but he was actually starting to enjoy himself high above the swells of the North Atlantic. Up on the mast, the deep blue horizon stretched out before him in all directions, giving Jamie a feeling of vastness that he had never experienced back on land. He also enjoyed how the fresh ocean air invigorated his exhausted mind.

Nighttime was even more spectacular. During his short breaks, he would simply lie back on the thick yardarm and take in the spectacular view of the starry sky above, counting the shooting stars and wondering if Ryan was staring up into the same sky with him at that very moment.

One night, as Jamie looked up to the black canopy of the night sky, his thoughts were suddenly shattered by a grief-stricken wail. He rolled into a sitting position and watched six crewmen carry out a wooden platform. On top of the platform were the outlines of two bodies covered in a single white cloth. Following behind was a distraught woman, a young girl, and the ship's chaplain. The strong ocean breeze rippled the thin, white cloth as the crew lined up the two bodies with the edge of the ship's rail. The young chaplain said a few quiet words, then nodded to the sailors. The woman collapsed to her knees as the sailors tipped their load, and two bodies, most likely a father and son, fell away and disappeared into the inky darkness of the waves.

Jamie closed his eyes and said a prayer for the family, both living and deceased. He had already lost count of the number of bodies he had witnessed go over the side of the ship. How many more would die before they reached Canada? He looked west, beyond the bow of the mighty sailing ship. The unending darkness made it feel as if they were sailing toward a dream, never in view and always just beyond their reach.

A sharp whistle caught his attention. Officer Keates was waving for him to come down. It was the end of his shift.

Jamie crawled along the yardarm and then slid down the ropes to the deck below. Officer Keates waited for him as a lad even younger than Jamie scurried up the opposite side of the mast to take his place among the sails.

"That's good work you're doing up there, Jamie," said the officer. "If you're ever in need of employment, we'll always have a place for you on board the *Independence*."

Jamie smiled. "Thank you, sir, but I still prefer my feet to be on solid ground."

"Now that your shift is over, why don't you head to the officer's mess and grab a bite to eat? Cook has whipped up a decent stew."

Jamie nodded, although his appetite disappeared as another covered body was brought up on deck, followed by the sobs of another tortured family. The ashen-faced young mother, with her young son in hand, followed the procession to the railing. Officer Keates and Jamie moved aside to allow the body to pass. A gust of wind caught hold of the fluttering white sheet and blew it sideways, exposing the face of the latest typhoid victim. Jamie shook his head in dismay.

"Not Brendan too … "

"Did you know him?" asked Officer Keates.

"We boarded the ship together. He was the one who waved to us below decks."

"Well then, you should know that their older son and daughter also passed away earlier this week."

Jamie looked at the officer, stunned, then to the wife at the railing. "And Erin, the mother, how is she?"

They stared at the young mother gently touching her husband's cheek one last time. "She's sick, as well, but not as bad as some. With a bit of luck, she might make it across to Canada."

Jamie looked at the officer, and then back to Erin. "I need to ask a favour."

"Anything. We owe you more than you know."

"I want Erin and her remaining child to have my berth in second class. It must be unbearable for her to remain in the same berth that has taken the lives of her husband and two other children."

Officer Keates nodded grimly. "I understand your feelings, but we have to consider the health of the other passengers, including yourself."

"I'm willing to sleep anywhere, even out on deck."

"I don't think that will be necessary. Perhaps the captain will bend the rules if you are willing to accept one condition. The woman and child must be kept under quarantine."

"Agreed."

"As well, she won't be able to access purser services for food or assistance. We can't afford any more sickness among the crew."

Erin wrapped her son in her arms as her husband disappeared over the railing.

"I'm sure that she will agree to the quarantine. And I will look after them myself between shifts on deck."

"Then you must take precautions for your own health. Typhoid is contagious."

"Don't worry. I'll be careful."

"So are they friends or family?"

"I've never met them before in my life."

"They're strangers?" Keates looked at him strangely, then shrugged. "I was going to offer you the extra cot next to mine, but I know the other officers would object to such arrangements once they learn you that are regularly visiting someone under typhoid quarantine. I'm afraid a sailor's cot is the only accommodation I can offer you."

Jamie shook his friend's hand. "That's more than a generous offer."

Chapter 5

Jamie ignored the black quarantine ribbon hanging from the latch of his cabin. He lifted the brass handle as he pulled up the handkerchief that hung around his neck until it covered both his nose and mouth. The oils in which he had soaked the cloth were herb derivatives known by the ancients to stop infection. Jamie would have to trust his health to the old Irish texts he had studied under the watchful gaze of the Brotherhood. He stepped quietly through the door.

Erin O'Connor lay under the covers of the bed. Her body was shivering beneath the single sheet. Her youngest son, Colin, was sleeping peacefully on the floor beside her. Hearing the door creak, she opened her eyes and managed to prop herself up on her elbow. She smiled weakly as Jamie presented a plate of bread, a slice of cheese, and a tumbler of water. Jamie tried to hide his shock at the worsening state of her appearance. In just hours, her skin had become milky white. Her voice was dry and raspy.

"You are an angel, Jamie Galway, even if you look like you are about to rob me."

He laughed, placed the food on the desk beside her, and pulled out the chair.

"Sorry for my appearance, but the cloth has to stay," said Jamie, sitting down beside her. "How are you feeling?"

"My head feels like it's swelling to the size of a watermelon and every single joint in my body is on fire. Other than that ... I'm as healthy as a horse."

Jamie admired her courage. "And Colin?"

Her voice quivered. "He seems fine, God bless him. I don't want him to go through what we went through. My heart simply couldn't take it, Jamie. Thanks to you, he might survive the crossing."

Jamie pointed to the porthole. "I'm happy to tell you that we are now officially in Canadian waters. We are only four days away from Quebec City."

"I don't know how I'm going to do it, Jamie," whispered Erin. "My husband and two children ... gone. How am I going to survive?"

"You'll do it for Colin," he said, looking down at the young boy still sound asleep at the foot of the bed. "When I was young, my uncle helped raise my brother and me. And our extended family helped him, just as yours will in Canada when you arrive."

She nodded as she wiped her cheek. "And you will find your brother. I know you will. Can I ask one last request, Jamie? It would mean the world to me."

"Anything."

"I'm so weak. I barely have the strength ... to talk anymore. If something should happen to me, can you make sure Colin finds his way to my sister Sharon's home? She lives in the town of Dundas, Canada West."

Jamie placed a gentle hand on her feverish forehead. "You can do it yourself, Erin."

He stroked the matted hair from her eyes, but her distant, hollow gaze confirmed that she was losing the battle with the disease. With a tremendous effort, she raised her head from her pillow. Her reddened eyes refocused on him in a desperate plea for help.

"Just … promise me. I need to know someone will look after my little Colin if I should die."

Jamie took her hand. "Of course. Colin will make it to his aunt's home. You have my word."

Grimacing in pain, she lowered her head back onto the pillow. "This is selfish of me to ask, but would you have another one of those special handkerchiefs?"

Jamie touched the cloth covering his face. "These medicines won't help you get better. It only helps those who haven't been infected. Otherwise I would have given one to you a long time ago."

"It's not for me," she whispered, out of breath. "It's for Colin. I would do anything to keep him from catching this sickness. Do you think your handkerchief might help him too?"

Jamie looked to the sleeping boy. He berated himself for not thinking of it sooner. "It might. I'll prepare one for him right away."

"You are an angel," she said softly, then drifted off into a feverish sleep.

The crew murmured with excitement as the ship pushed deeper into the narrowing valley of the St. Lawrence River. The end of the voyage was near and everyone was itching to get off the disease-ridden ship. Officer Keates told Jamie that Quebec City lay just a few hours ahead. He also said the crossing had been one of the worst in recent memory. Sixty-two passengers had succumbed to typhoid. A third of the crew was bedridden. Without the help of Jamie and several other willing passengers acting as crew, the ship could have found itself in serious peril during the dangerous final leg of the Atlantic crossing. Jamie stared over the railing at the distant shores on either side of the ship. He couldn't convince himself that they were actually sailing up a river. It was an absolutely enormous river, much larger than any river he'd ever crossed in Ireland. He would not have believed it had Officer Keates not lowered a bucket and offered him a drink of the gloriously cool, fresh water. Jamie surmised that Canada was indeed immense, in every sense of the word.

Captain O'Malley approached the two men at the railing. Jamie was surprised the captain wasn't at the wheel during their upstream sail, and from the lined expression on the captain's face, he sensed there was something wrong.

"I'm sorry, Jamie."

"Sir?"

"Erin O'Connor. We heard her son crying in your cabin. When a crewman went in to investigate, she was dead. I know you two had become friends. Again, I'm sorry."

Jamie hung his head in guilt. "I should have been there for her."

Officer Keates put a hand on his shoulder. "You did everything you could for her. There was nothing else you could have done, even if you had been there by her side. The ship needed you, too."

"Captain, I would like the honour of helping to carry her to the railing."

O'Malley shook his head. "We won't be performing an 'at sea' burial now that we're sailing up the St. Lawrence

River. The recent dead will be unloaded with any passengers heading to quarantine at Grosse Isle. She will be properly buried there. And don't worry about Colin. He seems healthy enough. Our chaplain is currently looking after him."

"Thank you."

"There is one more thing. This note was found lying next to the deceased. I believe it was for you."

Jamie carefully took the folded note from the captain. Not wanting to read it in front of company, he stowed it away in his shirt pocket. Captain O'Malley nodded, then walked back to the bridge.

Jamie turned to Keates. "Grosse Isle?" Jamie asked. "Is that part of Quebec City?"

"No. Grosse Isle is a quarantine station. It's an island in the middle of the St. Lawrence River where passengers suspected of harbouring infectious diseases have to wait before being allowed to step onto Canadian soil. With all of the sickness we've experienced on board, there will no doubt be some who will be asked to unload there."

"And it's supposed to help stop the spread of disease to the Canadian people?"

Keates shrugged. "From what I've seen, it doesn't work very well. If too many boats arrive at the same time, the facilities at Grosse Isle become overwhelmed and they simply send the surplus boats on to Quebec City or Montreal without proper quarantine. Because of this oversight, thousands of Canadian people have already died from typhoid or dysentery."

"I guess we Irish are not well-liked, then."

"Some understand that it's not the Irish immigrant's fault. But others are trying to keep new immigrants out of the cities — for fear that an infected newcomer might start a new wave of infection."

Jamie shook his head. "It seems that one can't escape disease or starvation on land or at sea."

"They go hand in hand, don't they? Starvation and disease are the Grim Reaper's two best mates."

"And how am I going to fit into all of this? I can't stay in quarantine for three weeks. I need to find my brother."

"Don't worry about Grosse Isle, Jamie. I'll get your name put on the crew manifest. That way, the captain can give you permission to stay on with us and sail to Quebec City after the identified passengers have disembarked." Jamie sighed in relief. "Thank you. That would be extremely helpful."

"After saving the ship a number of times, it's the least we could do for you."

A thought suddenly struck Jamie.

"But what of the *Carpathia*? Would it not also have to send some of its passengers to Grosse Isle for quarantine?"

Officer Keates thought for a moment and smiled. "Possibly. That means there is a chance you might see you brother today."

Keates slapped Jamie on the back then returned to his duties. Jamie was momentarily overwhelmed at the prospect of finding his brother in only a few hours. Then he remembered the note he had stuffed in his pocket. He walked over to the railing. A beautiful emerald shoreline floated past the ship, a land that Erin and her husband should have had the chance to see themselves, but never would. He unfolded the note. Her handwriting was faint and shaky.

*Dearest Jamie, I know I do not have long to
live. I can see Brendan, Neil and Patricia
waiting for me. You have done everything
you could to help us during the crossing.
I thank you with all of my heart. Please,
help Colin find Sharon and Robson...*

It was there the note ended.

Tucking the note back inside his shirt pocket, Jamie marched down the deck and opened the door to the chaplain's quarters. He found Colin sitting quietly on the side of the bunk while the chaplain filled out another death certificate at his desk.

"May I come in?"

"Yes. Please do," replied the young priest, standing up. "In fact, I'll go get some fresh air and give you two a little privacy."

The priest shut the cabin door behind him. Colin stared at the floor. Jamie crossed the room and sat down next to him on the bed.

"How are you doing?"

Colin sniffed and wiped a tear from his face with a dirty sleeve. Jamie put an arm around his shoulders, just as Ryan had done to him after the horrendous fire that took the lives of his parents.

"I miss her too. She was a good friend and an even better mother. She asked me to help you get to your aunt and uncle's farm in Canada West. How old are you, Colin?"

"Five."

"Colin, you need to listen to me very carefully. Somewhere out there, in this new land, you have a family that loves you and is waiting for you. You are not alone. You will be with your aunt and uncle very soon. Do you understand?"

Colin looked up, tears rolling down his cheek. "Can I go there now ... to my new family?"

"You'll have to be patient. It's a long journey to where your aunt and uncle live. There are also people who govern this country that want to make sure you are not sick before they let you join your new family."

"I have to wait?" sniffed Colin.

"I'm afraid so."

"How long?"

"I don't know."

"Will you wait with me?"

Jamie hesitated. He couldn't make a promise to this young boy that he couldn't keep. It would only break his heart even more. But if he told him the truth, that he had to leave him to go find his own brother, then that would surely shatter Colin as well. In the end, he said the only thing he could say.

"Yes, I will wait with you ... for a bit."

The ship anchored amongst a handful of wooded, picturesque islands. The crescent moon shape of the islands made natural harbours for the handful of anchored passenger ships as they waited for the arrival of the Grosse Isle medical inspection team. Grosse Isle was the largest of the river islands. From the port railing of the *Independence*, Grosse Isle dominated the view with rows of clean white tents and large wooden buildings decorating the length of the island's east peninsula. Jamie knew why Grosse Isle was the perfect location for a quarantine station. The river current here was so strong and the distance to shore so great that no one in their right mind would ever consider attempting a swim to the mainland.

Jamie, however, wasn't as interested in the islands as he was in the other five ships anchored nearby. He found Officer Keates on deck, barking out orders as the *Independence* prepared to disembark any identified passengers for quarantine.

"Is there anything I can do to help, sir?"

He smiled at Jamie behind his thick moustache. "No, lad. You've done more than enough for this ship."

Jamie pointed beyond the bow. "Do you recognize any of these ships as the *Carpathia*?"

Officer Keates shook his head. "No. The *Carpathia* is a smaller ship than any of those. It must have already sailed on to Montreal. But that doesn't mean that your brother is not on the island. If he was found to be sick by the station doctor, the doctor would have your brother disembark before the ship sailed on. Either way, they should have a record of the ships' passenger manifest on Grosse Isle, and your brother's name should be on it."

Jamie and Officer Keates turned to the port rail as a rowboat left the quarantine station. They watched its oars rhythmically propel it towards the *Independence*. Meanwhile, the ship's crew prepared a long line of wrapped bodies for transportation to the island. Captain O'Malley was wasting no time in his effort to rid himself of the recently deceased.

Jamie decided to check in on Colin. He found the boy sitting at Jamie's desk, busy drawing pictures with

Jamie's pencil. Colin smiled and held up the drawing for Jamie to see. Jamie walked over and ruffled the little boy's hair as he admired the piece of art. He could make out four stick people with wings on their backs. All four were standing on a cloud.

"Is this your family?" Jamie asked.

Colin nodded. "They're in heaven now."

"That's a beautiful picture, Colin. Can I fold up your art and put it in your bag for safekeeping?"

Colin nodded. Jamie had kept the best of the family's worn bags for Colin to use before the other contaminated belongings were disposed of at sea. Jamie had made sure that any of the meagre personal effects of Colin's parents, such as his mother's hair brush and his father's Bible, had been saved and stored. He also hung on to the family's travel papers. If he was to keep Colin out of an orphanage, he would need all of the required documents for the Canadian government, including the letter from his aunt and uncle that invited the family to stay with them in Canada West.

"Is it time to go?" Colin asked.

"Just a minute," Jamie replied. He wanted the body of Colin's mother to be well away from the ship before he took the lad out on deck. "Let me take a look at you first. I think we need to give your collar a fix. And now just a quick brush of your hair. There. Now you should be more presentable for the Canadian authorities."

Jamie opened the cabin door and led the small boy to the end of a growing line of passengers. Jamie was relieved to see that the bodies had already been removed from the ship's deck. The first to line the deck for inspection were the passengers with enough money to afford a cabin in first or second class. Colin looked completely out of place among the wealthy travellers. His filthy clothes hung from his thin frame and a tattered sack lay at his feet.

A stocky man with a handlebar moustache and high-collared coat climbed over the ship's railing and spoke briefly to Captain O'Malley. The captain pointed to the line of waiting passengers. The stern stranger stepped forward and addressed them.

"My name is Dr. George Douglas, and I am the medical superintendent for the Grosse Isle Quarantine Station. According to Canadian law, anyone who appears to be sick or is at high risk for sickness must disembark here and remain in quarantine before being allowed further travel. It is for the health and safety not only of the passengers on this ship but also for the citizens of Canada. If I deem it is necessary for you to disembark, you must immediately move to the ladder and be taken to Grosse Isle, where you will be processed and then have to fulfill a minimum quarantine period of three weeks."

The doctor moved down the line and quickly examined each passenger. Several men and a woman were pulled from the line and sent to the ladder. Those remaining gave a sigh of relief as they were given stamped permission on their travel documents to sail on to Quebec City. Dr. Douglas stopped at the couple next to Jamie. He peered into the eyes of the wife and examined her face closely.

"No discolouration. Good. Extend your arm, please."

She held out her hand. He manipulated the joints of her fingers. "Does that hurt?"

"No, doctor."

"Fine. Now let's have a look at your husband, shall we? Hmm, your eyes seem to be slightly sunken and your complexion is somewhat chalky. Hold out your hand, please. Now make a fist and squeeze."

The man's face contorted with pain.

"Yes, he is most definitely experiencing first stage symptoms. You will have to remain on the island."

Shocked, the couple looked at each other.

"But how can you separate us?" exclaimed the husband. "We are both expected in Montreal!"

"Your wife will have to make arrangements to meet you in Montreal after your three week quarantine period has ended. I'm sorry, but I must move on."

The husband was led away by quarantine staff. The doctor stepped up to Colin.

"Is this the one whose family all perished from dysentery?"

"Typhoid, sir," answered the assistant, looking through the thick pile of notes.

"He does look healthy, but he better have a stay on the island, just in case."

Jamie, standing behind Colin, couldn't believe what he was hearing. "But he's fine! Just look at him. He doesn't need to be quarantined. What he needs is to get to his family in Canada West. He's lost everyone else on the crossing."

Dr. Douglas looked up at Jamie. "And you are who, exactly?"

"Jamie Galway. I am a friend of the family, and I can firmly state that the boy is not sick."

"So you were in close proximity to the family during their illness?"

"Yes, I looked after them as I know a little bit about medicine, but I took care not to …"

"Then quarantine Mr. Galway, too."

Jamie was horrified. "Wait, you can't! I need to get to Quebec City as quickly as possible myself! Look! I can open and close my hands. No pain!"

Officer Keates overheard the heated conversation and pulled Jamie aside. The doctor ignored Jamie and moved on.

Officer Keates lowered his voice to a whisper. "Don't argue with the man. He has the power to put you on the next ship back to Ireland if you do not cooperate. I think I can help get you out of this mess. Tell the quarantine officers on the island that there was a mistake and you are a crew member of the *Independence*. I'll look after the paperwork at this end."

Jamie took a deep breath and tried to calm down as Dr. Douglas continued his examinations. It only took a second for Jamie to put his trust in his friend. Jamie took Colin's hand and led him to a long wooden ladder descending over the side of the ship. Climbing down, he helped Colin into one of the rowboats bobbing along the side of the hull. One of the sailors from the *Independence* sat at the oars and grinned at Jamie as he and Colin took their place on the bench.

"Hey, crewman," he said cheekily to Jamie. "Slacking off on your duties again? Sit yourself down over here and grab an oar."

Jamie smiled as he patted Colin reassuringly. "Sorry. Off duty, mate. I'm just here for the ride."

* * *

Jonathon Wilkes was shocked when he looked down the line and saw Jamie Galway ordered to quarantine. Even he could see the lad was as healthy as a horse. What was the doctor thinking? For a second, he had considered faking an illness himself in order to follow the lad onto the island. Thank goodness, common sense took over before the doctor arrived to examine him. He had been quietly keeping tabs on Jamie's conversations and had overheard that his brother had sailed on to Montreal. Why should he risk death at the quarantine station, surrounded by all those sick Irish peasants for three weeks, when he could just as easily wait in comfort for Galway to arrive in Montreal? Satisfied with his solution, he opened his mouth to the doctor and let him look into his eyes.

"Good colour. Eyes clear. Do you feel well enough to continue on to Quebec City Mr. … er, Wilkes?

"I have never felt better, sir. It must have been all of the fresh sea air from the crossing."

The doctor scribbled a note on his clipboard. "All right. That completes the first- and second-class passenger list. Now let's bring the other passengers up on deck!"

After fighting through the strong river current to the quarantine station's dock, the oarsmen tied the rowboat to the dock and helped many of the weakened passengers disembark. Jamie was surprised to see that the island was a bustling hive of activity. Dozens of families were spread out in little clusters along the rocky shoreline. Some were cooking over small campfires; others were washing their clothes in the cold waters of the river. Some of the children stopped their playing along the shore to eye the passengers from the *Independence* curiously as they made their way towards the wooden buildings. Several nurses dressed in the long white habit of a Catholic nun met the passengers at the end of the dock. One stepped forward and greeted the new arrivals.

"Welcome to Canada! Please stay in your family groupings and follow me to the immigration building where you will be processed."

Jamie and Colin followed the crowd into one of the smaller buildings and waited in queue for their turn to be processed. Finally, a man with spectacles and a long nose called them forward.

"Papers?"

Jamie handed him their travel documents. He also passed over the paper that Officer Keates had quickly created before he had left the ship. It was signed by Captain O'Malley himself.

"I'm a crew member on board the *Independence* and a friend to this boy," explained Jamie. "His family died during the voyage, but he has extended family living in Canada West. I was to arrange a meeting in Montreal in order to return him to his relatives."

The official glanced wearily over his spectacles. "I see from the list that his entire family died of contagious typhoid. He will have to stay here in quarantine for three weeks before he will be permitted to sail on to Montreal."

Jamie pushed Colin forward until he was on full display before the desk clerk. "Why quarantine? Just look at him. He's a healthy boy! There's no reason why he can't continue to travel on with me to Montreal."

The man shuffled through the papers. "I don't see a note among the papers that states that you, Mr. Galway, are a certified physician. This quarantine order was signed by Dr. Douglas himself. Neither you nor I have the power to change the order."

"He obviously made a mistake. Why do I need to be a physician to see that he's a healthy lad? You can see that for yourself."

The official gave Jamie an icy stare. "I'm a very busy man, Mr. Galway. You may go back to the ship, but he stays."

"But who will look after him if I leave?" Jamie demanded.

The official sighed. "We are not an orphanage or a babysitting service. He will have to stay in the quarantine building, where the nurses will feed him and keep an eye on him as best they can."

Jamie looked at him with disbelief. "Keep an eye on him? He just lost his entire family!"

The officer didn't bother looking up from the paperwork. At the top of Colin O'Connor's papers he slammed down a rubber stamp that stated FAMILY DECEASED.

"Mr. Galway, we've just had three large passenger ships dock within ten hours of one another. As you can see, we're a little overwhelmed at the moment. But don't worry, we will not lose the boy. Please drop him off with his papers at the quarantine building. It's the large building at the top of the hill. Next!"

Jamie stepped forward and placed his hands on the large oak desk. "Please, sir, just one more thing. I'm also looking for my brother who might have arrived here a few days ago. His name is Ryan Galway. Do you know if he is here in quarantine on Grosse Isle?"

"I'm a simple immigration officer, Mr. Galway. I don't have access to such information. Ask for him up in quarantine. Next!"

Jamie shook his head in frustration, grabbed the papers, and took Colin's hand.

"Come on, Colin. Let's go find the next building."

They left the office and climbed the low hill to a much larger building. Its two storeys stretched out across the island with its many windows facing out towards the St. Lawrence River. They climbed up the steps to the wooden veranda that ran along the face of the building, crossed the creaky planks, but froze as they stepped through the open double doorway. The nightmarish sight before them brought Jamie right back to the fourth-class compartment on the *Independence*. It seemed that every square inch of floor space within the building was covered in a carpet of humanity. Men, women, and children were huddled together, sick and shivering on the floor. Weaving in and out of the sick were a half-dozen nuns carrying either trays of medicines or mops. Jamie's nose twitched in disgust. The stench of the sickness simply poured out through the open door. Stepping over several patients, a nurse made her way towards them.

"Excuse me, but I have a small boy who … "

She glided past them in her long white habit as if she had not heard a word he had said. Jamie thought for a moment, then switched to French.

"*Excusez-moi*. Could I have your assistance, *s'il vous plaît?*"

She stopped in her tracks and turned around, amused.

"A French-speaking Irish boy?" she replied in French.

"I know a bit," he continued. "I'm dropping off this boy from the *Independence*. He has lost his family, and I was told to bring him here to quarantine."

She sighed and wiped her brow. "He can stay here by the door. After I tend to the other patients, I'll help settle him in."

A man leaning up against the doorframe doubled over in a heaving wet cough. His face was as pale as death itself. Jamie quickly moved Colin to the other side of the door.

"Should the boy really be in here? He's not sick."

The nurse shrugged. "We've brought up that very point with the doctor many times. The sick infect the healthy and that makes our job even more difficult. But the government insists that families stay together in quarantine. Some have chosen to keep away from the sick by living down on the shoreline. To tell you the truth, I cannot blame them. But this little boy is here by himself. He must stay in the building with us so that he can be supervised."

Jamie could see that she was exhausted. "Your duties seem to be unending. Are there really only six of you?"

"There usually are more nurses, but some have come down with the sickness themselves, and we are severely short-staffed. The only nurses in Canada willing to work here among the sick are other Catholic nuns. All other nurses in Canada refuse to come to our quarantine station for fear of catching disease."

"Then how do you survive?"

She mustered a smile. "I work all day long, but I try to catch a little sleep when I can. This is what I was meant to do. It's my calling. I'm sorry, but I must go."

A calling. Jamie understood. It was a calling from above that had brought him into the priesthood as well. The nun quickly approached a nearby family with eight children, all lying on their sides, writhing in severe pain. Jamie looked down at Colin, who was taking in the whole scene through huge eyes. His face showed no emotion. He had already seen so much death in Ireland and then on the ship as his family slipped away one by one. Jamie guessed he was probably now immune to it. Or perhaps he had decided that he was destined to be next. It wasn't fair that an innocent child had to see so much horror at such a young age. Jamie had him turn his back to the sickness and walked him across the veranda. Together, they sat down on the steps. The beautiful panoramic view of the sparkling St. Lawrence River stood in stark contrast to the bleak horrors that lay behind.

"I need to go talk to someone about my brother," said Jamie. "You wait right here on this step for me. The nurse will be back soon. If she arrives before I get back, do what she says and follow her. Don't worry if she moves you. I'll come and find you, I promise."

Jamie started to pull away, but Colin wouldn't let go of his hand. His eyes started to widen in panic. Jamie knelt down and smiled. "I'll be back very soon."

Slowly, Colin released his grip. It broke Jamie's heart to leave him alone, even if it was for just a few minutes.

Jamie needed to get his bearings on the island before he could start his search for Ryan. He swung behind the quarantine station and climbed up the hill until he reached the summit of Grosse Isle. The view of the huge river stretching east and west was breathtaking, with sailing vessels of all shapes and sizes plying its sparkling waters. He had never seen a valley as thickly wooded and lush as what banked either side of the distant river shores. On the far side of the hill was a scene that stabbed him in the heart. Large swaths of trees had been removed from the base of the hill and a small army of men worked spades into the earth, creating a series of long shallow pits. Other men were reaching into the back of a horse-drawn cart. The cart was full of shroud-covered bodies. The bodies were being carried to the long pits and unceremoniously dropped into the fresh earth. Another crew followed behind the cart and shovelled fresh dirt onto the mass grave. Jamie couldn't tear his eyes away from the horrific sight, for he knew Erin was among those currently being placed in the grave. He kneeled down and whispered a prayer of peace and deliverance for his friend and her family.

A grey-haired man led the horse and now empty cart back towards the dock. Jamie ran down the hill and intercepted the cart at the path before it reached the quarantine station. He clenched the old man's arm and pointed back to the graves.

"How many?" he asked, out of breath.

The old man glanced at him. "How many what?"

"How many dead are buried back there?"

He glanced back at the mass graves. "I'd have to say around three thousand are buried there now, but I'm not keeping a close count."

"Three thousand?" Jamie repeated weakly. His mind couldn't comprehend such a number.

"Sorry, son, but I need to move on. There are still a few more I need to pick up from the *Independence*."

For the first time, a wave of dread washed over Jamie. Could Ryan be one of the three thousand buried here at Grosse Isle? He ran back to the buildings and, after searching the compound, found the clerk's office. He burst in through the door with such force that the secretary nearly jumped out of her seat.

"Slow down, young man!" she chastised.

"I'm sorry," said Jamie, trying to calm down, "but I desperately need your help. I am trying to find my brother who should have arrived here in the last week or two. Can you help me?"

"And you are?"

"Jamie Galway. A sailor on the *Independence*."

She pushed herself away from the desk. "He's a recent arrival, then? I think I can be of assistance. Let me check the newest documents."

She turned to several wooden crates sitting on top of a low bookshelf.

"Name?"

"Ryan Galway."

She shuffled through a set of papers. The wait was excruciating, and Jamie began to pace. Finally, she turned around.

"We don't have any record of a Ryan Galway."

Jamie almost choked on his next words. "Do your records include both the dead and living?"

"Yes, they do."

Jamie's head was spinning. "I thought all ships arriving in Canada had to anchor at Grosse Isle."

"Not all ships do stop at Grosse Isle," the secretary explained. "If we are overwhelmed with new arrivals, and we have been very busy the past few weeks, the immigration department will send the smaller ships on to a port city. Did your brother have his proper papers?"

Jamie felt a chill run down his spine. "I'm not sure."

"It's hard to believe, but we sometimes receive deceased without any papers. With no way to identify the bodies, they are simply lowered into the island graves as unknowns."

"Do you know of the *Carpathia*? She likely arrived here last week."

"Sorry, I don't keep track of ship names, just the immigration papers."

Jamie grasped the door handle. "Thank you for your help, and I apologize for my abrupt entrance."

As Jamie stepped outside, he wasn't sure if he should feel angry or relieved. At least his brother wasn't in a mass grave here on the island. Or was he? Perhaps he never revived after the blows he received from the soldiers. Perhaps he died and was buried without proper papers. Perhaps his brother's ship had run into the same storm they had two weeks ago. Did the *Carpathia* sink with all hands in the Atlantic? Perhaps that was the reason there was no record of him ever arriving at Grosse Isle. His head was swimming with possibilities, and none of them were very hopeful.

Jamie could see a tender from the *Independence* bringing more passengers to Grosse Isle. Captaining the small craft was Officer Keates, who was waving to Jamie. Jamie ran to the dock to meet him.

"I brought word of the *Carpathia*."

Jamie held his breath. "Please, tell me!"

"The captain of the *Nautilus* told me that the *Carpathia* was ordered on to the city of Montreal, its final destination, just over a week ago. Being a smaller ship, a government official decided that the passengers were to go through immigration in Montreal, as Grosse Isle was filled to capacity."

Jamie paused. "Then my brother is in Montreal?"

"We're only sailing as far as Quebec City. We can drop you off there if you like. From there, you can catch another boat that will take you upriver to Montreal."

Jamie was torn. A part of him was screaming yes, but he couldn't stop thinking about Colin sitting on that step, waiting for him to return. If he didn't help that boy, who would? There must be a way he could get to Montreal while helping Colin at the same time. With only a moment's hesitation, Jamie reached forward and shook Officer Keates's hand.

"Thank you so much for your help, but I also need to make sure Colin O'Connor is well taken care of before I leave. Is there any possible way he can join us on the *Independence*?"

"Sorry, lad. But a five-year-old listed as crew would look a little suspicious. We also have our government licence to consider. What you are suggesting is called human smuggling. I'm afraid we can only bend the rules to give *you* a hand, not the boy."

"Then I will have to stay here at Grosse Isle."

Officer Keates raised his eyebrows but didn't seem overly surprised by the news.

"Just one last favour," asked Jamie, "if you don't mind."

"Name it."

"I noticed all officers on board the ship carry a small knife. Could I have yours? I can pay you for it."

Keates laughed and reached into his jacket. In his hand materialized a small pocket knife. The blade was stowed safely away within its metal housing. The officer offered it to Jamie.

"Keep this as a memento of your time on the *Independence*. And don't worry about the cost, I'll just dock it from your pay."

They both laughed. "Thank you."

The sailors pushed the empty tender away from the dock. Oars dipped into the water, and the small craft began its long trip back to the *Independence*.

"Sorry we couldn't help the young lad out," Keates shouted out over the stern. "The ship leaves in an hour if you change your mind!"

Chapter 6

Jamie sat on the edge of the dock, chatting with a large family about the pubs in Dublin as he kept one eye on the large woodshed nearby. Colin was having a nap on the veranda under the supervision of the nun who had befriended them. With the sun setting, Jamie watched the last of the labourers put a padlock on the shed door, climb into his boat, and sail home to the mainland for dinner. Even with the gentle waves of the river lapping beneath his feet and the animated chatter of the family surrounding him, Jamie could hear an endless shower of moans drizzle down from the quarantine building. He wondered how anyone could possibly sleep on this island without being haunted by constant nightmares.

Jamie excused himself from the conversation and meandered along the shoreline towards the wood shed. He was thankful that there were no official records of him on the island so he could move around the buildings as he liked. By the look of things, no one seemed overly concerned about the tracking of the quarantined immigrants anyway. The healthy families ignored official demands to stay inside the buildings. They preferred to take their chances outside in the fresh air and chose to camp out under the stars along the shoreline. Jamie couldn't blame them, for he would have done exactly the same thing if he had been in their shoes. Why put your family at higher risk for disease by sleeping with the sick?

Originally, Jamie had hoped to steal a small boat from the dock but he had to give the officials on the island some credit. All the boats were taken to other nearby islands or the mainland at night in order to prevent such an escape. So Jamie had to come up with another plan. He slid in behind the shed until he was under a small locked window. Using Officer Keates's knife, he pried out the pins holding the hinges in place, then quietly lowered the window to the ground. He then climbed in through the open window frame and lit a small candle. It wasn't hard to locate the things he needed. He grabbed a saw, glue, nails, a hammer, and some rope and threw them into a burlap bag. Before leaving, he spied an unfinished object on the workbench that could also prove to be very useful.

After lowering the bag to the grass, climbing out and repairing the window, Jamie worked his way past the families eating dinner on the shore until he found himself on the far side of the island and among the graves of thousands of his countrymen. Jamie fought his aching heart as he searched among the graves for what he needed. It was now almost pitch dark and he thought he remembered seeing one somewhere in this area. There it was! He had almost walked right into it.

The simple coffin was empty, thank goodness, and it was probably going to be filled in the morning with a dead body whose family had enough funds to avoid the mass burial. He dragged the wooden box around the rows of freshly covered graves until he found the water's edge. He put down the bag of tools, lit the candle, pulled up a fallen log, and got to work.

* * *

"Colin. Time to wake up."

Even in the dead of night, the quarantine building was awash in a sea of moans and coughs, punctuated with the occasional retching. He couldn't bear the thought of leaving Colin for three weeks in this disease-infested purgatory. He had been through far too much already. For once, Jamie had the power to stop another death, and he was going to do everything he could to save the young boy.

Colin's hazel eyes fluttered to life under the weak light of the oil lamps. The little boy's bed near the doorway was the wooden floor itself. Colin had used his meagre sack as a pillow. A passing nurse had covered the young lad in an old blanket. Jamie prayed that the blanket itself wasn't festering with sickness. Keeping an eye out for any movement, Jamie snuck Colin out through the door without incident. Jamie was proud of Colin. He was following perfectly the instructions for silence he had given him earlier in the day.

By looking at the position of the stars in the clear sky, Jamie estimated they had three hours of darkness left before the sun began to rise. They circled around the sleeping families near the shore and then angled away from the mass graves and Colin's mother's final resting place. Once they made it over the hill, the pair wound their way through a thick stand of trees to a small clearing beside the river. This was Jamie's temporary work station. He relit the candle on the log and sat the boy down.

"You did well, Colin. Now, do you want to get off this island as badly as I do?"

He nodded sleepily. "Is Mommy staying here?"

"Your mother will be laid to rest here, along with the others who didn't survive the crossing."

He looked up, concerned. "Can I come back and visit her?"

Jamie rubbed his head. "Sure you can. You can come back and visit Grosse Isle some day, but first let's find your living relatives. I know they want to meet you."

"But we're on an island."

"Ah, yes, you're right, lad. But not for long. All we need is a boat, and look what I made for you while you were sleeping!"

Jamie pulled the coffin out from behind the bushes. He had cut a large oval hole out of the top of the lid and an unfinished paddle lay across its makeshift bow. It was a bit of good luck that someone was making a paddle in the workshop on the night he broke in. Colin walked up to the box and touched its side.

"It's sticky."

"That's just the glue. It should be mostly dry by now. It will help keep the water out. And look at the name."

Colin looked at the letters painted in black. "I can't read."

"I've named our boat the *Good Erin*. Erin was your mother's first name and now she's going to help us go find your family."

Colin smiled and touched the name on the side.

"I think it's time to cast off. You hop in first. I've put a blanket down in front. You can go back to sleep if you want while I paddle us to shore."

Jamie helped the boy climb into the strange watercraft and then pushed it off the rocks and into the water. Taking the paddle, he climbed in and pulled at the water. He was pleased to see that the coffin moved silently away from shore. It was surprisingly stable. Digging in with greater confidence, Jamie set course for the northern shore of the St. Lawrence River.

The hidden sun was stretching its long, scarlet fingers across the early-morning sky. A light mist was forming on the water's surface. Jamie had been paddling for three hours yet the northern shore of the river was still frustratingly far away and he was starting to worry. The good news was that Grosse Isle was now a distant bump in the river behind them. The bad news was that the current of the St. Lawrence kept pushing them downstream, and further away from Montreal, the final port of the *Carpathia*. Rubbing his eyes, Colin poked his head up out of the hole.

"It's wet down here."

Jamie stopped paddling. "Are you sure?"

"See my hand?"

Jamie touched Colin's wet skin and grimaced. Although an early-morning mist veiled much of the far shore, he could tell it was still a distance away. An innate fear of the water danced in his mind, as the Brotherhood had taught him only the very basics of swimming.

"How bad is it?"

"My blanket is soaked."

Colin held it up, dripping wet. The glue! He had wondered if the glue was waterproof, but he thought that it would hold out the water for at least a short river crossing. He hadn't realized it was going to take this long to paddle across the channel. His miscalculation might end up costing them their lives.

"Colin, I need you to try and figure out where the water is coming from, then jam the blanket into that area and hold it there with your feet. Do you understand?"

Colin nodded, smiling, as if he was glad to finally have a task, and disappeared back into the front of the coffin.

Jamie dug furiously at the water. It was his idea to bring Colin with him for the crossing, and now he kicked himself for putting the boy's life in grave danger once again. Jamie shook his head at the irony. He was supposed to be saving Colin's life by taking him away from the island. If he had just left him there, at least he would not be in danger of drowning! Jamie tried his best to refocus his thoughts. There must be a way out of this. Death could not be an option.

Just ahead, Jamie could make out a large expanse of watery plants in the early morning fog. He hoped that the plants signified shallow water. If the coffin should go down in the plants, perhaps he could touch bottom. He pulled on the paddle with all his might, but he could feel the craft becoming more sluggish. Water was lapping up against his calves. He was sure that the coffin was going to sink very soon.

Colin re-emerged from the floating crypt. "I'm wet and cold."

"You did a fantastic job, Colin. Now why don't you come here, sit on my lap and try to keep out of the cold water."

Jamie was knee-deep in water when they reached the edge of the plants. The coffin was no longer floating, but ploughing through the water. They were still some distance to shore, but it seemed within reach. The plants brushed past the front of the coffin. Little brown bits from the plants rained down on the sinking lid of the coffin. It would be only seconds before they would have to abandon their lifeboat. With his last few strokes, Jamie reviewed everything he could remember about swimming.

"Colin, when I say, I want you to climb onto my back and hold on as if I were giving you a piggyback ride. Make sure you keep your head above the water. That's very important."

"Are we going to get wet?" he asked.

"I'm afraid so. I'm going to try and swim to shore."

"But the water's cold!" he protested.

"Our boat is not going to make it, Colin. But we're closer to shore now. I think we can make it if we swim."

Without warning, the coffin's nose dove under the water's surface. Colin clambered onto Jamie's back as the coffin completely submerged. Something moved ahead of them. Was it one of those large beasts he'd read about? A moose? Perhaps a person! He took his paddle and waved it frantically above his head.

"Help! Help us! We're sinking!"

Suddenly, the entire coffin dropped down to the bottom of the river.

"Colin! Hang on!"

"I'm scared!"

But the little boy did as he was told. He grabbed on to Jamie's shoulders and held on for dear life. Jamie had hoped the coffin might settle on top of the plants and give him a perch on which to stand, but the box kept sinking until he was treading water on his own. Having the weight of a five-year-old boy on his back didn't help matters. It was all he could do to keep his own chin above the surface.

Orienting himself, he set out, thrashing his arms, for the shore. Jamie had never had to swim through weeds. The plants wrapped around his arms and legs like hungry green tentacles, slowing Jamie's progress toward shallow water. Less than a minute passed before Jamie was exhausted. He knew they had barely gone anywhere. His feet could still not touch bottom. This was the end.

"I'm … sorry," he gasped. "I didn't … mean it…."

It was Jamie's last breath. With his remaining strength, he held the boy up to the surface with his arms. The weight of the boy suddenly lightened and disappeared altogether. Jamie's panicked mind could only assume that an angel had swooped down and lifted him up to heaven, saving the young Colin from any further pain. For a brief moment, Jamie smiled.

Then something gripped his extended arm. He was being pulled. Weeds tore away from his legs. His head broke through the surface! He gagged as river water spewed out of his mouth. His arm was pinned along the length of another small watercraft. He blinked the water from his eyes and looked into what had to be the face of an angel. A young woman with dark complexion and long, flowing black hair was gazing down at him. Colin was at her feet, wide-eyed and shivering.

"Give me your other arm," she commanded, in French.

"Angels speak French?" he asked, coughing.

"Now swing your leg over the side. Be careful you do not tip all of us into the water. I will lean the other way for balance."

Jamie threw one leg over the side of the craft and indeed nearly tipped everyone back into the St. Lawrence. The young woman threw her body over the far gunwale to help balance the boat against Jamie's waterlogged frame.

"Quickly! Climb in now!"

With his final ounce of strength, Jamie managed to pull himself up over the side of the boat and collapse onto its bottom. Colin threw himself into Jamie's shivering arms. Looking up into the early-morning sun, Jamie could only make out the silhouette of his rescuer against the rising sun. She was paddling hard for shore.

"I don't know who you are," Jamie sputtered, "but thank you."

He then collapsed on his side and passed out.

Chapter 7

Jamie groaned as his tired mind tried to figure out why he was lying inside a giant wasp nest. His confused thoughts began to settle and he came to realize that he was in an enormous wooden structure, a building unlike any he had ever seen before. The building itself was the shape of a long cylinder cut through its length and then laid on its side. The roof was wooden, no … not wood, but made of strips of bark! At either end of the building were small rectangular doors. Unused fire pits were lined along the centre of its length on the dirt floor. The large building was completely deserted.

Jamie himself felt as if he were wrapped in a luxurious cocoon. Extending his arms, he realized that he had been wrapped in a soft pile of furs. His body lay on a bench that stretched along the entire length of the building. Jamie suddenly panicked when he couldn't see Colin, but then he heard a shuffling sound beneath him. Peering over the edge, he was relieved to see the boy snuggled in another bundle of furs on a lower bench, still sound asleep. Jamie moved his aching body into an upright position. Next to him on the bench, a large wooden bowl held a selection of ripe berries, vegetables, nuts, and dried fish. Starving, Jamie gratefully dug into the food, being careful to leave enough for the sleeping boy.

He decided to try out his stiff legs. Getting his bearings, he quietly made his way to the nearest doorway and looked out into a sea of green. He had never seen such a beautiful, rich forest before, as the English had cut down almost all of Ireland's once legendary forests to build their ever-growing navy of ships. It was as if he had woken up and was still living inside a beautiful dream. He glanced up to get an idea of the time, but the canopy was so thick, he couldn't judge the angle of the sun.

Where was he? He started to look for other clues. There must be a connection between the woman who had rescued him and this structure. According to the books he'd read back on the *Independence*, this building was somewhat similar to the bark-covered wigwams that were used by Native people in the eastern part of Canada, but wigwams, he thought, were supposed to be much smaller and dome-shaped. Therefore, it seemed logical that if he had been helped by a Native woman, she was not of the Algonquin or Mikma'q Nations that were supposed to inhabit this part of Canada East. And why was this structure completely abandoned? Surely its size could shelter up to fifty families. Why was it not being used?

Perhaps some answers could be found at the other entranceway. Jamie went outside and circled his way around the entire length of the building, admiring its efficient construction, which used only the materials of the forest. When Jamie turned the far corner of the building, he walked right into a woman coming around the corner in the other direction. Jamie tried to spin away to minimize the impact, but he ended up only spiralling himself into a heap on the ground. The surprised woman put her hands on her hips and stared at him.

"Are you still suffering from your swim across the river?" she asked, in French.

Jamie sat up in the dirt and grinned. "Wasn't expecting to see you so soon, or so close."

"Grab my hand," she offered.

Jamie took her hand, and she easily pulled him off the ground. He was sure it was the same woman who had rescued them from the river. Perhaps a couple of years older than Jamie, she was tall and lean, wearing a cotton blouse buttoned up to her neck and a full length skirt. Her ebony eyes shone with a combination of amusement and concern.

"Thank you for rescuing me and the boy. We owe you our lives."

"I'm surprised you look so healthy."

"Why do you say that?" asked Jamie.

"I assume you were escaping from Grosse Isle. Either that, or you were planning on harvesting some wild rice."

"Those were rice plants I was swimming through?"

"I'm not sure I would call what you were doing swimming, but yes, those were rice plants. I was out on the river early harvesting rice for my village."

"What village?" Jamie asked, looking first at the building and then out at the surrounding forest.

She laughed. "This is not my village. My village is down that path. We only use the longhouse for traditional ceremonies. I'm by myself because the rest of my village refuses to see you, afraid that you carry the diseases that have ravaged our land. A dozen people in my village have already died from the scourge, including two of our elders."

"I'm sorry," replied Jamie. "I can promise you that the boy and I are healthy. If you knew about the diseases on Grosse Isle, then why did you help us?"

She laughed. "Anyone who could paddle across the St. Lawrence River in a sinking coffin could not be that sick. Say, you speak French very well for an Irish boy. How is that possible?"

"I spent two years studying in France." Jamie tilted his head and eyed her curiously. "This is my first time in Canada so forgive my ignorance but you are not of Algonquin descent, are you?"

"What makes you say that?"

"Just from what I read about this country." He pointed to the structure behind him. "And the fact you called this structure a longhouse and not a wigwam."

She nodded, impressed. "I'm Wendat."

"Wendat?"

"The name of my nation," she explained. "And my name is Tutuyak Lapointe."

Jamie smiled. "I'm Jamie Galway and my little companion over there is Colin O'Connor. I don't recall seeing the name Wendat on any of my aboriginal maps of Canada."

She shrugged. "It's because of our history. Our nation was pretty much wiped off the maps in the seventeenth century. My descendants are survivors from a war that took place in a land far away from here. I'm named after a great warrior who helped lead our people to the safety of this new land. Have you come to start a new life in our land as well?"

"Actually, I wasn't supposed to be here in Canada at all." Then Jamie explained to her that he was here to find his brother.

Tutuyak frowned when she heard the tale of Ryan's plight. "I understand the bond of family. You need to get to Montreal as soon as possible. The longer you wait, the harder it will be for you to find Ryan."

"Unfortunately, we lost everything in the coffin, except a little bit of money and a letter I had stored in my pocket."

"Why are you taking the boy with you to Montreal?"

Jamie looked towards the longhouse. "Actually, he was never part of my original plan. I witnessed his entire family die on the ship. *He* was healthy, but the doctor still placed him in quarantine. I couldn't leave him alone in that cesspool of disease over on Grosse Isle. I didn't know what else to do, so I brought him along."

"And you didn't know him before the voyage?"

"I had never seen him before in my life."

She stared at him. "You look like the other settlers, but there is something about you that is very different."

He smiled. "I'll take that as a compliment."

"You are wrong about your young friend. He is not healthy. He is sick."

"He is?" asked Jamie, alarmed. "Are you sure?"

"Yes. He is sick, but not with the pestilence that is sweeping through our two peoples. He has the ailment your people contract when they do not eat properly on a long voyage across the sea. Your people call it scurvy. I brought something to help him regain his strength."

She held up a small earthenware jug and led him into the longhouse. She reached over to a table, took a cup, and poured out a small amount of sticky brown liquid. She passed the cup to Jamie.

"You should have some as well."

He looked at the drink, took a sniff, then sipped it. It was thick, but it was possibly the sweetest, most delicious liquid to ever cross the tip of his tongue.

"It's wonderful! What is it?"

"It's a syrup my people make from the sap of the maple tree. When the boy drinks this, his spirit will once again grow strong."

He held out a hand towards the doorway of the longhouse. "Then I think it's time to wake up Colin."

They strode down the corridor of the longhouse and upon reaching the young boy, Jamie sat down next to him.

"Hey, lad. It's time to wake up."

"Jamie?" asked Colin, rubbing his eyes. "Where are we?"

"With a friend, and she has a special drink for you. It tastes like candy."

Colin had only had candy once before in his life, on a Christmas Day long ago. "Really? Candy?"

Jamie then noticed his gums were inflamed and a small sore was forming in his mouth. Tutuyak was right. He did have scurvy.

"Yes, delicious candy. Now sit up. Our friend Tutuyak has made it for you."

Tutuyak sat down on the other side of the boy and poured some more of the brown syrup into the cup. She passed it to Colin and he took a small sip. They both grinned when the boy's face lit up.

"Can I have more, please?"

Tutuyak nodded. Jamie rustled his hair. "Sure you can. But finish what you have first."

Colin happily sipped away on the syrup, using his tongue to get at every last drop.

"Thank you," he said as he passed the cup back to Tutuyak.

"*De rien*," she replied.

Colin looked to Jamie in confusion.

"She speaks only French," he explained.

Colin looked around at the strange building, then back to Tutuyak, noticing her dark complexion. "Where are we?"

"This is a building of Tutuyak's ancestors. She is Wendat, a Native person of this land."

Colin was staring at the pretty dark-haired woman next to him and was about to ask another question, but he hesitated, looked down at his delicious drink, and then back to his friends. His face scrunched up.

"Did we die and go to heaven?"

Jamie looked at Tutuyak, translated, and they laughed as Colin took another sip of syrup.

Chapter 8

Jamie luxuriated in his cozy cocoon of warm animal skins, but he simply couldn't fall asleep. Colin was curled up at his feet and covered as well in warm skins to help keep away the cool night air. Jamie was no longer worried about the young boy's health. Colin was already showing more curiosity and energy earlier in the evening as he explored the interior of the longhouse. Tutuyak's delicious syrup had done its job and brought Colin back to good health.

It was Ryan who weighed heavily on his racing thoughts. Was his brother hurt or sick? Did he still have the text? Had he died in the crossing? All the answers lay far away in a town named Montreal. He still had no clue as to the location of Tutuyak's village in relation to the rest of Canada East, the part of Canada that contained the cities of Quebec and Montreal. All of his maps had gone down with the coffin to the bottom of the St. Lawrence River. He fought the panic of being lost in an endless foreign land and trusted that both God and his newfound friend would help him find direction once again.

Finally, the sun lit up the early morning mist. Jamie jumped when he suddenly heard a loud snort come from just outside the doorway. Could it be a bear or moose prowling outside the longhouse? He had yet to see such creatures first-hand, but did not doubt the tales of their dangerous nature. He grabbed a long wooden pole from the floor and warily approached the doorframe. As he peeked outside, a large, flaring nostril sprayed him with a cloud of steam. Jamie jumped in surprise and banged his head on the frame of the door.

Tutuyak laughed. "Be careful. Your hard head might break our longhouse."

Jamie rubbed his head and smiled back at Tutuyak, mounted high up on a horse. "I think my head is going to break long before your longhouse."

Tutuyak was straddling a beautiful brown and white stallion. Its dark chestnut eyes stared at Jamie suspiciously. He stomped his hoof, and Tutuyak pulled back on the reins.

"Steady, Dreamer," she cooed. "Don't worry. He's a friend."

"You talk to your horse?"

"Of course. Don't you?"

Jamie scratched his head. "Actually, I've never had the chance to get to know a horse before. Where I come from, only the wealthy can afford them. But yours is the most beautiful horse I've ever seen. Do all women in Canada ride a horse like you?"

Tutuyak was straddling her horse wearing a pair of woollen pants, riding boots, and a loose cotton blouse. "I don't know about others, but this is the way I ride them. Why do you ask?"

"Because the women I've seen riding horses in Ireland wear skirts and ride side-saddle, with both legs on one side of the horse."

"As I see them riding in your towns down by the river," she said, understanding. "Then your women don't know how to ride a horse properly. How could you possibly gallop side-saddle?"

Jamie smiled. "That's a good point. Should I go wake up Colin?"

She nodded. "I have permission from the elders to take you to Quebec City. It is a day's ride from here. That is the best place to go if you and Colin want to get to Montreal as quickly as possible."

"We'll do our best to keep up with you and your horse," answered Jamie, hoping that Colin would be up for walking such a long distance.

Tutuyak smiled and put two fingers in her mouth. She blasted out a short whistle. A muscular mare with a flaming auburn coat, saddled and ready to go, trotted around the corner of the longhouse and pulled up next to Dreamer..

Jamie was awed. "How did you do that?"

"I train them. It's part of what I do for my village."

"A woman of many talents," he said. "Very impressive. And what's her name?"

"Falcon."

Jamie eyed the horse. "Falcon, eh? Does she eat meat? Should I keep my distance?"

She sadly shook her head. "And I thought you were a well-educated boy. She's named Falcon because of her speed."

"That's good to know." He smiled as he walked up to the horse and let her sniff his hand. "So Falcon, do you really like to fly? Well, please take it easy on me. We Irish break easily."

Tutuyak threw back her long hair. "We'd better go."

Jamie grinned with excitement. "I'll go get Colin."

* * *

The village of Wendake, Tutuyak's village, looked quite different from the Irish sod and thatch-roofed homes with which Jamie was familiar. Most of these buildings were either built of log or clapboard. Jamie assumed that so many houses were made of sturdy wood because of the fact that Canada was brimming with huge forests. With their Irish forests already plundered, the peasants of Ireland did not have the luxury of lumber and had to build their homes from the only materials that they could find: sod from the peat bogs for the walls and the fields of hay for the thatched roof.

Tutuyak kept Colin in her lap while Jamie trotted close behind on Falcon. Wendake, she explained, was named after Tutuyak's ancestral land that once stood on the shores of Georgian Bay in Canada West. Those who were out chopping logs or tending to the plots of vegetables behind their homes looked up and smiled at her as she passed, some even shared a comment or two with her in a language Jamie did not understand. Those, however, who glanced at Jamie, eyed him with silent suspicion. He couldn't blame them. Hadn't he eyed the English back in Ireland with the same prejudiced stare? European strangers had taken their land and inflicted them with disease. It was Ireland all over again, wasn't it? What other welcome could he possibly expect? All he could do was nod a humble thank-you in French.

Soon, they left the village and trees once again curtained the sky above the dirt road. Tutuyak leaned forward and whispered something to Colin, then she suddenly whooped and kicked Dreamer in the ribs. The stallion launched into a blurring gallop. Jamie was nearly thrown from the saddle as Falcon lowered her head and launched herself forward to keep pace. Terrified, Jamie did everything in his power to keep from falling off the galloping mare. Breathing hard, the two horses flew through the emerald tunnel of vegetation. It slowly dawned on Jamie that there was a recognizable rhythm to the horse's gallop. His legs started to match the bouncing by raising himself up in the stirrups with each beat of the hooves. He hunched his shoulders like Tutuyak and leaned forward. The wind whistled past his cheeks. Jamie could see why the horse was named Falcon. He felt as if he were flying low to the ground like an iron ball just launched from a cannon. For just a moment, he forgot all of his troubles, tilted back his head, and enjoyed the ride.

They galloped the horses hard until the forest finally began to thin. Tutuyak reined in Dreamer and the snorting horses slowed once again to a bouncy trot. Jamie couldn't stop grinning. He gave Falcon a good pat on her sweaty neck.

"Thanks for the ride of a lifetime, girl."

Jamie took a deep breath to clear his head then took in his new surroundings. On either side of the path, small plots of land had been hacked out of the pristine forest. Tiny one-room log cabins had been erected in a corner of each plot. Summer gardens were growing in the tilled fields. Jamie had no doubt that these were newly arrived settlers. The homes resembled the tiny farmhouses that littered the Irish countryside, except they were made of wood instead of sod or stone.

Tutuyak pulled up next to Jamie. Colin, sitting in her lap, was smiling from ear to ear. Jamie reached over and poked him.

"I take it you enjoyed the galloping."

"Can we do that again, Tutuyak?' Colin asked, looking up. Jamie translated.

"The horses need a rest now," she explained. "And the road will get busier as we get closer to Quebec. Sorry, Colin. No more galloping."

They passed several more farms. These were larger and more established. Women were in the field, either pulling out weeds or planting late seeds. Men were busy splitting wood for the coming winter. As they passed, some of them stopped their work to stare at them as they trotted past.

"Why are they staring at us?" asked Jamie.

"Because we are riding together," she explained. "An Irish man and a Native woman are rarely seen together. There is a tradition of French men and Native women marrying, especially further north along the trading routes. Their descendants are called Métis. But you are obviously Irish, and I have an Irish child on my lap. They are trying to understand why we are together."

"Do they think we are married?" asked Jamie.

Tutuyak looked to him, questioningly. "Possibly. Why? Does that bother you?"

He smiled. "Actually, I barely know you, but from what I've experienced so far, you're the first woman I've ever met that I'd consider marrying."

Surprised, she blushed, then smiled. "Sorry, Jamie. You're too young for me … and I'm not leaving Canada to live a life with you in Ireland."

At the next farm, Jamie waved and shouted at the staring woodchopper, "*Bonjour! Comment allez-vous?* Isn't my wife beautiful?"

Confused, the farmer shook his head and went back to work.

She shoved him, laughing. "Stop it! They know me."

Several children were working with a dark-haired woman in the next field. The children all had flaming red hair and freckles.

"If I didn't know better, I'd say those kids were Irish."

"They are," she confirmed.

"But I read that once the Irish arrive in Canada, most settlers move either to Canada West or travel south to the United States."

"I believe you are right. But those children are likely orphans, like Colin."

"You mean they've been adopted?"

"Not necessarily. I understand that the French and the Irish share a common religion."

"We do. We're both Catholic."

"I heard that the French Catholic church is helping to find shelter for the Irish orphans that have recently arrived in Canada. Many end up as workers on farms and then after some time, they are adopted into the families themselves."

"That makes sense. At least the children will have some place to call home."

"Perhaps the same will happen for Colin," she suggested.

"I hope not," replied Jamie. "He has an extended family living on a farm in Canada West."

"Are they meeting you in Montreal as well?"

He shook his head. "No. I haven't figured out that part yet."

Wagons full of summer hay, carts carrying fresh produce, and walking travellers were joining them on the dirt road. Jamie, Tutuyak, and Colin continued to get stares from the passersby, but Jamie didn't notice. He was preoccupied with figuring out the next step of their journey. His thoughts were suddenly broken by a tug on his pant leg.

He looked down in surprise at a girl, perhaps eleven or twelve, jogging alongside his horse. She had her wild ginger hair tied back in a loose ponytail, and her ghostly grey eyes seemed to stare straight through him.

"You're Irish, aren't you?" she asked.

"Yes, I am," he offered.

"Are you going to Quebec?"

"Yes again."

"I could use a ride into town if you would be so kind."

Jamie eyed the girl. "You're being quite presumptuous, assuming I would even offer you a ride. In fact, I don't even own this horse."

"But I can help you if you give me a ride!" she panted, trying to keep pace.

"And why do you think that I need help?"

The girl, out of breath, slowed to a stop and watched the horse trot off. "Because you are a member of the Brotherhood! You must be lost because why else would someone from the Brotherhood be out here in the middle of nowhere?"

Jamie pulled back on the reins and Falcon came to an abrupt stop. Tutuyak brought the stallion around in a sharp turn in order to see what had happened. Jamie narrowed his eyes and stared at the girl who jogged up to him with surprising confidence.

"What did you just say?"

"You are a member of the Brotherhood, aren't you?"

"Why would you say that?"

She looked at him slyly. "Give me a ride and I'll tell you."

The conversation with the young girl was happening in English so Tutuyak looked to Jamie for an explanation. He sighed and explained. "Somehow, this girl knows something about who I am back in Ireland. She won't explain herself unless I give her a ride into Quebec. Is that all right if she rides on Falcon with me?"

Tutuyak smiled at the wild-eyed girl, probably appreciating her precociousness as did Jamie. "I'm sure Falcon wouldn't mind. Tell her to hop on."

Jamie nodded to the back of his horse. A big smile flashed across the young girl's face as he held out a hand and gave her a swing up. Tutuyak and Jamie coaxed their horses forward while Jamie took a deep breath in vexation. First, he'd promised to look after a lad barely out of diapers and now a young girl was hanging on to his waist. What was he, the Pied Piper of Hamlin?

"This will be a very short ride for you if I don't quickly hear answers to my questions," commanded Jamie. "Understood?"

"All right," she said.

"First, what's your name?"

"Bethany Fitzgerald, but you can call me Beth," she said rapidly. "My parents called me Bethany, but I always preferred the sound of Beth. It just has a better ring to it, don't you think? All my friends call me Beth and I know if I ever have children, I'll let them call themselves any name—"

"Whoa! Stop!" shouted Jamie. *Lord, this one is a talker.* "Bethany, I mean Beth, keep the answers simple or again, this will be a very short ride for you."

"Oh, of course. I'm sorry. My parents always said that I ran on at the mouth and it's something of a bad habit that I've been working very hard to improve. I'll do my best not to say more than I have to, but my Aunt Sinead always said it's important to answer questions accurately, so I will try to—"

"Beth!"

"Sorry."

"Let's talk about the Brotherhood. What made you mention that?"

"Oh, you see, I'm very observant, at least that's what my mother always said to me, and I noticed that your fourth finger had the ring of the Brotherhood."

He looked back, surprised. "How are you familiar with my ring?"

"Well, my uncle Patrick had a ring just like it back in Ireland, and sometimes he would have these meetings at our farmhouse."

"Patrick Fitzgerald," muttered Jamie. "In Longford?"

"Yes! That's my uncle, and our home is in Longford! I wasn't supposed to listen in on the meetings. I was supposed to be asleep. But my bedroom was right next to where the meetings took place and sometimes I would hear the word "Brotherhood" being used. Then I noticed that the men at the meetings all wore the same rings. I notice things like that. My mother always said that I'm very observant."

"Yes, you already said that," sighed Jamie. "So what did your keen hearing and observations tell you about the Brotherhood?"

"I don't know, really. They mentioned ways of helping the poor a lot and many funny words I didn't recognize. It was almost like they made up the words. Or maybe the words were some sort of secret code. Maybe they had made up their own language! Wouldn't that be amazing, being able to speak a language that no one else could understand? Just think of …"

"Should I let you off right now?" Jamie groaned.

"Sorry."

"Where are your parents?"

"They died on the crossing."

Jamie paused, his exasperation suddenly fading. "I'm sorry."

"I'm an orphan."

"So am I. And so is Colin, the boy on the other horse."

"And who is she? She's so pretty. I wish I could have long, straight black hair like her. I really hate my hair. It's so curly, it's like a bird's nest. At least that's what my mother always said. If I had a choice, I'd …"

"That's Tutuyak," interrupted Jamie. "She saved Colin and me from drowning and now she's helping us get to Quebec."

"Quebec? That's where I'm going!"

"I know! You've already told me. Why are you going there?"

She hesitated, looking at Jamie, deciding whether she could trust him. She leaned forward and whispered in his ear.

"I'm running away."

"Why?"

"Two months ago I was taken from an orphanage in Montreal by Monsieur and Madame Viette. They wanted me to help them with their farm. We took a ship back to here, and I was expected to work all day long in and around the farm without any sleep! The farmer's wife, Madame Viette, was really mean to me. She would make me rest on the manure pile at night to keep warm and beat me with a willow stick if I didn't work my fingers to the bone! Here, look at my side."

She hoisted up the side of her blouse. Nasty red welts crisscrossed her side and ribs.

Jamie winced. "That looks painful."

"That willow stick sure hurts. I think they beat me because they lost two sons in the rebellion against the British lords a few years ago. I'm not British, I'm Irish, but I don't think they understand the difference."

Jamie looked over his shoulder, shocked by what he had just heard. "What did you say? The people of Canada tried to rebel against British rule?"

She shrugged. "From what I heard, both Canada East and West tried to rebel. I don't think it went very well. After all, the British are still in charge here, aren't they?"

"I didn't hear about any rebellions in my readings," Jamie muttered.

"I think my adopted parents hated me because I speak English. They also wanted a boy. I know they did, but Father McGivney gave them me. Boys are harder to get, you know. Everyone thinks that they are better workers, although I tend to disagree. They may be stronger, but I've noticed they often lack the dedication."

"Did anyone know you were being beaten?"

"No. We lived in the woods by ourselves. I'm sure Father McGivney didn't know that they were going to be so mean to me when he gave me to them. I know lots of other orphans that were taken in by caring families. I wish I could have been one of them...."

"Wait ... do you know Montreal?"

She nodded. "Of course. I stayed in Montreal for almost a year before being sent off to the Viette farm."

"And do you know the city streets? Buildings? Everything?"

"Oh yes. I'm very good with directions, at least that's what Father McGivney said. He sent me out on lots of errands around the city before I was adopted. Did you know that Montreal was built on an island? There is water going all the way around it! I think an island is a very silly place to build a city if you ask me. If I were to build a city, I would—"

Jamie interrupted. "Beth Fitzgerald. How would you like to come to Montreal with us? I've lost all of my maps and I think a knowledgeable guide might come in handy."

Her eyes lit up. "Montreal? Really? With you? But that's where the orphanage is. Someone might recognize me."

"Well, if you know the city so well, you should be able to stay far away from the orphanage."

"That's true," she agreed. "And I think the further away I get from my adopted family, the less likely it will be for them to ever find me again. Montreal is so much bigger than Quebec. It has lots of stores and roads as well as places to hide. Did you know that Montreal is as far as you can sail down the St. Lawrence River, because just after the city there is a large set of rapids and ..."

This time Jamie didn't try and stop her ramblings for his mind was already swimming in thought. Jamie started to feel more positive about what he first imagined to be an impossible task. He finally felt that he might have a shot at finding his brother and the lost text.

Chapter 9

They reined in the horses at the top of a steep decline that wound down to the northern bank of the St. Lawrence River. Below, the mighty river was constricted to a narrow channel and several large ships lay anchored in its glistening waters. In a large dry dock directly below them, Jamie recognized the streamlined hull of the *Independence*, lying naked in the afternoon sun. The punctured section of hull that Jamie had helped repair during their crossing had been stripped right down to the ribbing. To the right of the dry dock lay a large town. In the centre of a collection of buildings stood a tall, thin, silver spire shining among the mishmash of shingled roofs. On the far side of town, a huge military fort stood prominently on top of a cliff, guarding the area from attack by either water or land.

Tutuyak stared down at the European settlement. "That is Quebec."

Jamie dismounted Falcon and then helped Beth to the ground. "Thank you for your help, Tutuyak."

"Thank you," added Colin, giving Tutuyak a squeeze around her waist.

Jamie took Colin in his arms and lifted him off the back of her horse. Tutuyak smiled at the three young Irish travellers, her long, black hair flowing freely in the breeze.

"You have a strong spirit, Jamie Galway. You have chosen a difficult path to follow. I saw it in a dream last night."

"You've been dreaming about me?" asked Jamie, with a wry smile.

"Dreams help us make sense of things we don't understand," Tutuyak replied. "And you are an interesting man."

Just then, a falcon screeched from above and winged its way past them on the warm summer breeze. Jamie's horse whinnied in response, and Jamie laughed.

"Falcon thinks he's a bird."

"Their spirits are intertwined," she explained. "And it is also a sign for you. The falcon will help lead you to where you need to go."

"As will my faith," he added.

"Be true to yourself."

"I'll miss you," he replied. "Are you sure you don't want to come along with us?"

"Are you two in love?" asked Beth. "I mean, you kind of remind me of my older sister and her bonny lad just before they kissed. Now that was really disgusting! If you're going to kiss, warn me, please, because I had to run inside when they did, so I didn't have to look at it, but then I tripped over a bucket and fell on my face. My sister yelled at me and said I wrecked the moment, which I really didn't mean to.…"

Jamie wrapped a hand around her mouth and shook his head. "Can you take this one back with you?"

"I'm afraid your paths are intertwined as well." She laughed. "As you say, *bonne chance*."

She gave the horse a kick and trotted away, leading Falcon along behind her. Jamie led Beth and Colin down the steep hill and into the heart of Quebec. It was not as big as Cork or Dublin, but it still had the rhythm of a bustling community. There were bakers and tailors, blacksmiths and printers, all selling their wares behind the seemingly endless clapboard or stone facades. The children hungrily eyed the grocer's stand with its shelves of fresh fish and vegetables as well as several bakeries with their steaming loaves of bread.

"I'm hungry," said Colin.

"Keep your chin up," Jamie replied, picking up the pace. "I'm sure there will be a meal waiting for us at the cathedral."

The church towered before them. The large stone face and slim silver spire were quite different from the older, squatter Catholic churches found scattered across Ireland. Ignoring the main doors to the sanctuary, Jamie led the children around to the side of the church and the walled cloisters. Entering through a small gateway, they strolled through dark hallways to a wooden door. Jamie grabbed hold of a large iron knocker and rapped it several times. After a moment, it swung open and a thin priest with greying hair and an open, kind face examined the three Irish youngsters.

"May I help you?" he asked in French.

"My name is Jamie Galway," Jamie replied in French, "I am with the Brotherhood of St. Patrick, and I was hoping that you might give my young friends and me food and lodging for the night."

As they shook hands, the priest looked down at the ring on his fourth finger.

"Yes, of course. I am Monsignor Baillargeon. Please, do come in. A member of the Brotherhood, you say? I didn't realize members could be so young."

The priest moved to the side, allowing Jamie and

the children to enter the church office. The room was a small and comfortable study with shelves of books, a writing desk, and a set of cushioned chairs facing a log-burning stone fireplace. Lying on a bearskin in front of the fireplace was a little boy about two years old playing with a set of painted wooden blocks. He had light brown hair with playful green eyes and a halo of freckles across his nose.

"Little Simon," said the priest to the young child, "it's past your bedtime."

The priest scooped up the young boy, tickled him until he giggled, then walked him to a narrow flight of stairs that led up to a loft.

"Please, have a seat by the fire. I will return as soon as I put Simon to bed."

Jamie and Beth thankfully collapsed onto the chairs. Colin's eyes were locked on the collection of colourful blocks on the bearskin. He looked up to Jamie, who nodded his approval. Flashing a smile, the young boy flung himself down on the soft fur and began building towers.

"I didn't think priests could have children," said Beth.

"They don't," agreed Jamie. "But I doubt Simon is his child. They didn't look anything like each other."

She lowered her voice. "Please don't tell him that I'm a runaway! He might return me back to the orphanage! Or worse, they might send me back to the farm!"

Jamie paused in thought. "How are you going to get another family if you don't tell them what happened to you at the farm? I can promise that I'll do everything I can so that you won't be sent back to the same family."

"I don't want another family."

"What are you going to do, then, if not go to another family?"

She looked pleadingly at Jamie. "I'd like to stay with you."

Jamie raised his eyebrows. "I can't adopt you, and even though I like you, Beth, I'm not in need of a little sister just at the moment."

"Please? Just for a little while? I can help you find your brother. Remember what Tutuyak said? Our paths will be intertwined!"

Jamie examined her pleading face. "The one thing I will need when I get to Montreal is a nanny to look after Colin while I search for my brother. Would you be able to do that for me?"

She nodded eagerly. Before she could reply, Monsignor Baillargeon stepped onto the landing and made his way down the steps to his waiting guests. He joined them in front of the fireplace. In fear of being found out, Beth fell into an unusual silence.

"Little Simon is such a blessing, but he does take his time to fall asleep."

"Is he an orphan?" asked Jamie.

"Yes. He's one of hundreds I have in my care. I'm doing everything I can to find them safe places with families in the church. Simon I'm especially fond of. It gives me a moment to imagine what life could have been like as a father if I hadn't chosen to do the work of God."

Beth purposely looked away, but Jamie smiled in admiration. "That is a huge but noble task. Hopefully all will end up with loving families."

"Amen," said Beth, not looking up.

"I normally take travellers such as yourselves to the church hall for dinner, but I would very much like to talk to you, Jamie, in private. Why don't I serve up some of the bean soup and bread I have in my kitchen for Beth and Colin so that the two of us can talk in here?"

Jamie translated for the children. Beth and Colin jumped to their feet. "Yes, please!"

Monsignor Baillargeon led them through a small doorway and into a simple kitchen. On top of a small wood stove sat a pot of bubbling soup. The priest scooped some of the savoury-smelling broth into four wooden bowls, then placed two of them on a small table along with a piece of bread and mugs of sweetened tea. After the priest had blessed the meal, the children dug in hungrily. Jamie and Monsignor Baillargeon took their bowls of soup and tea to the study, making themselves comfortable in front of the fireplace.

The priest pointed his spoon at the young man. "So you are a member of the Brotherhood? I have only heard of the Irish Brotherhood through quiet conversation. Is it true, then? There is a group protecting the ancient knowledge of our early Christian brothers in Ireland?"

Jamie nodded. "Much must remain secret, but yes, the ancient knowledge has been kept safe for almost a thousand years."

Monsignor Baillargeon took a sip of the hot soup and shook his head. "How is it possible for such secrecy? A thousand years! And the knowledge being kept secret is all the more impressive considering your people have had to suffer through countless invasions. That is a tremendous accomplishment. So what brings a member of the Brotherhood to my humble abode in Quebec?"

Jamie put down his bowl. "There has been a terrible accident. My brother Ryan, who is also a member of the Brotherhood, was attacked by British troops near Cork. He was then shipped off, unconscious, to Montreal. To make matters worse, he also had with him a priceless document that the Brotherhood desperately needs to retrieve. I'm here to track him down and bring them both back home."

The monsignor thought for a moment. "Are you sure he survived the crossing?"

"At this point …" Jamie paused, "I'm not sure of anything."

He put a hand on Jamie's shoulder. "Try not to worry, my friend. We will do whatever we can to help you find your brother."

Chapter 10

After a hearty breakfast of ham and eggs, Jamie, Beth, and Colin were led down the cobblestone streets by Monsignor Baillargeon to the Port of Quebec. Three ocean-going sailing ships and two steamships were moored to the largest quay. Even at this early hour, wooden crates and pallets of timber were being loaded by crane onto two of the sailing ships, preparing them for their return voyage to Europe. The bishop led them to the smaller of the two steamships. It actually looked more like a schooner than a steamship with its long, low hull and typical two-mast sailing rig. A huge single paddlewheel was attached to its side and a black smokestack rose up between the two masts. A young man about Jamie's age was busy securing the hatches when the bishop called up to him.

"Young man, is Captain Nadeau aboard?"

The young man stood up and waved to the priest. "He's in the wheelhouse preparing to depart, Monsignor. I will go and fetch him for you."

"*Merci beaucoup.*"

He turned to the children and smiled. "Captain Nadeau is a personal friend of mine. We went to school together."

A grey-haired man with a patch over one eye appeared on deck and strode to the railing.

"Maurice! What are you doing down here on the docks? Do you need passage to Montreal?"

"Yes, but not for myself. It's my young friends who would greatly appreciate such an offer."

"Irish orphans?" he asked suspiciously. "I've already lost my engineer to typhoid. I can't afford to lose anyone else."

"They are all healthy. You have my word. They are trying to track down a lost brother who has recently arrived in Montreal. It's important that they find him quickly. The church has the desire to do what it can in order to help them in their search. Can you give them passage, Benoit?"

"Well, since *the church* supports their important quest," sighed Nadeau to his friend, "who am I to stand in the way? You have permission to come aboard, children, but you'll be put to work. This isn't a pleasure boat!"

"Fair enough," agreed Jamie.

The monsignor waved. "Thank you, Benoit. Chess, next time you are in town?"

"I'll give you white to give you a fair chance!"

Monsignor Baillargeon laughed then turned to Jamie and the children. "God bless you and your search."

"And you, Monsignor," replied Jamie. "You are an inspiration for what you are trying to accomplish with all of the orphans."

They waved one last time to each other before Captain Nadeau broke up the final salutation and welcomed them aboard. He directed Jamie and Beth to the bow, where they were put to work pulling in the lines from the dock. The cook took Colin by the hand and led him into the galley where he would stay out of trouble. The ship's large paddle began to churn and the craft slipped away from the dock. As the ship adjusted its course upriver, the captain yelled over to the two newcomers.

"Do not think that just because you're friends with the monsignor you're travelling first class on my ship!" he shouted, his English heavily accented. "Girl, what is your name?"

"Beth, sir."

"Beth, go to the galley and help the cook prepare lunch."

"Yes, Captain."

Beth disappeared through the cabin door. The captain pointed his finger at Jamie.

"And you, do you have any mechanical sense in that head of yours?"

"Some, Captain. I have helped repair a steam locomotive."

"That's good enough for me. With Henri ill in Montreal, we're short men in the engine room. Go down below and try not to blow up my ship."

Jamie smiled. "Yes, Captain."

As Jamie made his way to the stern of the ship, he glanced to his right to get a better look at the massive paddlewheel. The monstrous paddlewheel was bolted firmly to the side and the entire ship leaned slightly to port due to its massive weight. He found an open hatch and slid down the ladder into the engine room. The engine room was dark, hot, and noisy. A huge iron boiler powered a single giant piston that pushed the rod that turned the paddlewheel. The young crew member he had first seen on the dock was now manning the iron gate to the boiler; feeding the giant machine's monstrous appetite with giant shovelfuls of coal.

"Can I give you a hand?" shouted Jamie.

The man wiped his brow and looked at the new-comer.

"Sure," he said, throwing over the shovel, which Jamie caught in midair. "Another ten throws of coal should do it."

The young man took a pull on a waterskin as Jamie finished stoking the glowing boiler. Jamie slammed the iron door shut with his foot, then looked up at the huge chugging piston.

"Not much different from a steam locomotive," Jamie said thoughtfully. "Instead of the steam pushing a piston that's attached to the drive wheel of a train, it pushes that … teeter-totter thing up there."

The man laughed. "That 'teeter-totter thing' is called a walking beam. My name's Theodore Carbonneau."

He stuck out a greasy hand. Jamie shook it. "Jamie Galway."

"You've worked steam locomotives?" asked Theodore, impressed.

"I helped out from time to time," replied Jamie, "just like I'm doing here."

"They're talking about building a steam railway from Quebec to Montreal and then all the way down to Portland, Maine," noted Theodore. "When they complete that line, the railways are going to put all of our ships out of business."

Jamie tapped the boiler with the shovel. "So with a working paddlewheel, why are there still masts on this ship?"

"It doesn't make sense for us to use the steam engine when we're going down current and with the wind. The sails are just as fast as using this old engine and we save the cost of fuel."

Jamie was surprised. "Really? What is the top speed of your ship?"

Theodore laughed. "Six knots on a good day. See this dial above the boiler? If the pressure inside the boiler goes higher than the red line, we might get another knot or two out of her, but there's a very good chance that we'd also blow the boiler to bits. You and I would then be instantly steamed to medium-well and put on the cook's menu."

Jamie laughed. "I don't have enough meat on me to feed a child, let alone the ship's crew. I want to help make this journey a quick one. The faster we get to Montreal, the faster I'll find my brother and go home."

Theodore raised his eyebrows in surprise. "Go back to where? Ireland?"

Jamie nodded. "Ireland."

"I've seen hundreds come to Canada from Ireland, but you're the first I've heard that wants to go back."

"I've got a love for fourth class ocean crossings," said Jamie, dryly. "I just can't get enough of them."

Theodore gave him a look of disbelief then laughed.

"Welcome to the crew, Jamie Galway. Grab that shovel and let's get back to work."

Chapter 11

Beth led Jamie and Colin through the maze of warehouses that lined the port and out into the busy streets that crisscrossed the heart of Montreal. Jamie couldn't stop himself from gawking at the passing people. The wealth of the colony was on display, as a sea of well-groomed men strode the streets in dapper suits, with islands of women in elegant high-necked dresses chatting among themselves on the street corners. He could hear both French and English being used by the crowds. Feeling self-conscious, Jamie realized that he had not washed his one and only outfit since nearly drowning in the St. Lawrence. He made a mental note to do something about his haggard look at the next opportunity. The three made quite the sorry sight among the well-off in this prosperous city.

Beth didn't seem bothered by her ragamuffin appearance as she ploughed her way through the crowds along St. James Street towards the taller buildings of Montreal. An earlier summer downpour had turned the wide dirt road they were following into a sea of mud. Horses and wagons fought hard through the rutted glop while pedestrians tried their best to stay on the wooden walkways that lined the storefronts. Jamie couldn't help but notice several adults scowling at them as they passed. Were they afraid of possible disease? Did they hate the fact they were so obviously Irish? Jamie wished he could somehow put their worries to rest. Meanwhile, Beth rambled on about the city before them.

"Down that alley is a butcher," explained Beth, "and if you're really lucky, he might leave out some nearly spoiled sausages in a bowl behind his shop. If you time it right, you can sneak a couple of links out of the bowl before he lets his dogs out for dinner. But cook them well over a fire, because if you don't, you'll get a gut ache that will floor you for a whole week! And right beside the butcher is the fire station. The firemen are really nice and sometimes spray water on me and the other kids if the weather gets too hot in the summer. And do you see that building? They sell the prettiest clothes in town. Just look at the window! I used to think that any woman who had enough money to shop in that store must be a princess. And the store we're passing right now, this is a general store. The nicest owners in the world own this store. Whenever I had an errand to run to this store, the owner or his wife would give me a small peppermint stick! That's the best-tasting candy in the whole world! It was — Hey! Where are you going, Jamie?"

Jamie made a sharp turn and pushed open the door to the general store. The children looked at each other, Beth shrugged, and they followed him in. A small bell jingled as the door opened. The store was filled with shelves of products ranging from canned food to every-day household items. A large woman appeared behind the counter. She had her hair pulled back in a bun and around her waist was a white, frilly apron.

"May I help you? Oh, it's you Beth! I haven't seen you in so long!"

"Hello, Mrs. McCormick," replied Beth.

"I wondered what had happened to my favourite delivery girl."

"The rest of my family finally arrived from Ireland," she lied. "These are my brothers, Jamie and Colin."

Mrs. McCormick smiled warmly at Beth's new family. "My Jamie, you are certainly a handsome fellow. And look at little Colin! Red cheeks and all! So how can I help you three?"

Jamie pointed to a glass container on the shelf behind her. "I would like to purchase three of your best peppermint sticks, please."

Mrs. McCormick winked at Beth. "Coming right up!"

She reached up to the shelf lined with glass jars. Each jar was filled with different flavours of mouth-watering candy. "Beth, I think your brother likes peppermint as well. You two *must* be related."

She held the jar out, and they each helped themselves to a slender peppermint stick. Colin was delighted. He placed one of the coins that Monsignor Baillargeon had given him on the table. "Thank you very much."

The woman reached into a drawer and gave Jamie back his change. "You're welcome. Come back anytime. And Beth, it's so good to finally see you with your brothers. You really are a dear. All the best!"

"Thank you!" Beth grinned.

"Bye!" said Colin.

"Thank you, Jamie," Beth said as she curled her tongue around the candy.

"I thought you would enjoy it. Now, which way to the immigration station?"

"It's not too much further. Come on!"

Colin and Beth's beaming faces lit up the dreary afternoon sky as they licked their sweet. Seeing the children munching on a colourful candy seemed to placate many in the passing crowd. Surely, such smiling children sucking away on a candy could not be carrying sickness. Jamie was pleased to have killed two birds with one stone.

Beth turned a corner and led them away from the busy business district. Ahead was another collection of large wooden warehouses. Workers moved in lines through the huge sliding doors behind which were rows of neatly stacked crates. Some were being hoisted onto waiting wagons, likely destined for the port and then destinations overseas.

"All these warehouses are full of stuff to be put on boats," she explained. "The docks are just over there. Those warehouses are full of crates and crates of beaver, bear, and fox fur. That building over there is so full with lumber that it reaches all the way up to the ceiling!"

"How do you know all of this?" queried Jamie.

"I ran messages to all of the owners of the warehouses, asking if they were interested in hiring some of the older orphans as workers. They used to take in quite a few of us, but when the sickness returned, they refused to hire any new immigrant children. That's why I was shipped off to a farm. They said my job had become pointless since no one was hiring anymore."

Jamie smiled. "But now you're back."

She took a lick of her peppermint stick and nodded. "Now I'm back! It feels so good to be back, seeing all of those shops. I didn't think I would ever see Montreal again, you know. When I was sent off, I thought I would be surrounded by trees, corn, and grumpy farmers for the rest of my life."

She wrapped her arms around Jamie and squeezed. "Thank you."

Surprised, Jamie managed to wiggle out of her embrace. He decided to change the subject.

"Are we close?"

Beth scrunched her face. "Actually, I can smell that we're close. Can't you?"

Jamie sniffed the afternoon air. A foul stench tickled his nostrils. He hadn't smelled such a disgusting aroma since his time in the hold of the *Independence*.

"Is it going to be bad?" he asked.

She nodded sadly. "Worse. It's just behind that big warehouse across the street."

Jamie stopped and bent down to talk to the children. "Listen, we're blessed that we are still healthy. I don't want either of you two taking a chance of getting sick by going to the station with me. I'll go by myself. Beth, I need you to look after Colin until I get back."

"I'm tired of walking," complained Colin.

"You get to have a rest right now," Jamie explained. "Beth will look after you."

"We can't wait here," commented Beth, looking warily at the nearby workers. "Someone will think we are runaway orphans, and they will send for the police. We might get caught and put back into an orphanage."

"All right, then," said Jamie. "What do you suggest?"

Beth thought for a moment. "I know a nearby hiding place — if it's still there. Follow me!"

She led them away from the water and the warehouses to a pile of broken and discarded crates at the edge of an undeveloped field. They walked around to the back of the pile. Almost hidden was a narrow entrance-way to the interior of the jagged mountain of wood. Dropping to her hands and knees, Beth crawled through the opening and disappeared from view. A couple of seconds later, her head reappeared, grinning.

"Yep, the burlap sacks are still in here, just like I left them! They make a great sleeping mat."

Jamie studied the pile of crates. "Are you sure it's safe?"

She tapped the crates affectionately. "They haven't moved this pile of boxes in over a year. It's one of my favourite hiding places. I can't see it moving by itself anytime soon. Come on, Colin! I'm a mama bear and you're the baby. Follow me into our cave!"

Colin laughed and together they growled and scurried on all fours into the makeshift bear cave. Beth glanced over her shoulder at Jamie, her face flashing concern and hope at the same time.

"Good luck."

Jamie bent over. "Hopefully there will be two of us when I return. Keep an eye on that baby bear of ours."

"I will."

Jamie retraced his steps back through the ware-houses. The stench had risen to an almost unbearable level by the time he'd circled around the final building and found the entranceway to the quarantine station. There were not one but three massive buildings stretch-ing out towards the bank of the St. Lawrence. Guarding the fenced perimeter of the buildings was a company of armed servicemen. As Jamie approached, the soldier guarding the main gate stepped forward.

"Good day, son," he said, in English. "How can I help you?"

"Are armed guards really necessary for a quarantine station?" asked Jamie. "Most are too sick to walk, let alone try to escape."

The soldier guffawed as if that was the funniest joke he had ever heard. "We're not here to keep the sick imprisoned. We're to keep the locals under control. There has been more than one threat to burn down the entire quarantine station along with the hundreds of sick inside. Wouldn't want that to happen now, would we?"

Jamie was stunned. "Are you serious? That would be mass murder!"

"Some in town would claim the sick Irish have already committed mass murder on us Canadians. We've had over a thousand people die this year in Montreal alone of typhoid and cholera. Thousands more have died in the rest of the colony! So yes, considering it's the immigrants bringing the sickness to Canada, some would rather not have any immigrants on our land, if you get my meaning. Have you just arrived here yourself?"

"Actually, I am a new arrival, but I'm healthy."

"Can I see your papers?"

Jamie passed him the papers Officer Keates had passed on to him before leaving the ship.

"Everything seems to be in order."

"I'm looking for my brother who arrived in Montreal on a ship a week or two ago. Can you help me find him?"

"Not me, but I can point you in the direction of someone who can. See that small building beside the next gate? There should be someone inside who can access the records of new arrivals."

Jamie thanked the officer and walked along the perimeter of the fence to the small administrative office building. As he made his way along the fence, he glanced over to the entrance of one of the quarantined buildings. He shuddered as he saw rows upon rows of the sick and dying. The lines of cots were full, so many of the quarantined simply made makeshift beds out of straw and lay on the floor. The pungent smell of death wafting from the fenced-in misery was mixed with the sobs, groans, and screams of the still living. He could see only a handful of brave nurses trying their best to care for the overwhelming number of quarantined immigrants.

"Out of the way, boy!"

Jamie stepped sideways as a large horse-drawn cart rumbled by. Behind the driver, the wooden cart was piled high with a mound of canvas-covered cargo. The cart hit a bump and a waxy arm suddenly dangled out over its wooden side. Jamie turned away, bent over, and took several slow, deep breaths, fighting with all his might not to be sick.

"Ryan is still alive," he whispered, fighting for control.

He slowly straightened himself, took the final steps toward the office, and opened the door. At the far end of the office, a bespectacled bookkeeper was scribbling notes into a thick-bound book. A ring of stubbly grey hair crowned his intense face. He glanced up from his paperwork.

"May I help you, son?"

"I truly hope so," replied Jamie. "I've just arrived from Ireland and I'm trying to track down my brother.

He arrived in Montreal about two weeks ago."

The administrator stared at him over his spectacles. "And you believe he is here in quarantine?"

"Actually, I'm not sure. All I know is that he arrived two weeks ago, and I thought quarantine would be as good a place as any to start looking for him."

"Well, let's see what I can do. His name, please?"

"Ryan Galway."

"And any other tidbits of information that might help me narrow down the search?"

"I know he was on board the *Carpathia*."

The clerk's eyebrows rose. "The *Carpathia*?"

Something in his voice sent a shiver down Jamie's spine. "Do you know of the ship?"

"It ran into quite a severe storm during the crossing. I heard it's being repaired here in Montreal before it can return to service."

"And the passengers?" asked Jamie, anxiously.

The administrator removed his glasses and tiredly rubbed the bridge of his nose. "You should brace yourself for some disturbing news, Mr. Galway. It was not a good scene on board the *Carpathia* when it arrived in the port of Montreal. A quarter of the passengers had died at sea. Some were washed overboard by the storm. Many who did survive the crossing were placed in quarantine while in very poor condition. I'm afraid some of those people have already passed away. But let me check the records. Certainly there must have been a few passengers who were able to walk away from the crossing."

Jamie had to force himself to breathe as the old man shuffled through the files beside his desk.

"Ryan Galway … that name seems familiar. There was an older man, an uncle, in here a couple of days ago looking for the same last name."

Jamie shook his head. "I'm afraid I don't have an uncle here in Montreal. In fact, I don't have any family in Canada, except for my brother."

"Strange. I could have sworn that was the name he enquired about. Galway, Galway…. Ah, here it is."

Finding the proper file, he flicked through the papers until his eyes came to rest on two attached sheets. He looked them over several times and then walked the file over to Jamie. He held it out for Jamie to inspect. The first was a death certificate with his brother's name on it. The second was a letter that Ryan had in his possession from a priest at Limerick Abbey. Jamie felt his blood turn to ice. The old man placed a comforting hand on the boy's shoulder.

"I'm sorry, son."

Chapter 12

Colin rubbed his eyes. "But I don't want to go to sleep. Tell me another story about the baby bear and the moose. The moose is so funny!"

"I think you've had enough stories for one night," said Beth, tucking him in with a burlap sack.

"Will you tell me another story tomorrow?"

Beth kissed him on the forehead. "You bet I will. I will have lots of stories for you after we help Jamie find his brother. Tomorrow, I'll tell you how Moose met the crafty old — Did you hear that?"

Colin listened. "Hear what?"

"I thought I heard something outside."

"Is it a bear?"

"No. Bears don't come into the city. You still have a lot to learn about Canada."

"What is it then?"

Beth hoped it wasn't a police officer. "Stay here and don't make a sound. I'll go find out."

She put a finger to her lips and Colin responded by hiding his freckled face under a sack. Beth quietly crawled through the maze of boxes until she reached the secret entrance and peered out into the cool evening air. Something rustled to her right. Moving as slowly as she dared, Beth slid low to the ground and peered around a broken crate from the Hudson's Bay Company.

Only an arm's length away was a tall man staring up

at the cloudy night sky. The stranger had a cloth sack in one hand. Her shock quickly evaporated when she recognized the familiar dark silhouette. She leapt to her feet.

"Jamie! Oh, it's you. I thought it might have been an animal, a police officer, or even worse, an orphanage inspector! I told Colin that on my signal we would have to make a run for it, should the need arise. He's been ever so good, little Colin. He first had a nap and since he woke up, I've been telling him stories that I had learned way back in —"

Beth stopped when she realized there was something very wrong. Even in the dark, she could tell that Jamie's eyes were red, hollow, and lifeless. He turned and she shivered when she realized that he was looking through her instead of at her. Instinctively, she reached out and wrapped her thin arms around him. She had seen that look too many times already in her short life.

"I'm so sorry, Jamie."

After a moment, she backed up, tears trickling down her cheek.

"Are you sure?" she asked. "Sometimes they make mistakes, you know. I've seen them do it."

He shook his head slowly. "They had a personal letter of Ryan's attached to the death certificate. He was the only one who could have had the letter. It had to have been him."

"I'm so sorry." She wiped away a tear with the back of her hand. "What do we do now?"

It took a moment for Jamie to fight through the pain and organize his thoughts. "Do you know of a place where the captains of ships like to go after a long voyage?"

"Most of the captains head down to the pub by the docks. I often went down there to see if any captains needed older orphans for crew. They mostly refused, thinking the orphans might be sick, and they didn't want to infect the rest of their crew. It's a scary place at night. It's better to go down there during the day."

"I need you to take me there right now."

"Why?"

"I need to track down the captain of the *Carpathia*."

Her eyes widened. "You're not going to do anything to him, are you?"

"I'd be lying if the thought hadn't crossed my mind."

A tear spilled down Beth's cheek. "Please don't! I don't want to see you go to jail, or worse, be killed!"

He smiled half-heartedly. "Don't worry. I'm a priest."

She took a step back. "Really?"

"Yes, I am. And I won't take you back to the orphanage. Being a priest also means that I won't hit anyone. Besides, I can think of much better ways to deal with scum like the captain of the *Carpathia*. But right now, all I need to do is go talk to him."

She glanced down the darkened street. "So we're going now?"

He nodded. "Go get Colin."

Beth dove in among the boxes, blew out the tiny candle, and led Colin through the wooden maze back to Jamie. Colin was tired. but he held his tongue, sensing an anger in Jamie that he had never felt before from his friend. As they walked along, Jamie passed out two small loaves of bread to the ravenous children, which they hungrily ate. Beth led them through several dark alleys until they reached the river's north bank.

The long docks that jutted out into the dark waters of the St. Lawrence River wrapped themselves around the berthed ships like the giant tentacles of a wooden sea monster. The children carefully made their way through a hive of filthy men loading timber into an enormous ship. Jamie then spied a smaller ship behind the one loading lumber. Pieces of the deck had been removed and its long masts were lying horizontally on the quay beside the hull. He felt a flash of rage as he read the name on the bow. *Carpathia*. The ship of death.

Across from the ships were a collection of several small, ramshackle buildings. Rough-looking men staggered out through the doors of the largest structure. They were holding on to each other for balance, and they threw slurred curses at the men who followed them out with crossed arms, watching them leave. A pair of women lurking in the shadows strutted up to the departing sailors and, putting their arms around the men's waists, joined them in their weaving walk back toward a collection of cheap hotels. Jamie wondered whether Beth was right. Was it wise for him to take young children into such a shady establishment? Now he had no choice. It was better to stick together than for him to leave the children outside in such a rough area.

They entered the noisy building from which the sailors staggered. Jamie gagged on the thick fog of tobacco smoke that filled the pub. Rude and raucous voices cut through the blue haze as a piano player banged away on an out-of-tune upright piano in the far corner. Several gruff sailors eyed Jamie and the children suspiciously as they stepped into the melee.

Cautiously, Jamie made his way through the rough crowd, and after checking to make sure the children were right behind him, tracked down the bartender.

"I'm looking for the captain of the *Carpathia*," Jamie shouted over the din of the unsavoury customers.

"Never heard of him or the ship." The bartender shrugged.

Jamie slid a few coins to the bartender. "I'm not here to cause trouble. I just want to ask him a few questions."

The bartender stared at Jamie for a few seconds then down at the children he had in tow. He shrugged and took the coins. "See the back table by the window? Black beard and cap. That's Captain Jack Chamberlain. He sails the *Carpathia*."

The bartender walked down the counter to serve another customer as Jamie turned and sized up the table in the corner. Four men sat around the small round table, ales in hand. All were older, broad-shouldered and craggy-faced, but only one wore a cap, the captain. The captain of the *Carpathia* was leading the conversation, arms waving in amusement and voice booming like thunder. As Jamie got closer, he could make out some details of the story.

"… and the wave, bigger than I had ever seen in my life, curled its ugly fangs above my bow. We went soaring up its face like we were going to be launched into the heavens itself! I tell you, it was the first time I had ever feared that the ship might actually flip nose over tail! Can you imagine the size of this wave? Then the crest came down on us in a torrent of white foam! Several of my best men were washed clear off the decks by the surge! I hung on to the wheel for dear bloody life and somehow survived as her bow finally slammed forward and we flew down the backside of the swell."

The conversation came to an abrupt halt as Jamie stepped up to the edge of the table. The men coldly stared at Jamie and the two children.

"Are you Jack Chamberlain, the captain of the *Carpathia*?" asked Jamie.

"What is it to you?" shot back a huge black-bearded man next to the captain.

"My brother, Ryan Galway, died on the ship during your last crossing," Jamie said, not taking his eyes off Captain Chamberlain.

The other three burly men pushed their chairs back slightly and clenched their fists above the table where Jamie could see them. Their icy stares left no doubt that they were capable of killing. They had dealt with vengeful relatives before.

Captain Chamberlain coolly raised his pipe to his mouth and took a puff. "Lots of people died on the crossing, lad. Shame about your brother."

"I'm not looking for trouble, Captain. I know I can't get him back, but I'm in desperate need of one of his possessions. He had with him an old Celtic book. It was with him in a leather pouch when he boarded your ship in Cork."

Jamie detected a flicker of recognition before the captain's face hardened once again.

"I don't think I can help you, lad. I'm not a land-lubbin' librarian."

His comrades relaxed slightly and gave a hearty chuckle at the captain's joke. Jamie placed his hand on the table and let drop a handful of large coins. He pushed the money towards the captain.

"This is all the money I have, Captain. It should buy you gentlemen at least a few more rounds before closing. Please, can you give me any idea of where that book might be?"

The captain collected the coins then rubbed his thick beard in thought. "Now that I think about it, I seem to recall my first officer mentioning that he found an old leather-bound book among the unclaimed items after the voyage. He said he might take it down to a bookseller on St. James Street to see if it had any value. What happened after that, I have no idea. That's all I can tell you, lad. Now get those snivelling children away from us. Who knows what diseases they may be carrying."

"Thank you, Captain," Jamie replied. "And one last thing. My brother, Ryan Galway. Can you tell me how he died?"

"Galway?" the captain repeated, looking up to the smoky rafters. "I recall him now. He died early on, typhoid I believe, second week of the voyage. Buried him at sea."

Jamie took a moment to digest the news then nodded to the cold-eyed captain.

"I saw your ship at the dock. Is it in for repairs?"

"Nay, lad. The old girl is being decommissioned, or put to rest you might say. She's too small to make good money doing the Atlantic run, so she's being sold for scrap."

"I'm sorry to hear that," Jamie lied. "So does that mean you're out of a job?"

"Me?" Captain Chamberlain guffawed. "Out of a job? Never! In fact, I've been promoted to the captain of the Western Shipping Line's newest ship! She's due to hit the waters in the town of Prescott in a few days' time. In fact, I've already insisted we name her the *Carpathia II*."

"Prescott? Isn't that above the rapids?"

The captain growled. "Give him a cigar! The lad knows his geography! It's a new route the company wants to open to Lake Ontario. I'll be taking the immigrants who disembark in Montreal onwards to the towns in Canada West. A very lucrative route it is, and they want their best manning the helm."

"The best at what?" one of the men snorted, and they all burst into raucous laughter.

Jamie nodded solemnly to the men, grabbed the children's hands, and led them out of the pub. As Jamie reached for the door handle, Captain Chamberlain's voice could be heard booming across the room.

"Men, I tell ya, nannies don't come any homelier than that."

The pub exploded into guffaws as the door slammed shut.

From his vantage point at the bar, Jonathon Wilkes watched Jamie Galway and the children leave the raucous pub. Wilkes took a sip from his ale and wondered how Galway had managed to get that little boy out of quarantine in such quick order. He congratulated himself on not taking any chances. A less detailed man might have waited for the end of the three-week quarantine before beginning the surveillance of the

Carpathia crew. His attention to detail, as always, was going to pay off in spades.

He knew if Galway was going to track down his brother, he was eventually going to have to come here and talk to the captain of the *Carpathia*. Wilkes had already checked the Montreal quarantine station for the Galway lad and while playing the part of a distressed uncle, had discovered the news of Ryan Galway's death. Without his brother, Jamie Galway would need to talk to the crew in order to track down the book. Sure enough, Galway showed up, just as planned. He didn't know who that ginger-headed girl was with him, but it didn't matter. By moving further down the bar and listening in, he managed to hear just enough conversation over the boisterous crowd. The boy was unknowingly going to lead him to the book and his next fortune. Since he didn't know what the book looked like, he would need the help of the young Irish priest to find it. He threw some coins on the bar and pushed away his half-empty mug.

"Leaving early tonight, Mr. Wilkes?" asked the bartender.

"I'm afraid so," he said, smiling. "I have some unfinished business to attend to."

Beth led them once again to St. James Street. The crowds were thin as the shops had already closed for the night. Jamie threw Colin up on his shoulders as they hurried to the address of a bookseller given to him by a passerby. Four streets later, they arrived at a tiny establishment with a store window displaying everything from popular author Charles Dickens to a new children's story titled "The Little Mermaid" by Hans Christian Andersen. The name "Kessler Books" was written in big letters on the awning above the door-way. Jamie was surprised the door was unlocked. As they stepped through the doorway, the distinct smell of musty old books brought Jamie right back to the old Irish church libraries where he'd completed his years of study. He glanced at shelves of reading material, recognizing many of the books as classics.

"Hello?" a deep, friendly voice called out from the backroom. "I'm sorry, we are presently closed for the night."

A man with wire-rimmed glasses and a thick, grey-ing goatee shuffled out the door. His eyes were kind and curious as he inspected the young shoppers.

"It's a bit of an emergency," explained Jamie. "I was hoping I could ask you a question before you close your shop."

"All right then," the shopkeeper replied in a friendly voice. "Does it have to do with a book?"

"Yes, it does, and I must say, sir, you have an impressive selection of reading material."

"Do you read quite a bit?" asked the old man.

"Whenever I can. The last story I read, *Wuthering Heights*, I found to be quite a passionate tale. It was so different from anything else I have ever read."

The old man looked at the boy over the steel rims of his glasses, surprised. "*Wuthering Heights* by Ellis Bell? An excellent read, but the first addition just arrived in my store a few weeks ago! Only stores in Britain would have had copies before me. Have you just arrived from overseas?"

Jamie managed a smile. "Very recently. In fact, that is why I'm here. Someone illegally removed property from my deceased brother during a recent crossing, and I'm desperate to reclaim the item. It is an old family heirloom. I was told it might have been brought to you recently for purchase."

"I'm so sorry to hear about your brother. I'll certainly try to help. Could you describe the book for me?"

"It's a very old book, centuries old, and one that would be extremely rare for anyone, especially in North America, to ever see outside of a museum. The scriptures within were written in a combination of Celtic and Latin. Most of it would probably seem like nonsense scribbling as the text was often written in code but the penmanship and artwork throughout the pages were outstanding. Have you seen it?"

The old man's eyes widened. "That was your book?"

Jamie felt a surge of relief. "Yes! You do have it, then!"

Mr. Kessler sat down on his stool in amazement. "I had never seen a book like yours in my entire life! It had the most exquisite penmanship I had ever seen, as if angels themselves had written the passages. It was an indescribable honour to hold such treasure in my unworthy hands. In fact, the term 'book' does not do it justice. It was a masterpiece made during the Irish Golden Years of the fifth or sixth century, if I'm not mistaken. Extremely rare; in fact, priceless would be a better word to describe it! I'd seen pictures of the Book of Kells that resides under lock and key in Dublin, Ireland. That might be the only text in the world that comes close to the workmanship I saw in your book."

Jamie anxiously stepped forward. "May I please see it?"

Mr. Kessler removed his glasses and gave his temples a rub. "Ah, yes. Now there we have a problem. After I bought the masterpiece for a ridiculously low price of a pound from that ignorant and foul-mouthed captain of the *Carpathia*, I took it to Angus McCall, the head librarian of the Canadian National Library at the parliament building. Together, we sat for hours and gazed in wonder at each and every beautiful page. McCall didn't hesitate in purchasing it for the National Library. He gave me a hundred pounds for the text, saying it was an absolute steal for the price, and said it would soon become the jewel of the Canadian collection! So that is where your book is residing right now I'm afraid — in the parliament building library."

Jamie's face fell. "Do you think Mr. McCall would return it to me?"

"With the proper documentation, I'm sure he will. He is merely a humble librarian, not a private collector. He understands the rights of ownership. But if I were you, I would look after that manuscript a little bit better. I know of collectors who would pay thousands of pounds, if not more, to have a piece like that in their private collection."

Jamie nodded. "Thank you for your help. Would Mr. McCall still be in the library at this hour?"

The old man chuckled. "Oh no, I think not. Haven't you heard? There are protests in front of the parliament buildings as we speak. It's been going on for hours. There's quite a bit of anger in the crowd, and rumour has it the parliament building might remain closed for days until the matter is resolved."

Jamie shook his head at his growing dilemma. "Why are the crowds so angry that they would have to close a House of Parliament?"

"You really aren't from around here, are you? The English-speaking loyalist population in Montreal is furious with the government. Our government wants to compensate those who lost property during the rebellion several years ago."

"Why is that so controversial?" asked Jamie.

"Because the law that just passed parliament states that those who were directly involved in the rebellion will also be compensated. Citizens loyal to the British crown are furious that their tax money will be spent compensating those who fought against British rule. Fearing violence from the mob, the government sent home all of its government workers, including those in the library."

Jamie frowned. "I can see why the crowd is angry."

"It's certainly a crazy situation," agreed the bookkeeper. "Being paid for trying to overthrow a government…. Who knows how it's all going to end? There's insanity all over Canada right now. If it's not the anger over new government laws, it's the irrational resentment towards Irish immigrants."

"I've heard that some want to burn down the quarantine station," added Jamie.

Mr. Kessler shook his head. "That's just the tip of the iceberg."

Mr. Kessler stepped behind his counter. He bent over and picked up a copy of the morning paper. He held it up for his visitors to see while he read the headline out loud.

"*Irish Immigrants in Toronto Incarcerated on Quay.* Can you believe it? A mob of angry citizens rounded up any and all the Irish they could find in Toronto, recent immigrants or already settled, sick or healthy. Then forced them at gunpoint to gather on the Toronto harbour quay! They then fenced them all in like a herd of cattle! They've told the penned-in Irish that they're no longer welcome in Canada and to go home. Can you believe that? It isn't the immigrants' fault that they've arrived in such a disastrous state of health. And what insanity could push them to gather as well the Irish who have lived here for years?"

Beth paled at the thought. "That's a terrible thing to do to anyone!"

Mr. Kessler went over and opened his till and returned to the small group. He gave Jamie a large sum of money.

"It's not fair that I'm the only one to profit from your beautiful book. This is my payment to you for giving me the honour to gaze upon its exquisite pages."

"Thank you," Jamie replied, glancing down at the generous amount of cash. "You don't have to do this."

"I insist, lad. It looks like you three could use a helping hand anyway. Perhaps you could put some of the money towards some new clothing. Is there anything else that I can do for you?"

"Actually, I could use some help with a map," Jamie said. "With the parliament building shut down, I was wondering if you could show me the location of the library within the parliament building. I want to get inside as quickly as possible when the building does reopen."

"Certainly. I can show you a map of the building. It's in the back of this book."

The bookkeeper pulled a book from the shelf and opened it up to a detailed diagram of a large building. He showed them the front entrance and the route through the corridors to get to the large rectangular-shaped library located just behind the House of Commons. After memorizing the map and thanking him once again for the money, Jamie led the children to the door.

"Good luck," called the bookseller as the door swung shut.

"He's a nice man," said Colin, waving goodbye.

"You're right," replied Beth. "He was very kind and helpful."

"Can you lead us to the parliament building?" Jamie asked her.

"Of course," replied Beth. "It's one of the biggest buildings in town. It's between Commissioners and Foundling Street, just three streets down and to the right."

Jamie looked down the street in the direction she was pointing. "Good. All right, here's the plan. I need you to take Colin to your friend at the general store. Tell her we need her to look after Colin for a few hours. You can give them this money for their troubles. Then meet me in front of the parliament, but stay well behind the protesters. We don't need to get mixed up in that mess. Understand?"

She nodded. Colin squeezed Jamie's hand. "But I don't want to go!" he protested.

Jamie got down on one knee. "I need you to be a big boy, Colin. Beth and I have to get my book back. You'll have fun at the store. In fact…." Jamie reached into his pocket, "here's a coin for another peppermint stick. You can have it while you wait for us."

Colin nodded. The thought of another peppermint stick in his hands had brightened his mood considerably.

Chapter 13

The imposing parliament of the province of Canada was two storeys high and constructed of well-cut stone. It sprawled out symmetrically in either direction from a central multi-stepped entranceway, with rows of windows giving government workers an impressive view of Montreal and the St. Lawrence River. Stretching out over two city blocks, the massive building dominated the core of Montreal.

But dominating the attention of the entire city and a handful of overwhelmed soldiers was not the impressive building itself, but an angry, torch-wielding crowd that swarmed the building's entrance like a colony of angry wasps protecting a hive. With a cheer, they stormed through the meagre line of soldiers and marched their way up the wide marble steps to the parliament building's carved oak doors. A man with a tall black hat climbed up onto the wide stone railing, opening his arms to the crowd below.

"Are we just going to sit back and let our elected representatives give our hard-earned tax dollars to those who fought against King and Country?"

"No!" shouted the crowd.

"What I have behind me is a mockery to the concept of democracy!" he continued. "We will not allow *our* government to reimburse those who fought against the crown with our tax money! Instead of paying the traitors compensation, send those conniving, treacherous criminals to jail and throw away the key!"

"Or better yet," someone else shouted, "line them up for their rightful punishment at the town stockade and shoot them!"

"Give them what they deserve!" another yelled.

The crowd went into a frenzied chant.

"We Want Justice! We Want Justice! We Want Justice!"

People started pelting the first-storey windows with sticks, rocks, and garbage. A window shattered under the hail of missiles, and the crowd cheered again.

Beth couldn't believe what she was seeing. In her young life, she had never seen so much anger in a crowd, and it scared her. She backed further away and nervously scanned the stores that faced the parliament building for a familiar face. As another shattering of glass echoed through the night air, Beth couldn't stay still any longer and decided to jog along the road, looking anxiously down every darkened alleyway and hidden doorway. Finally, she saw a shadowy figure waving to her. The man was sitting on a rain barrel at the side of a grey stone townhouse. She ran towards him and was relieved to find it was Jamie.

"Jamie, I'm scared! I've never seen a crowd like this before."

"This is getting uglier by the minute," agreed Jamie, eyeing the angry mass in front of the parliament building.

Beth noticed a large coil of rope, a sack, a big crowbar, some long sticks, and a large metal hook piled up beside the rain barrel.

"What's all that, Jamie?" she asked.

"Just a few items to help make our task a little bit easier," he said, glancing up at the dark sky while collecting the equipment. "Pick up the rope and follow me."

He led her away from the crowd and into the shadows of the alleys that paralleled the length of the parliament building. Eventually, they circled around to the side of the massive government building. Jamie then took her into a tight cul-de-sac between a work shed and a blacksmith's shop. After dropping the equipment on the ground, Jamie reached into the burlap bag and removed a stick of charcoal. He rubbed the stick into his palm until it became black with soot.

"Now don't move," he said to her.

He rubbed his blackened hand across the bridge of her nose until her splash of freckles became as dark as the night sky. He then smudged the charcoal across her bright cheeks and neck. She stared at him, curiously.

"What are you doing?"

"Darkening your skin so you won't be easily seen."

"Why?"

"We're going on a bit of an adventure. Have you ever been to the mountains?"

"I'm from Ireland, lived in Montreal, and worked on a farm. I've never seen more than a steep hill in my entire life, let alone the mountains … although I've always dreamed of the mountains. Wouldn't it be wonderful to live among beautiful peaks and valleys? I've always wanted to raise a herd of goats and a mountain would be—"

"Then this will be a first for you," interrupted Jamie. "And no more talking unless absolutely necessary.

There. That's better. All right, it's your turn to do me. Just be careful that you don't get any in my eyes."

She smiled as she took the charcoal. "This should be fun."

Soon the two of them looked as if they had just finished a shift in the coal mines. Night had draped its dark cloak over Montreal as the two quickly crossed the street and approached the back corner of the House of Parliament. Not a soul could be seen as the noisy demonstrations had attracted all the onlookers to the other side of the building. Moving behind a row of bushes to help conceal their location, Jamie inspected the rough texture of the stones and mortar with his fingertips. Satisfied, he threw the coil of rope over his shoulder and then turned to Beth, passing her the heavy bag, loaded with all of the other items.

"When I get to the top, I'll lower the rope down to you. Tie the bag to the rope and I'll bring it up to the roof first, then you'll be next. Just put your foot in the loop, hang on to the rope, and relax. I'll do all the work."

She looked up to the roofline far above their heads. "I'm going up there? What do I look like, a pigeon? And how are you going to get up?"

He smiled. "See you soon."

Jamie put his fingers into the crevices between the stones and started climbing. Beth was amazed to watch him move up the building so quickly. He had a natural rhythm to his climbing, like a spider feeling its way along its web. In only a few minutes, Jamie had disappeared from sight. All alone, she jumped in fright when a coil of rope suddenly thumped onto the ground next to her. She quickly tied the bag to the end of the rope, then gave the rope a tug. The bag jumped off the ground and raced skyward. It was only another minute before the rope fell to the ground a second time. She spied the loop that Jamie had put into the rope. Taking a deep breath, she put her boot into the loop, gave the rope another tug, and held on. The rope tightened and, before she knew it, she was rising off the ground.

She tried not to look down as the building slid past her body. Above, she watched the rope running past a thick stone protrusion that jutted out from the top of the wall. Her fingers were just about to get crushed by the edge of the stone overhang when she desperately made a grab with one hand over the stone lip. Thankfully, she was able to grab on to the rope once again before she lost her balance. As Beth continued to rise, she bent her body around the stone lip then threw her free leg up over the edge of the roof, allowing her body to roll onto its flat surface.

Jamie grabbed Beth by the shoulders. Concerned, he looked down at her still body, her eyes tightly closed.

"Are you hurt?"

"Please tell me going down is a lot easier than going up."

He laughed. "Much easier. Come on. We don't want to be up here any longer than we have to be."

Beth managed to get to her feet. As she stood up, she caught her breath at the sight of Montreal from up high. The entire town twinkled magically as if lit up by the light of a million tiny fireflies.

"Oh, Jamie. Montreal is beautiful! I didn't know things looked so different way up here."

"It *is* impressive," he said, glancing over the edge. "Now don't forget the rope."

The roof was unimaginably huge. They jogged perhaps a city block, or what Jamie guessed to be a third of the roof's entire length, before they came to a metal hatchway. Jamie lowered the bag and waited for Beth to catch up.

"So what are we doing here?" asked Beth, dropping the rope.

"I don't have time to wait for Canada to sort out all of their rebellion issues before I retrieve my book. Plus, I don't have the paperwork to prove the book is mine. So this is the quickest way I know to solve the problem."

Beth watched Jamie put a crowbar to the hatch. "You mean we're going to steal it?"

He glanced up, smiling. "Well, it's not really stealing if you already own it. I'm a priest you know. That would be breaking one of the Ten Commandments."

"But we're breaking into the parliament building! Surely that's in the commandments somewhere!"

"I'm doing this for the greater good."

She put her hands on her hips. "You are the strangest priest I have ever met."

"Can you lend me some of your muscle, Beth?" Jamie grunted. "This hatch is tougher than it looks."

Reluctantly, Beth grabbed on to the crowbar with Jamie and pulled. Suddenly, the hatch sprang open with a metallic snap as they tumbled backwards onto the roof's cold black tar. Lying together on their backs, trying to catch their breath, she glanced at him.

"We could go to jail for this."

"You're too young to go to jail, and I'll tell them I forced you to help me. I'll tell them that I wouldn't give you back the peppermint stick I took from you until you helped me break into the most important building in all of Canada."

She giggled. "With a story like that, I'm sure the judge will be very understanding."

Jamie jumped to his feet and helped her up. They peered down into the gaping hole in the roof. It was dark inside the vacant building, but Jamie and Beth could make out stacks and stacks of books.

"The library," Beth whispered.

"Hats off to Mr. Kessler. His drawing was right on the money. Hmm. Unfortunately, I don't see a ladder up here that we could lower down to the floor. It looks like I'm going to need your help again."

He quickly took the specially rigged poles he had brought with him and arranged them into a pyramid above the hatch. He then took two pulleys out of the bag, hooked one up to the apex of the pyramid and quickly threaded a rope through the other. Back and forth he went between the two pulleys until he gave the make-shift rigging a final tug. Satisfied, he passed the loose end of the rope to Beth.

"I'm going to need you to lower me down into the library."

"Me?" she cried. "I can't lift you, let alone lower you down by rope!"

"Don't worry," he said. "You have more than enough muscle in those farming arms of yours. The pulleys will make the task easy. We need to lower the bag down first anyway. With the crowbar in it, it's quite heavy, so you'll get a chance to practise."

He pulled out a pair of leather work gloves from his back pocket and passed them to her. Skeptically, she pulled the gloves on and took up the rope. Jamie then placed the crowbar back into the bag, hooked it up to the lower pulley, and dropped it through the hatch in the roof. Prepared to be thrown off her feet by the weight of the bag, Beth was amazed at how she could barely feel its heavy weight on the rope. She let out the rope slowly and the bag soon dropped out of sight.

"Wait, Beth," he said, taking the rope from her. "Make sure you wrap the rope around your back like this and then hold the rope on either side of your waist. Let it slowly slide through your gloves. This way you will always keep control of the rope. That's it. Good! We'll turn you into a mountaineer yet."

"When have you been in the mountains?" she asked.

"While in France, I visited an abbey high in the French Alps."

"Oh," she muttered as she let more rope slide through her hands.

Jamie peered through the hatch. It took a while before the bag finally clunked onto the marble floor below.

"You did it. Now play out a little more rope and the bag will fall off the hook. There! Good! Now haul the hook back up!"

After a minute of hauling rope, Beth raised the lower pulley and hook back up through the hatch. Jamie didn't hesitate to sit on the edge of the hatch, add a length of looped rope to the hook and then place his foot in the loop. He looked over to his young friend, who was turning pale with fright.

"I don't think I can do this," she muttered. Her knees were shaking. "I'm going to kill you!"

"I know you can do this, Beth. I need that book. Without it, my life is meaningless. In fact, all of Ireland needs that book. If I don't get it, I might as well die tonight, right here and now. But don't worry, I promise that this rig is safe. Really, it won't be any different from lowering the bag down to the floor. Just think of me as a gigantic sack of potatoes."

Beth managed a giggle and nodded weakly. "I'm ready, I guess."

Jamie lowered himself into the hatch. The wooden pyramid groaned at the added weight and Beth had to dig her toes into the raised lip of the hatch, but everything held. Slowly, she eased her grip on the rope and she could feel the coarse fibres slide sideways against her back. Amazingly, Jamie was right. It really wasn't that much worse than lowering the bag. After a minute of slowly releasing the line through her gloved hands, the rope finally went slack. She didn't dare let go, however, until she felt several tugs from below. Taking a deep breath, she let the rope fall to her feet. She clambered over to the edge of the hatch and looked down. In the darkness, she could see Jamie waving at her. She waved back and watched as he disappeared out of view. Perhaps it was the tremendous excitement of the moment or the concentration required to track Jamie through the distant library gloom, but Beth was completely unaware of another presence joining them on the rooftop, and that it was moving silently towards her.

Jamie had been in enough libraries to know where to start his search. He moved quickly through the gloom.

He ignored the rows of periodicals and rushed past the long oak study tables. There! He spied a glass door hiding among the impressive stacks of printed knowledge. As he approached, he could make out a sign on the door: ANGUS MCCALL — HEAD LIBRARIAN. Taking his crowbar, he unceremoniously shoved it into the door jamb and heaved. The wooden frame made an ear-splitting crack and the door popped open. It only took a brief search before he found an oil lamp sitting on a corner table. He quickly lit it and his heart fell. The office was far bigger than he'd expected, and there were books everywhere. There was a large mahogany desk to the left while rows upon rows of cupboards and cabinets lined the remaining walls. Where should he start looking?

Take a moment to think this through, Jamie thought to himself. *If I was the head librarian, where would I store a priceless item that I just recently purchased?*

He examined the office again.

I would keep it as close to my workplace as possible.

Jamie went straight to the desk. All of the drawers were locked. It was a beautiful piece of furniture, but Jamie didn't hesitate to jam the crowbar into the first drawer and send splinters of mahogany flying through the air, snapping the drawer open. He rummaged through numerous papers and letters. Nothing. He broke open the remaining two drawers with the same frustrating results. Where should he look next?

Suddenly, a loud bang erupted from somewhere deep in the building. Jamie froze. He ran back out into the main library. In the distance he could hear voices … angry voices. His worst fears were realized when he heard thunderous footsteps rushing down the hallway. Torchlight suddenly flickered through the cracks beneath the library's locked oak doors. He sprinted back to the rope, the hatch far above.

"Beth!"

"I'm here!"

"There are people inside the building! I think the mob has broken in through the front door! Quickly! Pull up the rope and keep it up with you until I call for it! Then close the hatch almost all the way. We can't let anyone know we're here! Understand?"

"All right!" she shouted back.

The rope and pulley quickly ascended up toward the ceiling.

Jamie ran back into the office. As quickly as he could, he started to snap open the nearest locked cupboards. Files, more letters, and books that were in need of repair filled the shelves. Just as he was about to jam the crowbar into a smaller, locked cabinet, the library's doors exploded open and the vast room was inundated with a tsunami of enraged shouts and flickering firelight. Jamie blew out the lamp and dove under the desk. He could hear men shouting instructions. People were knocking over shelves and throwing irreplaceable collections onto the marble floor. Then, to Jamie's horror, the dim flickering light in the library began to grow in intensity.

The mob was setting fire to the library! This was insanity! Jamie had always bemoaned the fact that the great library of Alexandria had been destroyed by pillaging Roman armies in what was considered the greatest loss of ancient knowledge in human history. He had always chalked up such insanity to the fact that it had happened almost two thousand years ago.

He had assumed that human nature had grown and matured since then, that a repeat of the destruction of the library of Alexandria could never be repeated in today's nineteenth century.

But at this very moment, he was being proven wrong. The records of an entire nation were being put to the torch! Suddenly, it became crystal clear to Jamie why the ancient Irish had kept their sacred texts hidden from the general population. If a modern society could do this to a library, it didn't deserve the irreplaceable works of knowledge and art that were hidden in the Irish countryside. His thoughts were interrupted as a large man stomped into the office. He threw a torch onto the pile of papers and books that Jamie had made next to the desk and then ran for the hallway. The clamour of insanity faded away from the library and was slowly replaced by a much more ominous sound, the snaps and crackles of a growing fire. Jamie crawled out from under the desk and got to his feet. He almost died from the horror of what he saw.

Tongues of fire were already licking bound volumes of reading material all over the library. Centuries of written records and Canadian history were turning to smouldering ash. The thrown torch had also set off a small fire in the office. Jamie whipped the sweater off his body and used it to whack the flames. With a combination of determination and panic, he managed to extinguish the fire in the office, but there was nothing he could do about the rest of the library.

Desperately, Jamie returned to fetch the crowbar, and with it he cracked open the small cupboard. Loose papers filled the shelves. He moved on to the next locked cabinet. The crowbar threw the doors open wide, and Jamie collapsed in relief. There, sitting on the bottom shelf, was his beautiful, leather-bound Irish text. He plucked it gingerly off the shelf and placed it against his chest, wrapped his arms around it, and wept. He wept for his brother. He wept for Ireland. He wept for the destruction of knowledge happening all around him.

The collapse of a burning shelf of books snapped Jamie back to reality. He wrapped up the text in a special oilskin, then turned to leave the office. But suddenly more voices echoed from the outer hallway. He dove behind a shelf next to the office as several men ran in through the library doors, aghast at the sight of the growing inferno.

"Quick! Grab what you can! We must save some of these volumes!"

Jamie ducked as about a half-dozen men poured into the library, filling their arms with irreplaceable volumes of Canadian history.

"Mr. Curran! I hear a gas leak!"

"Then everyone out! We have to leave before this whole building goes up in a ball of flames!"

The men staggered out of the library, their arms filled with as many books as they could carry. Jamie tucked his book into his shirt, and then ran through the burning periodicals until he was below the hatch. He looked up to the glowing ceiling.

"Beth! Lower the rope!"

Beth opened the hatch and peered over the edge. "Oh, Jamie! Thank heavens you're safe! We have to hurry! There's fire everywhere!"

The pulley quickly descended to the floor. Jamie clipped on the bag.

"Quickly, Beth! Take the bag up, then send the pulley down again for me!"

"Why the bag? Why not you?"

"We need the bag!" he shouted. "Hurry!"

The bag shot upwards and disappeared through the hatch. He waited impatiently for the pulley to return. Instead of the seeing the pulley reappear above his head, Jamie heard a terrified scream. Shadows moved on the roof, but the small hatch didn't allow Jamie the chance to see any other detail.

"Beth! What's going on? What's wrong?"

Suddenly, instead of the pulley, Beth herself fell through the hatch screaming and tumbled through the air towards the floor far below.

With the bag in hand, Wilkes ran for the edge of the building. He knew it would be only a matter of seconds before the building exploded like a giant bomb. He had to get off this roof or he would not be seeing that huge payday that was so tantalizingly close now that he finally had the book in his hands.

He didn't much like the thought of killing a child, but if it meant he could leave undetected with one of the most valuable books in the world in his possession, then it was an easy choice for him to make. Besides, a fall from that height would be a quick and painless death for her. He looked at it as doing her a favour, compared to the other options he could have chosen for her.

He placed the bag down at the edge of the roof. He didn't need all of the climbing equipment in the bag for his escape. He had already rigged up his own escape rope, which lay just ahead. He was an expert climber, and he could descend the wall in a blink of an eye. All he needed now was the book. He ripped open the bag and began to pull out the equipment. He threw aside the crowbar, the hook, two more coils of rope, and some clothes. His hands searched for more. The bag was empty! Where was the book! He turned the entire bag inside out in desperation. From the top of the parliament building, Jonathon Wilkes cried out in unbridled anger.

"No!"

Chapter 14

Jamie watched in horror as Beth fell through the hatch high in the ceiling towards the hard marble floor below. He threw himself directly underneath her falling body, extending his arms to catch her, bending his knees and readying himself for the impact.

Two things saved both Jamie and Beth from major injury. Beth was as light as a feather from her mistreatment on the farm, but still, the violent impact of her body knocked Jamie violently backwards. The other miracle occurred when their bodies crashed not onto the marble floor but into a large pile of leather-bound books that had been knocked over by the earlier rampaging crowd. As Beth landed hard into Jamie's chest, the careening couple sent volumes of statistical reports flying in all directions.

For a moment, the two of them lay stunned on the floor. Ignoring the fiery pain from his shoulder and with the wind still knocked out of him, Jamie managed to roll awkwardly onto his hands and knees. Beth lay beside him. She wasn't moving. He crossed himself, said a prayer to the Virgin Mary for help and, with a shaking hand, touched her face. Just then, a massive explosion shook the entire building. Bits of plaster fell from the ceiling like a violent summer hailstorm. Jamie threw himself over Beth to protect her from the crashing debris. His back was pelted with chunks of plaster. In the remaining dust cloud, he pulled himself off and checked her again. He sighed in relief when she moaned and her eyes fluttered to life.

"Beth! Thank God! Are you all right?"

Beth looked around, confused. "What happened? Where am I?"

"You fell through the hatch and now you're in the library with me! This whole place is about to blow up! We have to get out of here!"

She sat bolt upright, remembering, then flinched in pain. She grabbed her shoulder, her eyes wide. "Someone took your bag from me, then threw me down the hatch! Jamie, he tried to kill me!"

He took her hand and helped her to her feet.

"The rope ..." she looked up.

"It's gone. We can't go back up. We'll have to find another way out. Come on!"

A second, closer explosion ripped through the air. They crashed hard into a bookshelf but kept their feet and made it to the library entrance. They stared down the hallways, dismayed at the growing inferno. The tongues of flame seemed to be coming at them from all directions.

"Which is the fastest way out of here?" he muttered.

"Is that the main entrance down there?" she pointed.

"Good!" Jamie agreed. "Let's go!"

Together they ran hand in hand through the burning hallway. They coughed as the heat and smoke burned their lungs. The main entrance still seemed impossibly far away when a third, larger explosion ripped through the building. A giant fireball hurtled out of a door halfway between them and the main entrance. Huge sections of the upper floor collapsed like an avalanche into the hall. Beth screamed as Jamie pulled her sideways through an open doorway. As he landed, he kicked the door closed with his feet. A sudden whoosh of heat and light sizzled past the glass door. They gasped for breath on the relatively cool floor of the darkened office.

"It's the gas lines," coughed Jamie. "The fire is igniting each one as it moves through the building. We don't have much time before the gas lines at this end of the building ignite as well."

"Can we make it to the entrance?"

"I don't think so. We need to move back toward the library and find an office with a window. We'll smash it and hope the fire crews can get us down."

They staggered to their feet. Jamie felt the door. It was warm but they had no choice. He once again took her hand. Beth was scared, but Jamie admired the look of determination on her face.

"Are you ready?"

She nodded. He pulled the door open, and they both gasped at the heat that smacked them as they crawled into the collapsed hallway. They backtracked toward the library and Jamie grabbed the first handle they came to. He yelped in pain.

"Can't go in there. Keep moving!"

He tried a door on the other side of the hallway. The handle was just as hot. Beth tugged on his shirt. Through the glass, they could see that all of the offices were aflame.

"The stairs!" she cried.

Jamie and Beth sprinted for the staircase. They descended as fast as their legs could carry them through the thickening smoke. When they reached the ground level, they were horrified to see it was even worse than upstairs. Beautifully carved wood panelling glowed with tongues of fire. Flames licked at the crumbling ceiling. Smouldering plaster rained down onto the floor.

Beth yanked on his arm. "Keep going down!"

"But that's the basement!" Jamie protested. "There's no way out!"

She squeezed his hand. "I have an idea! It might be our only chance!"

Left with no choice, Jamie followed her down into the darkened basement. The air was slightly cooler and much less smoky. They were both drenched in sweat and soot. Jamie took a second to gather his thoughts. He figured they only had a precious minute or two before the growing inferno collapsed the entire structure down upon their heads.

"So what's your idea?" he asked.

Beth was already on her hands and knees, crawling around, feeling the floor. "Help me look for it!"

He joined her on the floor. "What exactly are we looking for?"

"This!" She banged her hand down on a metal grate.

Jamie looked at her, confused. "Why? So we can go deeper?"

"Exactly."

Jamie shook his head. "But what good is a hole in the ground going to be to us if the building collapses? It will only trap us down here."

"Or," she gasped, "it might be another way out of the building. Come on! Help me lift the grate."

With no choice, he helped her grab hold of the iron rods in the grate. Together, they managed to lift the heavy grate and slide it to the side.

Beth smiled, waved, and jumped into the circular hole feet first. With no other choice, Jamie stuck his own feet into the hole in the floor and lowered himself down as well. He fell almost six feet but landed on his hands and knees in the bottom of what appeared to be a stone well. He was all alone in the pitch darkness.

"Beth? Where are you?"

"Over here."

Her voice echoed to his left. In the gloom, he could just make out a narrow pipe leading out of the well.

"Come on, follow me!" he could hear her say from inside the pipe.

Jamie lowered his head and followed her voice into the tight confines of the pipe. Crawling and slipping, Jamie made his way through the slimy enclosure as best he could. The pipe suddenly took a turn downwards. Jamie's hand slipped in the muck. Suddenly sliding head first and out of control, Jamie yelled as he was launched into the air, crashing down hard into a flowing stream of ankle-deep water.

"Jamie! Are you all right?"

In the pitch darkness, Jamie felt Beth's hands on his leg. He moaned from the impact as his side exploded with pain. Gritting his teeth, he rolled over into a sitting position. Wherever they were, this dark place smelled awful.

"I think I'll live," he groaned. "Where are we?"

"I think this is Montreal's main sewer," she answered.

"A sewer? You mean an underground canal for taking away rain and human waste? I've heard of them recently being built in some cities, but I've never actually been in a town with a sewer before."

"Montreal built their first sewer a few years ago. I know it stinks in here, but it's safe. My friends and I sometimes hide in it to escape the police, in case they're in the mood for tracking down orphan runaways. They never bother to follow us in here."

"I can smell why."

She gave him a shove. "Hey, at least we're safe now, right?"

He paused and lowered his nose near the water. He started to gag.

"What is it?" she asked.

"I don't think we're safe at all. Gas is heavier than air, and I think it's building up inside the sewer. The gas line above us must have been ruptured in the fire and now the gas is sinking down into the sewer. One spark from above and this sewer turns into an inferno. We have to get out of here! Which way do we go?"

"We follow the running water," she explained. "It will take us to the river."

Jamie felt the water flowing by his boots with his fingertips. "Then it's this way!"

They reached for each other's hand in the dark and then ran as fast as their legs could carry them through the huge cobblestone pipe. Luckily for them it was as straight as an arrow.

"When does this thing end?" asked Jamie.

"I don't know! I've never been this far inside it!"

Far behind them, they heard an ominous *whoosh!* A flash of yellow light was followed by an orange fireball rushing up the sewer towards them at unimaginable speed!

"Run faster!" screamed Jamie.

But it was too late. A huge pressure wave knocked

Jamie and Beth right off their feet. Fortunately, they had almost made it to the end of the open sewer. The long, straight underground structure acted like a giant rifle barrel as Jamie and Beth were launched out the end of the sewer like a pair of human bullets. A gigantic fireball burst out of the pipe right behind them, igniting the night sky in a stunning explosion.

Tumbling head over heels, Jamie and Beth landed with tremendous splashes in the St. Pierre River, the river just deep enough to soften their spectacular landing. Jamie thrashed about in the water until he could finally find his feet. Trying to keep his balance in the waist-deep water, he spun in all directions.

"Beth? Beth! Where are you?" Jamie yelled.

Jamie searched frantically in the water. He saw some ripples nearby. He splashed over as fast as his legs could carry him and dove into the water. Grabbing hold, he hauled her up off the bottom of the river. She gagged and coughed, grabbing hold of him in a panicked embrace.

"I ... I didn't know which way was up!" she spluttered.

"It's all right," he said, hugging her. "You're all right."

He carefully put her down feet first in the river, holding on to her arm until she got her balance. Much to Jamie's surprise, she suddenly burst out in laughter.

"I can't believe that we're still alive!"

"Those are the prettiest stars I've ever seen," said Jamie, looking up at the clearing sky.

She squeezed him. "Thank you so much for catching me. I would have been dead in the library if you hadn't broken my fall."

"We would both have been dead if you hadn't thought of the sewer."

They sloshed their way toward the nearby river-bank. "I still can't believe what happened to you in the library. Who could have been on the roof with us and then intentionally tried to kill you by throwing you through the hatch?"

Beth tried to collect her thoughts as they finally stepped onto dry land and collapsed together on a large, flat rock.

"I only caught a glimpse of him, Jamie. He was tall and thin, with a long, hooked nose like an eagle. Before I knew he was there, he had snatched the bag out of my hand. In the next instant, I had been whisked off the ground, lifted over the hatch, and thrown down into the fire. It all happened so quickly. I saw him as I fell through the hatch. I'll never forget that cold face staring down at me from above."

Jamie shook his head. "You say he grabbed the bag first. That must have been what he was after. He must have been trying to steal the bag, and then decided to murder you so there would be no witnesses."

"Was he after your book?"

"It seems to be the only thing that makes sense, but how could he have known about it?" asked Jamie.

"You could have been followed," she offered.

"All the way from Ireland?" said Jamie, pondering the thought. "There have always been treasure hunters sniffing around the Brotherhood, hoping to find more Celtic masterpieces. I suppose it's possible. In fact, that's why my brother and I had to move the book to Cork in the first place. Well, at least your killer believes we're dead in the fire. It will be the last time we'll have to worry about him."

Beth leaned up against him. "I'm so sorry, Jamie.

You've lost your brother and now your book! This has been a complete nightmare for you."

"Not a complete nightmare," countered Jamie. "I met you and Colin."

"Thank you," she said, smiling.

"And I also still have this."

Jamie unbuttoned his thick shirt and after reaching down inside, he pulled out a large, folded, waterproof oil-cloth. Beth caught her breath and leaned in closer as Jamie unfolded the cloth. A beautifully bound leather book materialized on his lap.

"Your book?" she gasped.

"Once I had it in my hands, do you think I'd ever separate myself from it again?"

Beth laughed. "I guess not."

Jamie smiled. "Do you want to see it?"

She nodded enthusiastically. Jamie carefully wiped his hands then opened the cover. By the light of the half moon high overhead, she gasped at the first page. The intricate Celtic designs and words blended into an exquisite piece of colourful artwork. As he carefully turned each page, Beth was awed by the wonderful depictions of animals, trees, and symbols.

"I wish I could read. I want to know what it says!"

"You would have to know Latin and ancient Celtic to read the text, I'm afraid."

"And the story has the clue for finding the treasure?"

"Yes, but even I don't know what it is exactly. You would need the other keys back in Ireland in order to decipher it properly."

On turning the final page, much to Jamie's surprise, a single piece of paper fluttered down to his feet. He carefully closed the book, picked up the mysterious paper, and unfolded it. By the moonlight, it appeared to be a series of sketches. Beth could see a bunch of rectangles, side by side, ascending in a slightly staggered pattern. Lines and numbers were sprinkled around the diagram. In the corner, a picture of a ship had been sketched into one of the lower rectangles. At the top was the title *How to Get a Ship over a Mountain*. Jamie's eyes scanned the sheet several times, and then he suddenly jumped to his feet.

"I don't believe this!"

"What is it?"

"I don't believe this!" Jamie pumped his fist and whooped with joy.

Beth grabbed his arm. "Tell me! What does the paper mean?"

"I'm not sure, exactly, but I know this is my brother's sketch! And look here at the bottom. Do you see it?"

He tapped the paper with his trembling finger.

"Those numbers?"

"Yes, Beth! It's a date! He dates all of his work! And this sketch was dated only *three days* before the *Carpathia* reached Montreal. Don't you see?! The captain said he died just two weeks into the crossing. This proves he was alive just before reaching Montreal! Therefore, there's a chance he might still be alive! The captain made a mistake in identifying a dead body!"

She threw her arms around him. "I'm so happy for you!"

"Come on!" he said, bursting with excitement. "We need to get back to Montreal!"

After wrapping up the book and tucking it back safely into his shirt, Jamie and Beth strode away from the river and back into the city. The glow of the still-burning parliament building illuminated the centre of town in an eerie yellow light, as if the city were celebrating some ancient pagan event with a giant bonfire. The bells of fire wagons could be heard congregating to do battle with the towering flames that lit up the early-morning air. To the east, the sky was just starting to glow a faint crimson, signalling the start of a new day.

Upon reaching the main road, Jamie reached into his pocket and gave Beth a handful of coins. "Take the money and go get Colin. Give your friend an extra tip for keeping him overnight, then buy some breakfast for the three of us. I'll meet you back at the bookstore in an hour. We have some research to do."

Beth was just about to run off on her errand, but instead turned to face Jamie, her face beaming with hope. She bounced up and down a few times then flew towards him and wrapped her arms around him in excitement.

"I'm so happy for you! Ryan might still be alive!"

Then, with the flash of a smile, Beth disappeared into the brightening dawn.

Chapter 15

Jamie towelled off his hair and then threw on the brand new shirt he had purchased a day earlier from a St. Denis clothing store. The face in the mirror staring back at him looked completely different from the one that had been there only minutes earlier. Gone were the sweat-stained smears of soot and charcoal across his face. His hair, instead of smelling of smoke and sewer, glowed with a fresh, soapy scent that he hadn't experienced in a very long time. In a way, it felt as if he had almost washed away the memories of last night's horrific fire and Beth's near murder.

He left the bathroom, walked down the short hallway of the small but tidy apartment, and then opened the door that led into the back of the small bookstore. Mr. Kessler and Beth were poring over books on a table while Colin sat on the floor with a paper and pencil, having fun drawing pictures of the huge fire he had seen from the window of his sitter's home in the early hours of the morning. Jamie pulled up a chair.

"I feel as if I've been reborn."

"I hadn't had a proper bath in so long," agreed Beth, looking fresh and cheery with her strawberry hair neatly braided and a starched blue cotton dress setting off her clean freckled face.

"If I hadn't offered you my tub," chuckled Mr. Kessler, "that smell of fire and sewer on you two would have chased away all of my customers for at least a week."

"Don't worry," added Jamie. "I've thrown all of our old clothes into the garbage bins outside. Your store should be back to smelling like its musty old self well before the noon meal."

The three shared a laugh as Jamie bit into an apple Beth had purchased earlier in the morning. A hearty breakfast of fresh buns, cheese, nuts, and a jug of milk was laid out on a side table. While Jamie ate, Mr. Kessler shook his head in disbelief.

"Jamie, when I saw you standing outside my shop window with the ancient text in your hands, I almost fainted in disbelief. I thought everything had been lost in the awful fire. I'm still in shock that we have lost our parliament building. And all of those precious books … gone forever."

"It makes me think back to the library at Alexandria," said Jamie.

Mr. Kessler nodded. "Two thousand years later, I can see that we're no better than the Romans. And to think that you both almost died in that inferno. Beth, well done to think of the sewer system! You are a brilliant young woman!"

She blushed. "I've been called lots of things, but never smart."

"Well, you'll be hearing a lot more of that in the future, I'm sure," praised Mr. Kessler.

"She will indeed," agreed Jamie. "We'd both be dead if it wasn't for her quick thinking."

Jamie and Beth looked at each other knowingly. They had decided not to tell Mr. Kessler about the attempted murder.

"I think I'm getting closer to solving the mystery of

your brother's sketch," added the bookkeeper.

Jamie and Beth leaned in to look at the open books on the table.

"These tiny measurements along the side of the staggered rectangles are measurements in feet, so the structure that Ryan sketched is, in fact, a huge project. And with the picture of a typical Great Lakes boat at the base of the sketch, I've come to the conclusion that it must be a diagram of a lock system."

"A lock?" queried Beth. "Like the one you find on a door?"

"No, a different type of lock," Mr. Kessler explained. "The word 'lock' is also used to describe a method of raising a boat to a higher elevation in a man-made canal so that it can avoid any rapids found in a natural waterway."

"So why then does the title here say a mountain and not rapids?" asked Beth.

"A great question," replied Mr. Kessler. "Why would anyone in their right mind want to lift a boat over a mountain? The logical starting point in searching for an answer would be to find all of the recent or proposed canal projects in this part of North America. Here, take a look at these books, Beth."

He passed her several books with drawings of waterways and labelled canals. Jamie stretched over for a closer look. "This one here is the Rideau Canal. It connects Kingston to Bytown, and it opened only ten years ago. Although there is an impressive drop in the topography here at Jones Falls, I think it would be a stretch to call this particular landform a mountain."

Mr. Kessler pointed to a second book. "This book shows a diagram of the Erie Canal in the United States, not too far from the border with Canada West. Again, it is a very impressive piece of engineering, joining the Great Lakes to the Hudson River, which flows south to New York City, but really, nothing in the canal's vicinity even hints at a mountainous environment. Right here in Montreal, there are dreams of bypassing the Lachine rapids with a series of canals. Still, the land surrounding the southern shore of Montreal is as flat as can be."

"Which brings us to this project," said Jamie, tapping a third book.

"Right. This is a diagram of the Welland Canal. It is a vital water link between Lake Ontario and Lake Erie, and it allows sailors to avoid the dangerous waters that flow over Niagara Falls. The first attempt to build a canal around Niagara Falls began in 1825. It involved using a long series of wooden doors and beam boxes to raise a boat up and over the rising topography of the local area. Horses then pulled the ships along the length of the canal until the journey to Lake Erie was complete."

"Wait!" said Beth. "I've heard of the Welland Canal! A few months ago, I was sent to search all of the orphanages in Montreal for older boys who were strong enough to work on its construction."

Mr. Kessler nodded. "I remember the papers mentioning that there are a large number of Irish labourers working on that particular canal project."

Jamie smiled. "And the interesting thing about the Welland Canal is that it does take a boat over a mountain."

"What?" exclaimed Beth.

Jamie pointed to a map of Canada. "Between Lake Ontario and Lake Erie is the Niagara Escarpment. Looking up from Lake Ontario, I bet the escarpment would appear to be a mountain. A canal would have to go up and over it to reach the shores of Lake Erie."

Mr. Kessler smiled. "My thoughts exactly."

Beth eagerly leaned over the book. "A canal carrying a boat over a mountain! Fantastic! But why are they wanting to build another canal if one already exists?"

Mr. Kessler examined the book. "According to this recent publication, the original canal is in dire need of repair. The company that owns the Welland Canal wants to make the system more efficient so that larger ships can pass between the two lakes. They also want to increase their revenues by using the water in the canal to power local factories. To achieve their goals, they decided that they might as well start from scratch and build a brand new canal. It would take some brilliant engineering to pull it off, but if they could build it, the company would stand to make a great deal of money."

"And that now explains my brother's sketches. Ryan is an excellent engineer. He helped design a repair to an old aqueduct back in Ireland. I'm thinking that he was trying to help someone on board the *Carpathia* with a problem associated with the building of the new canal. See these lines coming out the bottom of each rectangle? I bet those are the pipes that will bleed water from the bottom of the highest locks in order to help power the factories at the bottom of the escarpment."

"So Ryan drew a sketch of the Welland Canal just before he reached Montreal," summarized Beth. "What do we do now, Jamie?"

"We follow the only lead we have. We go to St. Catharines, the town located at the bottom of the Welland Canal, and see if we can track him down."

"And how do we get to St. Catharines?"

"Leave that to me," said Mr. Kessler, smiling. "I have a friend who owes me a favour."

They all stood up from the table. Beth leaned down and lifted Colin to his feet. Mr. Kessler extended his hand to each of them. "It's been a pleasure to meet each and every one of you. Jamie, I wish you all the best in finding your brother Ryan."

Jamie nodded. "And thank you for your help once again, Mr. Kessler. We would not be planning to go to St. Catharines if it wasn't for your assistance. Before we go, could I ask for just one more small favour?"

"Certainly, Jamie. Name it."

"Can I buy a copy of that newspaper you showed us yesterday, the one with the headline from Toronto?"

Mr. Kessler went behind the counter and retrieved the paper. "It's a day-old paper, so please, keep it. No charge."

Jamie tucked it under his arm. "Thank you so much."

"Now could I ask for one more small favour from you?" asked the bookseller.

"Anything," replied Jamie.

"Could I just look at your ancient text one last time?"

Jamie smiled, reached into his leather bag, removed the *Book of Galway*, and passed it to the old bookseller. Mr. Kessler sighed happily as he carefully turned each page of text and admired the glorious masterpiece. He carefully closed the book and passed it back to Jamie.

"Now I am a happy man," he murmured.

After saying their good-byes, the young travellers stepped out into the blinding morning sunshine. The store owners were busy raising their awnings and preparing for the new business day. Pedestrians carefully worked their way along the rickety wooden sidewalks. Everyone was buzzing about the razed House of Parliament, still smouldering in the centre of the city. The smoke from the massive fire hung in the morning air like a fine fog. Jamie pulled Beth and Colin into a bakery doorway.

"Where are we going?" asked Beth.

"We go back to your hideout near the docks and sleep."

"Sounds good to me," agreed Beth, who yawned and looked ready for a nap after being up all night with Jamie. "Then what?"

"How quickly can you round up a dozen strong, smart orphans?"

She looked at him. "Do they have to be boys?"

"Not necessarily. They just have to be the best."

She brightened. "Sneak them out of the orphanages without anyone knowing?"

"Yes."

"It would be harder in the daytime than it would be at night."

"Tonight is fine. How fast can you do it?"

"Before midnight," she said, confidently.

"Good. After the sun sets this evening, go get me those orphans."

She crossed her arms. "Are you going to tell me why you need a dozen more orphans? You can barely handle two."

"Because," he smiled, "it's time to go borrow something else, and this time it's going to be a lot bigger than a book."

Chapter 16

Like the Pied Piper of Hamlin, Jamie led the four-teen Irish orphans down to a small beach located in the deserted southwest corner of Montreal. Jamie explained his audacious plan to the teenagers as they marched along the gravelly shore. No one was being forced to come along. At this point, he gave them all the choice to return to the orphanage, because in a moment it would be too late to turn back. To Jamie's surprise, not one hesitated in agreeing to help him.

Mr. Kessler had arranged the midnight rendez-vous with his friend on the beach. The children could hear the gentle rumble of the Lachine rapids only a few hundred feet upstream from where they stood. Boats would rarely sail this close to the dangerous hazard, especially at night, so the orphans were safe from being seen. After what had happened to Beth on the roof of the parliament building, Jamie was not going to take any more chances.

All eyes turned toward the river as the bows of four huge canoes quietly materialized from the moonless gloom. The crafts glided silently through the water until their pointed bows ground up gracefully onto the grav-elly beach. The bowmen jumped out and secured their craft while the men in the stern climbed forward to join their mates on dry land. Jamie approached the tallest of the men. He fit Mr. Kessler's description perfectly.

"I'm Jamie Galway. You must be John Rice."

The faint moonlight made it difficult to see, but Jamie could discern his giant-like frame, broad face, and long, braided hair. The man's hand engulfed Jamie's like that of a hungry shark swallowing a minnow.

"I am. Call me Big John." He looked over at the children, noticing their fair skin and freckles. "Are there any sick among you?"

Jamie shook his head. "You have my word that they are all healthy. They've been out of quarantine for months."

"I have a ship leaving Kahnewake in two hours time. It's heading to Kingston to pick up timber for export, but we can drop you off at Prescott along the way. Mind if I ask what you are doing with fourteen children?"

Jamie smiled. "I'm taking them on a tour of Canada West. We hear it's beautiful this time of year."

Big John raised an eyebrow. "A tour?"

"What did Mr. Kessler say was the reason for our need of transportation?" asked Jamie.

"He wouldn't tell me, but he said it was important that I pick you up at night, and that there were to be no questions asked. Being a friend, you'd think he'd trust me with the reason to start your, um, tour, in the dead of night."

"Perhaps he's being a friend by choosing not to tell you," countered Jamie.

"That's not good enough."

"I can share this with you, Big John. Someone tried to kill one of these innocent orphans yesterday, and I don't know why. An unseen departure was the only way I could ensure everyone's safety."

Big John looked over to the children. "Attempted murder? All right, now I understand the secrecy. Just tell me this. You or these children haven't done anything illegal, have you?"

"Not yet."

He laughed. "That's good. As long as it wasn't you that burned down the House of Parliament yesterday."

"I swear to you it was not I that burned down the House of Parliament. Seeing that beautiful library go up in flames actually brought tears to my eyes."

"Just tell me we won't get into any trouble with the law by letting you on my ship. I have permits that need renewing at the end of the year."

"You won't have to worry about a thing from the law."

"If I find out that you've been lying to me, you and your orphans will be in more trouble than you can possibly imagine."

"I understand." Jamie passed him an envelope. "Here is your payment for services rendered."

Big John held up his hand, refusing to take the money. "I owed Mr. Kessler a big favour and he cashed it in on you. Keep the money. My ship isn't Queen Victoria's royal yacht. Do we have a deal?" Big John stuck out his hand.

Jamie clasped it. "We have a deal."

"The only thing you need to worry about is feeding your young sightseers for two days until we reach Prescott."

Big John Rice turned the worn wooden wheel with the affection of a proud parent as his ship ploughed through the waters just south of the village of Cornwall. The midday river was busy with boats of all shapes and sizes running the profitable route between Montreal, Canada West, and New York State. More often than not, Big John would recognize a fellow boat captain, give two short rings on the tarnished brass bell that hung outside the wheelhouse, and wave. The captain on the passing boat would smile and return a similar salute.

"The *Kentson* is my first steamship," he explained to Jamie, patting the wheel. "On these waters, she and I have seen too many joys and tragedies to count. The ghosts of twenty years of hauling cargo, moving passengers, and avoiding almost certain disaster … all of those memories have permeated the railings and bulkheads of this old girl. It's just too bad a ship is like you and me, she can't live on forever."

Jamie saw the imposing captain admire his rusting ship the way he had seen many priests admire their dilapidated abbeys. Jamie understood Big John's emotions perfectly.

"It sounds like you're getting close to giving her up."

Big John sighed. "You're right. In fact, this is the old girl's last run."

Jamie leaned back on the rail. "Really? Then I guess you'll have to tell me a little bit more about her."

"Her Boulton and Watt engine was built in 1817 and saw duty on two previous ships before I purchased it right off the dock in the Port of Montreal. It took me a year to modify this ship to take on the engine's enormous bulk and the twenty-foot paddlewheel on her portside. But in the end, it was all worth it. I've built up enough capital over the years of running goods up and down the St. Lawrence to go out and buy a new ship with a proper propeller."

Jamie raised his eyebrows. "I've never seen a propeller-driven ship."

The captain laughed. "It's the future, lad! Soon, all the ships will have them. The best thing about my beautiful new ship is not the propeller though, it's the engine. My new compound engine is kept in the stern, which translates into a doubling of my ship's cargo space. With so much cargo capacity, I'll also be doubling my profits in no time."

"And then you'll be happy?" asked Jamie.

"You have to think big, son. This is how you do it. You take your profits from the one ship you own and then invest the money into purchasing two or three more ships. Next, with your greater market share, you run your competition into the ground by lowering prices. Then, you buy even more ships until you dominate the industry. My goal is not just to be the biggest shipping company under Mohawk ownership, but the biggest shipping company in all of Canada!"

"I wish you all the best with your dream. Did you say you're Mohawk? I read that Mohawks are part of a larger Iroquois nation."

He nodded. "We're one of six tribes that make up the confederacy. Our land is just southwest of Montreal."

The conversation was interrupted by an older man in grease-covered overalls entering the wheelhouse. With massive arms and a barrel chest bursting out from a torn shirt, the mechanic ambled over to the captain and slapped him on the back.

"Thanks for sending those kids down to help me in the engine room. They're as smart as whips, and they're making our lady's last run real easy."

"Easy enough to leave them down there, all on their own?" growled Big John.

He laughed. "Don't worry, Captain. Jonesy is down there, keeping an eye on them."

"Well, don't thank me for the idea, thank Mr. Galway here. He's the one who wanted to send his kids all over my ship in order to help out with its operations. Jamie Galway, this is my chief engine man, Russell Summers."

"A pleasure to meet you, Mr. Summers. And thank you for taking the time to explain to the children how to operate your steam engine. Having this experience may help them find work when they're older."

"Call me Hawkeye, and no thanks needed. They're doing a terrific job. In fact, Big John might want to consider taking them on as apprentices once he purchases one of those new ships of his."

Big John laughed. "A crew of Irish kids on a Mohawk ship? Why not? What do you think of that, Mr. Galway?"

Jamie smiled, but something hanging around Hawkeye's neck caught his eye. "I think they would be thrilled to have the opportunity. Are you Mohawk, too, Hawkeye?"

"Iroquois yes, but not Mohawk. I'm Oneida. My tribe is from the southern shore of Lake Ontario."

Jamie squinted and moved closer. "Say, what's that around your neck?"

Hawkeye held out his chain for Jamie to see. Jamie's eyes widened as he recognized the pendant hanging from the chain as a finely carved Celtic cross. "That's a beautiful Celtic cross you've got there. Where did you get it?"

"Actually, my grandfather gave it to me. He says it's been in the family for generations. There's a story attached to the cross, and he said he'll get around to telling me about it, someday."

"I bet there is," said Jamie, surprised at its similarity to the legendary St. Patrick cross he had seen in illustrations back home.

"Well, I better get back to work before the boss here sees that I'm slacking off."

"Too late," growled Big John as Hawkeye disappeared from the wheelhouse. "So you still want me to drop you off in Prescott? What could possibly be in that small town for you and fourteen Irish orphans?"

"I hope you understand, but it's better you don't know."

Big John grinned. "A task that is too secretive to share with your good old buddy Big John? I really don't gossip ... much."

"Trust me," said Jamie, seriously. "It's better for everyone this way."

As the men stood in silence, a piercing cry carried through the open door and into the wheelhouse. Jamie stuck his head outside and shielded his eyes from the midday sun.

"I thought I recognized that call," muttered Jamie. "He's following us."

"Who is?" asked Big John.

"There's a falcon up there, following the boat."

"So?"

"A Wendat friend told me not long ago that a falcon would help show me the way. With our flying friend leading us forward, I'm starting to feel a little better about the crazy plan I'm hatching."

* * *

Denny Ferguson strolled along the dock of the Prescott Shipbuilding Company whistling a tune he had heard at the county fair earlier that afternoon. It was too bad he couldn't have spent the evening at the fair as well. His wife's gooseberry pie was up for tonight's judging, and he hoped she would win the contest for the second year in a row. Another blue ribbon would look fine on the mantelpiece, and he could once again crow to all his friends that after work he was lucky enough to have a beautiful wife *and* the best desserts in the county waiting for him at home.

The setting sun was shimmering scarlet on the river, and the colour reminded him of gooseberries, just like the ones in that slice of pie in his lunch pail back at the gatehouse. She had slipped it into his dinner before he'd headed off to work. She gave him a kiss at the door and said the slice would bring her luck at the fair. Although his mouth was watering at the thought of his treat, he decided that he could resist temptation until the sun went down. Until then, he had better finish his patrol.

He walked along the shipbuilding company's long dock and examined once again the three moored ships. The smallest and furthest from shore was the high-bowed fishing boat *Daytripper*. The boss was doing a friend a favour and had repaired its hull in dry dock after the boat had run aground on a shoal near Brockville. The second ship was the *Mary Jane*, a Great Lakes cargo carrier that had been brought to them by the York Shipping Company. They were willing to pay

Prescott Shipbuilding a handsome sum to convert her from sail to steamship. She was next in line to use the company's dry dock.

The nearest boat was the pride and joy of the Prescott Shipping Company: the *Carpathia II*. Built and designed right here in Prescott, her sleek silhouette shimmered in the twilight sky. Freshly painted twin smokestacks rose up from behind its streamlined superstructure. Between the smokestacks, two imposing walking arms were poised and ready to pump power from brand new steam engines into the two massive paddlewheels that were mounted on either side of the ship. The pilothouse rose up like a proud forehead above its graceful wooden bow. Lines of portholes marked the comfortable berths that would soon carry passengers for the owner, the Western Star Shipping Line.

Denny strolled up to the new ship and rubbed his hand along the side of her spotless white hull. Everything was quiet, as it always was at this time in the evening. He listened to a bass splash in the water beside the dock as it leapt high in the air for an evening snack. The hungry fish reminded him of the gooseberry pie. Turning, he strolled back toward the gatehouse. He could see Rodney, his partner, sipping on a freshly made cup of tea. *A spot of tea and a slice of pie on a cool night like this will be the perfect start to the shift*, Denny thought to himself as he reached for the door.

Beyond the gatehouse, a wire-linked fence cut across the dock in order to keep trespassers at bay. Three young teenagers, a girl and two boys, were fishing off the dock on the other side of the fence. They'd been at it since he'd first arrived.

"Don't you think it's time you youngsters head back home to your parents?" Denny called out. "It's getting late."

"We'll be going soon," shouted the girl. "I first want to try out this new night jigger. My pa made it out of balsa wood last week!"

"Good luck, then," replied Denny, twisting the handle.

Denny had heard about these new night jiggers. He made a mental note to give one a try next time he went out with his own rod and reel.

"Hey Rodney, do you mind pouring me ..."

"Whoa! It's huge! Oh my gosh, don't let go of the rod! Help! We need help!"

Denny stuck his head back outside the door. "Are you kids all right?"

The girl and boy held the second boy by the waist. "He's got a monster fish on the line! Maybe a muskie! He's going to fall in!"

Dennis hesitated. "A muskie? Are you sure?"

Just the mention of a mighty muskellunge, the St. Lawrence's number one prized fish, got his attention. He'd hate to see this kid lose a once-in-a-lifetime fish. Must have been the lure. He had to get a look at their magical night jigger while he had the chance.

"Rodney," he called into the shack. "I'll be right back."

"All right, Denny," the other man replied. "I'll have the tea waiting."

Denny jogged to the fence while fumbling through his key chain. Quickly unlocking the gate, he ran over to the children. The boy's rod was bent right over and he was fighting the fish like crazy. The other two had their feet dug in and were still hanging on to his waist.

"I can't hold on!" cried the boy. "Please, sir, help me land him!"

"Sure, son, let me grab ahold of the rod. Good. All right, I got it!"

Denny took the rod, expecting his arms to be pulled out of their sockets, but surprisingly, it didn't happen. In fact, it just hung there like the hook was attached to a sunken log.

"Hey, kid, I don't think … whoa!"

Distracted by the rod, Denny didn't see the three kids quietly move in behind him and with a terrific push, they sent the night watchman flying off the dock. A second later, there was a tremendous splash in the river below.

Rodney Leary had just finished making the second cup of tea when he heard the splash.

"Help!" called a girl. "The guard has fallen into the river!"

"What?" called Rodney, confused. He stepped out the door and saw the open gate.

"Denny, where are —"

Rodney's world went black as something heavy was thrown over his head. Suddenly, dozens of hands were wrestling him to the ground while his wrists and ankles were bound with rope. The soggy night watchman was also rescued from the water, blindfolded, and tied up beside his partner in the gatehouse. Jamie Galway strode around the room and congratulated all the orphans.

"Well done. And don't worry, these men will be released by the workers when they arrive in the morning. We don't have much time. Follow me."

As the collection of youngsters made their way out of the gatehouse, the oldest of the orphans, Daniel Kenny, leaned down to Beth.

"I thought you said Jamie was a priest."

"He is."

"So far he's sprung a dozen orphans out of an orphanage, abducted a pair of night watchmen, and now we're going to steal a full-sized steamship?"

She smiled and pointed up. "All for the Greater Good."

Daniel guffawed. "I don't recall a story like this in the Bible."

"Look, Jamie explained this all to me. We didn't hurt the watchmen, and we're only borrowing the boat. This shipping company owes us one. He told me how many hundreds of Irish have died on their ships coming over from Ireland, including probably some of our parents. And we're not stealing it. We're going to give it back to them when we're done."

"And what are we going to do with this steamship?"

She shrugged. "He said something about killing two birds with one stone. He seems to like that expression. I assume one of the things has to do with finding his brother."

"I've never met a priest like this before."

She grinned. "Neither have I, but if you'd prefer to go back to Montreal, we're not going to force you to get on the boat."

Daniel jumped onto the gangplank that led to the *Carpathia II*. "Go back to the orphanage so I can miss this adventure of a lifetime? Forget it! I'm in!"

* * *

Jamie realized that if the heist of the *Carpathia II* was to work, they would have to be well away by first light and then manage to stay ahead of the authorities, who he was sure would be hot on their trail. He took the six oldest orphans down into the boiler room. The brand new twin engines gleamed in the light of the freshly lit oil lamps. The six young teenagers had spent the entire trip on Big John's steamship below deck in the engine room, learning how a big steam engine operated — with the help of the *Kentson* crew. Now Jamie was banking everything on the hope that their brief education had taken hold.

"But there's two of them!" protested Daniel, the self-designated chief engineer, pointing to the two huge boilers.

Jamie shrugged. "So you just double everything. Two boilers, two pistons, two walking arms, and two paddlewheels. Just do everything twice! Here, let me help you get things started."

Jamie divided them up into two groups of three. He then pointed out the boiler doors, the coal, the shovels, and the lighter fluid.

"So, Daniel, you're in charge of the boiler on the right and Laura, your group can take the boiler on the left. Talk to each other. Everyone will need to work together as a team to make this work. Now I need to head topside. Give it your best shot. We're counting on you."

"Aye, aye, Captain," replied Daniel, saluting. The other orphans burst into hysterical laughter. After months in a boring orphanage, it was like Jamie had just given them the best Christmas present imaginable. Jamie looked back from the stairs.

"All right, start stoking those boilers and get them fired up as soon as possible. We need to get this bucket of bolts moving."

"Aye, aye, Captain!" they all shouted in unison, followed by a salute and another burst of laughter.

Jamie shook his head, smiling, as he disappeared up the stairs. Beth was waiting for him at the top. Behind her were three girls, two boys, and Colin. "We've gone through the entire ship. They must have been just about ready to sail — the cupboards are stocked full of food. There's no bedding yet in the staterooms so we'll have to sleep on the bare wooden frames. Other than that, everything looks good."

"That's great news," said Jamie. "See if you can find anything soft to throw on those bed frames. We'll need to get rest in shifts at some point. This is going to be a long trip. And remember, don't carry candles or oil lamps on the open deck or anywhere near the windows. We need to run dark until we're well away from Prescott. Someone might see our escape and alert the authorities."

The children hurried off toward the passenger berths.

Daniel poked his head up the stairs from the engine room. "The boilers are lit and the steam pressure is starting to rise. I think we can get started in a minute and increase speed later on as the pressure continues to build."

Jamie could smell the thick smoke flowing out from the stacks above his head. "Brilliant work, Daniel. I think we better get going before someone smells that burning coal."

Jamie walked down the elegant, wood-panelled corridor towards the bow. He reached the first mooring rope and unlashed it from the cleat. With the bow free, he could feel the river's current begin to push the front of the ship away from the dock. He quickly ran along the outer walkway to the stern and pulled in the stern line. Another run along the length of the ship and Jamie headed up top to the wheelhouse. Just as he had hoped, the current had moved the nose of the boat a good ten feet away from the dock while the stern stayed close. Getting around the moored ships should now be easy.

Standing in front of the large polished oak wheel, Jamie pulled twice on the rope that hung next to the wheel, thereby ringing the bell in the engine room to get Daniel's attention. He grabbed the brass handle on the round telegraph and pushed it forward until it read *Ahead Slow*. A different brass bell on the other side of the wheel rang twice in response, and a small brass arrow on the inside of the telegraph also moved to *Ahead Slow*, acknowledging the order from the bridge. The ship gave a shudder as the pair of huge walking beams began to tilt slowly back and forth like gigantic teeter-totters. The shafts at the end of each beam pumped the paddlewheels. The paddlewheels slowly slapped at the dark, moonlit water and the *Carpathia II* steamed away from the dock.

Hawkeye Summers joined the captain in the wheelhouse as the first of the Thousand Islands began to glide past the old steamship. Hawkeye saw his captain absentmindedly rubbing the worn wheel as he hummed a tune.

"You're going to miss her, aren't you?"

Big John looked around the rusty old wheelhouse and nodded. "A lot of memories in this old girl, but we're going to give her one heck of a send-off."

Hawkeye's eyes lit up. "You're still planning on shooting her down the Lachine Rapids?"

He smiled. "As soon as I drop off my cargo in Montreal, we'll head out to the rapids. I can't wait to race her through those rapids like a bolt of lightning. I've canoed and paddled those rapids for over a week, planning out the perfect route. We're going to retire this girl in style."

"Every captain in the area will be out at the rapids watching. They've been talking about it in the pub for weeks, even putting wagers on whether she'll make it down the rapids in one piece. No one has tried shooting those rapids in a ship this size."

"And what did you put your money on?" asked Big John.

Hawkeye laughed. "On you making it, of course. Can I ask a favour of an old friend?"

"Sure."

"Can I be up here in the wheelhouse with you when we shoot the rapids?"

Big John slapped his friend on the back. "Of course. I wouldn't want you down in the engine room anyway, just in case I do lose your bet."

Two loud dings from a nearby bell broke their conversation. Big John knew it had come from a nearby ship, but where was it? There wasn't a ship in sight.

"Do you see a ship?" he asked Hawkeye.

Hawkeye ran to each window. "Wait, ah … there she is. Look behind us to port!"

Glancing out his port side, Big John yelped in shock. Only thirty feet from his stern, another paddlewheeler was pulling up alongside his boat. It was a beauty of a ship with a double set of brand new paddlewheels. Big John had to work hard to control his temper. What idiot would sail a brand new ship so close to his and risk a collision?

"Uh, Captain, you better leave the wheel and come over to see this."

"What's that idiot of a captain doing now? Cleaning the dirt out from under his toenails?"

"No. He's waving to you."

"Great. A friendly idiot. Well, I'm not in the mood to wave back."

"You might want to. And he's not the only one waving either."

"What?"

"I'll take the wheel, Captain. You have to come and see this for yourself."

Fuming, Big John handed the wheel to Hawkeye and tilted his head out the portside window. His jaw nearly hit the floor. Waving to him from the wheelhouse of the stunning new paddlewheeler was Jamie Galway. A half-dozen of the orphans whom he had dropped off in Prescott were laughing and dancing on the open bow as if they were at a party. He tried to make out the name of the ship on the bow. A new piece of wood had been placed on top of the original. In still-wet paint, which must have been written by the hand of a child, read the name the *Flying Irishman*. On the deck, the children recognized Big John and waved to him excitedly. He sheepishly waved back.

"Hawkeye," he said. "Keep the helm. I'm heading out on the yardarm."

"Yessir, Captain," Hawkeye replied with a chuckle.

Big John stepped outside the wheelhouse door and leaned out over the port yardarm railing. To his further shock, he saw Jamie Galway hand the wheel over to that young girl named Beth. Jamie walked over to his starboard yardarm railing and waved across the small expanse of water that separated the two ships.

"How you doing, Captain?"

Big John threw his arms in the air. "Jamie! What the heck are you doing on that ship?"

"Taking the kids on a tour. Remember?"

"That cannot be your boat! It looks brand new!"

"Actually, we're just borrowing it. The captain owed me and a lot of other Irish immigrants a big favour."

"And where are you planning to go on your tour?"

"West," Jamie replied cryptically. "Quite far west, actually."

"I don't believe this," muttered Big John.

Jamie pointed ahead. "According to my map, I think we're about to enter the Thousand Islands. I was hoping you could help lead me through the narrow channels. It looks a little tricky, especially with the currents and night coming soon. To tell you the truth, this is the first time I ever skippered anything bigger than a rowboat."

"The first time he's ever skippered anything bigger than a rowboat," muttered Big John to himself, shaking his head. "He's got the newest ship in all of Canada under his command. and he's asking me for help."

"So what do you say, Captain? Can you help me out?" called Jamie.

Big John pointed one of his huge fingers at Jamie. "I don't know you and you don't know me. Got it?"

Jamie scrunched up his brow. "I'm sorry, what's your name again?"

"Very funny. And stay a good distance behind me. Your sleek ship has twice the speed of mine so the last thing we need is a collision at night. Once we get to Kingston, son, you keep going west and you've made it to the open waters of Lake Ontario. From there, you're on your own. Got it?"

"Yes, sir!" Jamie saluted. "And thank you, Captain."

Big John returned a weak salute and watched as Jamie gave the telegraph a signal to the engine room to slow her speed. The *Flying Irishman* started to slow down and then drifted in behind the *Kentson*. She took up her position at the rear of the procession, as ordered.

"Is that entire ship being run by children?" asked Hawkeye incredulously.

"We didn't see anything," corrected Big John, still shaking his head. "And go tell the rest of the crew they didn't see anything either."

Chapter 17

A sombre Jonathon Wilkes waited in queue at the Western Star Shipping Line ticket booth. He had been so close to having the *Book of Galway*, his next fortune, in his possession, and now he had to return to England empty-handed. He wondered how he could have blundered so badly. The book, he was sure, was now lost in the massive fire that had consumed Canada's House of Parliament. He felt no remorse about being responsible for the death of the two Irish children, but he found the burned-out shell of the parliament building strangely disturbing. In all of his travels, he had never experienced a local population torching their own legislature. This Province of Canada is going nowhere, he surmised. The crowds have no respect for authority, and the leaders can't even protect their own government buildings from riots and arson!

"May I help you, sir?" asked the ticket clerk.

"Yes, I would like a first-class ticket on the next Western Star ship leaving for London, England, please."

As the clerk scanned the schedules, a door burst open at the back of the office. An irate fellow with a thick black beard stormed out of the office, and he was quickly followed by a tall man dressed in an immaculate business suit. Wilkes suddenly recognized the black-bearded fellow as Captain Chamberlain of the *Carpathia*.

"Richard, you need to calm down!"

"Calm down? You want me to calm down? How can I? You just told me my new ship has been stolen right off the dock of your Prescott shipyard!"

"We will find the ship shortly, I assure you. Surely, a bunch of troublemaking children can't get too far. They have no training in the operations of a steamship. They likely beached themselves in a nearby marsh."

"It was a bunch of Irish children, you say?"

"The authorities say witnesses saw a group of young Irish children near the shipyard the evening the boat disappeared. The two night watchmen confirmed their descriptions and said the ringleader was a tall Irish lad with brown hair and a leather satchel over one shoulder."

Chamberlain slammed his fist on a desk. "I bet it has something to do with that lad I met at the pub. He was towing along two Irish brats. I told him I had sold his old Celtic book at the bookseller on St. James. This must be revenge for his brother! I can guarantee that when you find my boat, he will be the one behind it! I want him arrested and the keys to his cell thrown away!"

Seeing his customer distracted, the ticket man cleared his throat. "The *Europa* has a first-class berth available, and she is leaving Montreal for London in three days' time. Can I interest you in purchasing a ticket?"

"Perhaps in a moment," said Wilkes, excusing himself from the line.

Captain Chamberlain, the mention of Irish children, and the theft of a boat was simply too much of a coincidence. Jamie Galway survived? Surely the girl had died from the fall, but perhaps the boy had survived the fire with the priceless text still intact! Wilkes made his way to the side of the ticket booth, found the door into the office, and stepped through the doorway. He approached the heated argument continuing between the captain and the company man.

"The authorities are already alerting all of the ports and shipping lines along the St. Lawrence. It's not like a ship the size of the *Carpathia II* can hide anywhere. We will find it, and when we do, we will arrest the perpetrators, and she will once again be all yours."

"You'll find her half-sunk on a shoal, that's what you'll find when you catch up with her," yelled Chamberlain. "My ship captained by children! This is outrageous!"

"Excuse me, gentlemen," interrupted Wilkes.

"And who in blazes are you?" stormed Chamberlain.

"My name is Jonathon Wilkes. I'm a private investigator."

Wilkes pulled out his wallet, shuffled through the various fake business cards and pulled out the one he was looking for. *Jonathon Wilkes. Private Detective for Hire. London. Paris. New York.* He passed it to the director.

The company man glanced down at the card. "My name is Walter Reeves, director of operations for Western Star Shipping Lines".

"I just finished a case here in Montreal," lied Wilkes, "and I happened to overhear your conversation regarding a missing ship. I feel that I can be of assistance in tracking down and retrieving the *Carpathia II*."

"As if anyone needs help tracking down a stolen three-hundred-passenger steamship!" scoffed Chamberlain.

"I'm sorry," said Reeves, "but I feel it's a situation that is best left to the authorities."

"Have you not been following the newspapers, sir?" Wilkes countered. "The authorities are completely overwhelmed at the moment. If they're not dealing with the spread of sickness throughout the country, they are having to control angry mobs, such as the one that burned down your own parliament building two nights ago. I'm afraid that a search for a stolen ship might simply overtax their already strained capabilities."

Reeves considered the argument while Chamberlain simply huffed in irritation. "And what's your fee, Wilkes?" asked Reeves.

"Our agreement will be simple. I will not accept any form of an upfront fee. Payment for services will only take place upon the reacquisition of the *Carpathia II*. However, I will require access to all of the information you receive regarding tips as to the location of the *Carpathia II*, plus coverage of any transportation costs that I might incur as I track down the ship's location. My finder's fee will be a flat fifty pounds plus a royal suite ticket to London, England, on a Western Star ship. Are these terms acceptable?"

"Are you saying I will not have to pay anything until you find my ship?" repeated Reeves, surprised.

"That's correct."

"I can certainly live with those terms. Welcome aboard, Mr. Wilkes."

The men shook hands.

"Now then," said Wilkes, leading Reeves and Chamberlain back into the office, "let's see what information you already have that will help me track down your naughty little Irish children. I'm very good at my job, Mr. Wilkes, and tracking down missing items is my speciality."

* * *

Big John Rice spun the wheel to the right and pointed the nose of the *Kentson* toward the busy harbour of Kingston. Tall masts and steamer smokestacks rose from the shore-side docks like the posts of an enormous fence protecting the skyline of the bustling waterfront town. Only the impressive dome of an elegant stone building rose above the collection of moored ships. Grey smoke from a departing steamboat fogged the calm morning air. The *Chippewa* churned its single paddle east toward the mouth of the St. Lawrence River. Big John knew the captain well and waved to him as the two ships passed.

Looking over his other shoulder, Big John could see the *Flying Irishman* veering off on a southwest heading down the channel between the town of Kingston and Wolfe Island. Beyond Wolfe Island lay the open waters of Lake Ontario. Big John knew only too well the summer storms that could blow up at a moment's notice on the wild open waters of Lake Ontario. Did Jamie have a clue as to the dangers that could be awaiting him as he attempted to cross the great lake?

Still, Big John couldn't help but grin as Jamie stepped out of the wheelhouse one more time and waved thanks, finishing off the gesture with a big salute. Big John saluted back. That kid had managed to successfully steer his ship through the narrow channels of the Thousand Islands, and on a cloudy night to boot. Perhaps the young lad would be all right after all. The *Flying Irishman* belched thick grey smoke as it accelerated toward the open water. Lord knows what that crazy boy and his crew in diapers were planning to do with a brand new steamship. He then remembered Jamie's words. Perhaps it *was* better not to know.

"Good luck to you, boy!" he shouted, and gave his brass bell two mighty rings.

Chapter 18

Brimming with excitement, Chamberlain pushed the stranger through the office door. Together, they strode up to the men sitting at the table. The stranger sported a shock of white hair and a face so craggy it would have made the cliffs of Dover proud. Jonathon Wilkes and Walter Reeves gazed up from a large map of the St. Lawrence River.

"This is Captain Sanderson of the *Chippewa*," said Chamberlain. "I was down at the pub asking all of the newly arriving crews and captains whether they might have seen our missing ship, perhaps abandoned or wrecked somewhere along the St. Lawrence. I think the captain here has a story that you both might find interesting."

"Thank you for coming," Reeves stated. "Any help in retrieving our missing ship will be greatly appreciated. Tell us, what did you see?"

"Well, sir," Sanderson answered in a thick Scottish accent, "I was pulling out of Kingston harbour with a full load of timber when I spied my friend Big John Rice and his ship the *Kentson*. As she turned in toward the harbour, a second ship suddenly appeared off its portside. Lower and sleeker than the *Kentson*, it was a brand new double-stacked wheeler. The only ship I've ever seen like her was that new ship of yours, the *Carpathia II*, while she was tied to the dock up in Prescott. I thought she wasn't due out of the shipyard yet, but I just assumed that I was wrong and she must be out on her first run into Lake Ontario. Deciding to check her out with my looking glass, I was thrown by the strange name I saw on the bow. It was blurry, probably hand-painted, but I thought it said something like the *Flying Irishman*."

"The *Flying Irishman*?" questioned Reeves. "What in blazes is my ship doing with that name?"

"A little humour from the children would be my guess," chuckled Wilkes. "I think we may have found our pint-sized Irish thieves."

Fuming, Reeves slammed a fist on the table. "I don't care if they're the funniest comedy team on the face of the Earth. They have stolen company property and I want it back! The president of the company himself is breathing down my neck and said he is holding me personally responsible for the safe return of his ship. If that ship is damaged in any way, I'll be fired!"

"It's not your fault the ship was commandeered," countered Wilkes.

"He blames me for not having more watchmen on the dock that night," Reeves mumbled.

"At least we know where it is," said Wilkes, pulling out a new map. "The east end of Lake Ontario."

"I can't believe those little Irish brats managed to sail it all the way through the Thousand Islands," commented Chamberlain. "That's a tough piece of navigation."

"Are you *complimenting* them?" shouted Reeves.

"Look at it this way," said Wilkes to both men. "At least your boat is still in one piece. That means you both still have your jobs."

"You're right," agreed Reeves, sighing. "We need to catch them before they destroy that ship and my future."

"And what about the chase ship?" Wilkes asked Chamberlain.

"The *Maid of the Rideau* is approaching the Port of Montreal as we speak," said Chamberlain. "We'll load her up with fuel and fresh food as quickly as we can. With no cargo to haul, she'll almost be as fast as the *Carpathia II*. We won't be too far behind her. Perhaps three days, no more."

"I'm coming with you," stated Reeves. "I'll offer the both of you an extra thirty-pound bonus if you can also bring me back the children responsible for this outrage. I want to charge them with so many acts of piracy that they'll be locked away for the rest of their lives!"

Wilkes felt the weight of his hidden pistol holstered under his jacket. "You need not worry, Mr. Reeves. We'll make sure those children get what they deserve."

Huddling with his family under a rain-drenched tarp, Shane Beckett had never felt such utter hopelessness and despair. It had been over a week since he had woken up on his wife Chloë's lap and found that they and their two children had been forcibly confined to a guarded pier, trapped like condemned dogs, with dozens of other Irish families. With his forehead sporting a huge goose egg and his mind foggy, he had to be reminded by Chloë of what had happened. She told him how they had been attacked on Yonge Street by an angry mob. The weapon-wielding gangs were determined to stop sickness from spreading through Toronto. The gang leaders decided to round up all the Irish they could find and hold them inside a fenced waterside quay like cattle destined for slaughter. It didn't matter that he was an established watchmaker who owned his own small store on Yonge Street. It didn't matter that his family had been living in Toronto for over five years.

He still remembered his desperate pleading with the armed guards at the gate to their pen that first day.

"Excuse me, sir! There's been some kind of mistake! My family and I were attacked as we were walking home on Yonge Street. We've been living in Toronto for five years. Look at us! We're not sick! Keeping us penned up here won't do anyone any good, and my wife and children are scared. Can you please let us out?"

The man with the loaded rifle ignored him.

Shane felt a touch of panic. "Can't you hear what I'm saying? My family shouldn't be in here!"

The guard wheeled around in anger. "I can tell by your accent that you're bloody Irish. My mother died from cholera last week. We don't want your kind here no more, and I don't care whether you're sick or not. We're going to keep you locked up until the government sends us a boat to ship you all back to Ireland, back to where you belong! So stop your snivelling. You and your family are not going anywhere!"

Stunned, Shane stepped back from the gate and slowly returned to his family. He broke the horrible news to his wife.

"This is complete madness!" Chloë whispered, as Shane sat down heavily next to her. "They're trying to ship us all back to Ireland? Doesn't he realize we're more Canadian than half the population of Toronto?"

As the days passed by, church groups and other concerned strangers brought the detainees tarps, tents, and food, but the Irish remained locked in their make-shift jail, guarded by the unforgiving pack of vigilantes. A Toronto police force, sympathetic to those who had lost loved ones, simply looked the other way. Everyone waited for the Canadian government to make a decision on the prisoners. With the government still reeling from the burning of their parliament building, a decision regarding the illegal detention centre in Toronto was not about to come anytime soon.

As the days passed, the Beckett family continued to huddle in quiet despair at the far end of the pier, in the corner farthest away from the sick and dying. Already eight people on the pier had died from a combination of exposure and disease. The guards at first had refused to take the first body away. With no choice, Shane had enlisted the help of three other men, who then wrapped the body of the deceased man in an old canvas tarp and lifted it over the fencing. A large splash echoed along the quay as the body hit the water of Toronto Harbour.

The enraged guards screamed at them to stop, claiming the drinking water would get contaminated from the disease, but nevertheless, they refused to open the gates for fear of starting a prisoner stampede. Instead, the guards had to remove the discarded body from the water using a fishing net and a collection of small dinghies. Since then, the guards had reluctantly agreed to have the dead passed over the gate for proper burial.

Shane fought back the tears as he looked at his tired children huddled at his feet. He took Chloë's hand. She leaned against him, and he listened to the rhythm of her beating heart. What was to become of them? Left exposed on the dock, it was only a matter of time before they too would get sick and die.

"Please Lord, help us find a way out of this hellish purgatory," he whispered, looking up into the endless blue sky.

In what seemed like an answer to his prayers, a loud bell rang in the waters behind him. Puzzled, he turned around to see a sleek white steamship rounding the western tip of the Toronto Islands. With its double stacks belching out black smoke and the bow aimed directly at their quay, the ship closed the distance between them in short order. Shane raised himself to his feet. Were his eyes playing tricks on him? Through the haze of the afternoon sun, it appeared that the entire ship was being run by children! A teenager was at the helm while two young girls manned the bow lines. A boy no older than six stood on the stairs leading up to the wheelhouse, waving to everyone on the pier. Not knowing what else to do, Shane waved back. He could make out the name of the ship, the *Flying Irishman*, painted in childish lettering on the bow. The young "captain" stuck his head out of the wheelhouse window as the ship began to slow.

"Is this the quay where I heard Irish families are being held against their will?"

Shane raised his arms. "Yes, it is! We're all Irish and they won't let us leave the dock!"

"I don't suppose that you would fancy a ride away from your dilemma?"

Shane looked at the crowd gathering behind him. All that still had strength to stand were staring at the bow of the huge ship in disbelief.

"And who are you?" asked Shane.

"A friend. My name is Jamie Galway."

"That's a wonderful offer, Mr. Galway, but we have a slight problem — this fence that has us trapped in here like caged animals."

"Ah, the fence!" shouted Jamie. "It shouldn't be a problem for very long. And your name, sir?"

"I'm Shane Beckett."

"Beth, Laura, pass Mr. Beckett those bow lines. Mr. Beckett, if you would be so kind, could you tie those bow lines to the fence?"

Shane's face lit up with understanding. "It would be my pleasure, captain!"

The boat approached the dock nose first.

Shane started to wave his arms. "You better slow down! You're going to hit—"

The portside bow crunched into the end of the pier. Metal and wood screeched and groaned as the ship ground itself along the wooden quay. Everyone on board the ship stumbled forward from the impact. Jamie left the wheelhouse to look over the railing at the bow of his ship.

"Oh dear, did I scrape the paint? And I promised father I would bring it home without a scratch."

Shane shook his head in disbelief as he took the thick ropes from the girls. With the help of three other men, they quickly knotted the thick ropes to the fence. "Is your whole crew children, Mr. Galway?"

"Indeed they are! I like to call them the Lost Boys, although some are indeed girls. Please back away from the fence. I've never tried this before. Actually, I've never tried sailing a ship before! Here we go!"

Jamie signalled the engine room to give the ship full reverse. Dark steam and smoke poured from the smokestacks as the paddlewheels dug into the waters of Toronto harbour. The fence pulled away from the quay as easily as paper torn from a wrapped Christmas present. The Irish prisoners gave a whoop of joy! The guards, taking in the improbable scene from the far end of the fenced quay, were furious. Some shouted to the prisoners to back away from the boat. Others ran off to get reinforcements.

A larger boy appeared at the bow of the ship wielding a fire axe. A large chunk of fence was now dragging through the water in front of the ship. He swung the axe sharply down on the taut bow lines. The axe sliced through them cleanly, which allowed the submerged metal fence to sink to the bottom of the harbour. The paddlewheels changed direction and began to push the ship forwards, back towards the quay.

"I might need a bit of help landing this ship," Jamie shouted out. "First time docking as well!"

"Patrick, Ethan, Brian, Kyle!" shouted Shane. "You heard the lad! Get over here and help him land his ship!"

Shane turned back to the ship and cupped his hands. "You're coming in too quickly! Turn hard to port, reverse the engines and slow yourself down!"

Jamie nodded, ducked back in the wheelhouse and took the wheel back from a girl no older than twelve. He pulled back on the telegraph. Within moments, the big paddle wheels started slapping the water in reverse, bringing the turning ship up against the end of the wharf. The ship slowly sideswiped the dock, and the impact eventually brought it to a screeching stop. Chips of white paint snowed down on the Irish onlookers like flakes of Christmas snow. Shane and the men grabbed the tossed mooring lines and together they wrestled the giant ship up against the dock. The paddlewheels ground to a halt. The young captain clambered down a ladder to the ship's deck and, with the help of the child crew, threw the gangplank across to the quay. He then stepped across the gangplank and strode up to Shane.

"Thank you for your help in landing my ship, Mr. Beckett."

They shook hands.

"Pleased to meet you, uh, Captain Galway. Now do you mind telling me what a young lad like you is doing with a ship like this?"

"I volunteered to take the ship on her first run through Lake Ontario. While passing, a little bird told me that there might be some Irish folk here in Toronto who would like to join us on our maiden voyage. So, are there are any takers for our fine promotion? A free cruise to all interested Irish citizens! This once-in-a-lifetime offer has been brought to you by your good friends at Western Star Shipping Lines."

Shane stared at him as if he had two heads, then burst out laughing. He turned to his fellow countrymen. "This lad wants to take us on a free cruise around the lake. What say you?"

A huge cheer swelled up from the desperate crowd.

"Jamie Galway," said Shane, as he wrapped his arms around his wife and children, "I don't know where you came from, but in my books, you're an angel sent from Heaven."

Chapter 19

Up in the wheelhouse of the *Flying Irishman*, Jamie Galway and Shane Beckett quickly became friends. As the city of Toronto faded into the mist behind the stern of their ship, Jamie explained to Shane everything that had happened to him since leaving Ireland; his harrowing trip across the Atlantic, his escape from Grosse Isle, nearly losing his life in the fires in Montreal, and then stealing the ship from the company that had caused his brother and hundreds of other Irish so much misery. Jamie played down the significance of the old Celtic book that rested in his satchel, simply saying it was an invaluable artifact for the church.

Shane couldn't help but be impressed by the young priest's determination. It was obvious that Jamie had no regrets regarding his many unorthodox, perhaps criminal actions. Given how Canadian law had abandoned his own family this past week, Shane himself had no issues with steaming a stolen ship across Lake Ontario in order to reach a safe haven for his family.

Before them, the bustling town of St. Catharines grew ever closer. The docks to the town lay just to the north of the city. Shane had offered to dock the ship for Jamie. Shane had spent his younger days fishing with his uncle in the Irish Sea. Jamie laughed and gladly offered him the title of "captain."

"This time, it would be best if we brought her to the dock with some semblance of professionalism," agreed

Jamie. "We don't want to bring any undesired attention to our arrival."

"So what are your plans, Jamie, once we reach the dock?" asked Shane.

"I'll comb through every work party along the entire length of the Welland Canal and see if my brother is among them. If he isn't there, and I can't find any more clues, then I'll have no choice but to head back to Ireland with the book."

"And what of this ship?"

He shrugged. "Now that I've made it to St. Catharines, I was going to simply set her adrift in the night and let Western Star salvage her out on the open water."

Shane thought for a moment. "If you do that, the authorities will soon be all over St. Catharines looking for the culprits who stole her. They'll have you arrested before the end of the week. You and your brother will never get back to Ireland."

"I was going to head by land for the American border as soon as possible to avoid being caught," explained Jamie. "But I see your point, especially if the search takes longer than a day or two."

"To get into the United States by land, you will need to cross the dangerous Niagara River. Don't even think about swimming it, lad. Everyone who has tried has drowned. You've never seen a river like it. It truly is a frothing white monster of death and a perfect borderline between two countries."

"I was hoping I wouldn't have to swim," agreed Jamie, thinking back to his near drowning at Grosse Isle.

"The only way across is through Canadian government checkpoints at ferry crossings. By then, the authorities might have a description of you. They'll be waiting at the crossings for you with half of the British army."

"A very good point," said Jamie, discouraged. "You've successfully pulled apart my only escape plan. Do you have any suggestions?"

"I think after you leave the ship, you should let me sail the *Flying Irishman* to the United States."

"Your family wants to go to the United States?" repeated Jamie. "Why?"

"I can tell you that many of us on board have no desire to return to a city that treated us like animals. We have relatives already in Boston and New York City. I have a cousin on Long Island who has begged me to move closer. My family and I will go to New York and start our lives all over again."

"And the orphans?"

"I've already talked to the other families. We'd be more than happy to adopt one into our family and the other families have agreed to do likewise. They all seem to be wonderful children."

"That's fantastic news! But how will you get there? You can't sail the ship all the way to New York City."

Shane smiled. "I've heard in the Toronto pubs of a little-used dock near Rochester, New York, that has been used in the past for smuggling Irish across the border. We'll tie her up there in the evening twilight and quietly drift off into the American night. We'll then likely catch a ride up the Erie Canal to New York City."

Jamie could see the plan coming together. "Because the ship will be found deserted in American waters, it will likely be seized by American authorities. That will cause Western Star Shipping Lines a huge headache to get her back."

"And Western Star should have no idea that you disembarked from the ship here in St. Catharines. Hopefully in all their confusion of finding their ship in American hands, the company will be completely thrown off your trail. They will think that you moved on with us to New York City. They will then have to give up their search."

Jamie smiled. "All right. You've convinced me of your plan so far. But I myself still have to get across the border. The British might still look for me at the border crossings. How will I get into the United States?"

"Leave that to me," Shane smiled. "I owe you an escape plan. My family and I will gladly wait for you in Tonawanda. It's a village just across the Niagara River from the head of the Welland Canal. At exactly midnight, send me three quick flashes then two slow from the Canadian shoreline, and I'll come over with a boat to pick you up. After that, my family would be honoured if you joined us on our journey to New York City. You'll find plenty of ships heading back to Ireland from there."

"That's a kind offer, Shane, but the search for my brother might take a while."

Shane clapped him on the back. "We'll wait in town for two weeks before heading off to New York City. It's the least I can do for a young priest who's half off his rocker but has a heart the size of Canada."

Jamie shook his hand. "Then I hope to see you again soon."

Shane pulled down the telegraph until it read "Ahead Slow." The brass bell rang in confirmation. He stepped aside and offered the wheel back to Jamie. "We still have a couple more minutes before docking. I'll let you have your last turn as captain while I go and tell everyone below our plan."

Captain Shane soon returned to the wheel and the *Flying Irishman* came to a much less dramatic docking in St. Catharines. Shane was right. Only a small handful of people rescued from the quay decided to stay in Canada. Jamie, Beth, and Colin huddled low amongst the group of Irish that disembarked, hoping not to be noticed by the gathering crowd. The locals were wandering down to the water's edge in order to gawk at the sleek new steamship. They were surprised when the gangplank retracted as soon as the passengers had disembarked. The crew then pushed her away from its moorings and Jamie dared to sneak a quick glance at the now familiar superstructure of the *Flying Irishman* turning her nose seaward. The steam thickened over the twin smokestacks, and she set a course due south for the American border.

Jamie, Beth, and Colin parted ways from those heading back north to Toronto and instead turned south for the town of St. Catharines. The trio soon found themselves strolling along St. Paul Street in the heart of St. Catharines. They admired the many shops that catered to the large work crews rebuilding the Welland Canal. Jamie finally spied the door for which he was searching. Avoiding a carriage and several piles of horse manure, the three made their way across the street and into the town post office.

"I think it's high time we wrote a letter to your relatives, Colin. What do you think? Would you like to finally meet your aunt and uncle?"

The young boy nodded enthusiastically. Jamie sat on the steps of the post office and wrote a letter with a pen and paper he had removed from the captain's quarters of the *Carpathia II*. Colin climbed up to the top step and looked over Jamie's shoulder at the writing.

"What does it say?" he asked.

"It says there is a handsome young lad by the name of Colin O'Connor who would very much like to meet his aunt and uncle. I'm going to tell them that we should meet right here in front of the St. Catharine's post office in one week's time. Luckily, the town of Dundas is only a day's ride away for the letter. Is there anything else you would like me to say to them?"

Colin looked up at Jamie with his big blue eyes. "Can you tell them that my mommy and daddy and my sister and brother are not here any more?"

Jamie gave Colin a hug. "Of course, I will. There. All done. Now, can you take this envelope and money up to the postman and say it is going to your aunt and uncle in Dundas, Canada West?"

The boy nodded enthusiastically and opened the door to the post office. Beth leaned into Jamie. "I'm going to miss that little guy when he leaves."

"Me too. He reminds me so much of myself, right after I lost my parents."

Beth eyed the distant construction snaking up the side of the escarpment. "So what are we going to do now?"

"It's not that complicated a plan, really. We just start at one end of the canal and work our way to the other, asking every single person we meet if they have seen my brother."

Hundreds of men could be seen milling about the long, narrow worksite, popping in and out of the scar like a colony of ants tending to a massive nest.

"This search is going to take a while," whispered Beth.

As Colin skipped back to the steps empty-handed, Jamie stood up. "You're right, Beth. So I guess we better get started."

The first three days they spent searching for Ryan Galway ended with frustrating futility. Jamie meticulously interviewed every single worker that was on the lower end of the project; from the stonecutters and sappers working hard to turn the deep trench into a functional canal, to the engineers and supervisors who were poring over various drawings and calculations in the scattered foreman offices. Not surprisingly, many of the labourers were Irish. Most were sympathetic once Jamie explained his plight to them. It was all too common a story among those at the canal, as everyone had stories of family members who had been separated from each other either in Ireland, at the quarantine stations, or, more tragically, by the hand of death. Jamie could only hope that someone would either know Ryan's name or perhaps recognize their facial similarities, for many who knew them in Ireland said that except for the difference in hair colour, it was easy to tell that they were brothers. Jamie prayed for that next clue that could help lead them to his brother's whereabouts … but so far, no sign was forthcoming.

Colin had quickly tired of canvassing. As a gift to his younger companions, Jamie went into town and purchased both Colin and Beth fishing rods. Jamie first showed them how to scavenge for worms under rocks and logs, skewer them on a hook, then how to select a good section of a nearby creek for fishing. The two young travellers quickly found a suitable rock from which they could sit and dangle their lines into the fast-flowing water. With Colin content, Jamie left Beth in charge of the boy while he continued his search for Ryan further up the mountain.

It didn't take long for Beth and Colin to get the hang of the sport. In no time, they were bringing back pan-sized speckled trout for the evening dinner. Fascinated, Colin watched every gory step while Jamie cleaned the catch with Officer Keates's pocket knife. Jamie quizzed Colin and Beth on the fish's internal organs, explaining their function to the children as each organ plopped out from a sliced belly. Beth would then happily pan-fry their catch over the open campfire. A makeshift tent on the other side of the fire was their temporary home.

By the fourth day, Jamie had worked his way up to one of the most impressive feats of engineering he had ever seen. It was a series of twenty-five locks being built one after the other, straight up the steep-est part of the mountain. Jamie took the sketch he had kept since Montreal out of his pocket and compared it to the massive construction effort before him. It was a rough match. With growing enthusiasm, Jamie could simply sense that Ryan was nearby, drawn here by the immense engineering challenge of the project. Sending a ship up the side of a mountain would have been an engineering challenge that would have attracted Ryan like a bee to honey.

But that was just the thing … it had been eating away at Jamie ever since he had first found the diagram in Montreal. Why would his brother be here, working on a canal, when he knew how important it was to get back to Ireland and fulfill his obligations to the Brotherhood? Was he in need of money for the return trip? Did he not yet have the energy to make the taxing journey back home? Was he suffering an injury to the head? There was no way for Jamie to know the answer to his nagging questions. He just had to keep his faith that he would soon find Ryan and finally discover the truth.

Halfway up the giant staircase of locks, a group of a dozen workers was setting huge cut stones into the bottom of a lock. The crews were completing the locks from top to bottom. The highest locks were already finished, complete with stone facades and massive wooden doors. The lowest locks of the twenty-five were not much more than naked holes held in shape by wooden retaining walls.

Jamie avoided the crane and crew as they lowered a huge stone into the base of the lock. He stepped closer to the edge until he could clearly see the group of masons busily setting each stone into place. He stood and admired their work until the crew took a short break. Jamie then cupped his mouth and shouted down into the lock.

"Excuse me! Sorry to interrupt."

The men paused and looked up at the lad high above them.

"How can we help you?" asked the foreman of the group.

"Has an Irish worker arrived in the last few weeks by the name of Ryan Galway? He's two years older than me, and we look quite similar."

The older man shook his head. "Haven't heard of anyone by the name of Galway."

"He does look something like Patrick, though, doesn't he?" commented one of the crane operators, listening in on the conversation.

"And didn't Patrick arrive about three weeks ago?" said another.

"Yes," agreed the crane operator. "He did arrive three weeks ago but his name is Patrick Kell, not Ryan Galway."

"And where might I find Patrick Kell?" asked Jamie.

"You can usually find Patrick near the engineering hut at the top of the mountain," said the crane operator. "We're glad he arrived when he did. He helped solve a conduit problem that has plagued our construction site for six months. We were just about to start laying off workers when he got us back on track."

Jamie thanked the men and hiked up towards the top lock. Along the way, he interviewed three more groups of workers. Many agreed that he did look eerily similar to Patrick Kell. Upon reaching the top, Jamie took a moment to catch his breath and looked back over the massive engineering project that descended to a sparkling Lake Ontario far below. A cool breeze brushed across his brow. For just a moment, Jamie closed his eyes and allowed his imagination to take him back to his homeland. He saw the cobblestone streets and thatch-roofed cottages of his family's village. He smelled the rose-scented gardens and heard the moans of the oxen plowing patches of field for spring potato seeding. His family milled about, chatting about the day's events, sharing a laugh. He could even hear his brother guffawing with them in his own unique style. Jamie blinked hard in the bright sun. The guffawing was not coming from his imagination! Jamie spun around. Much to his disbelief, Ryan, his brother, walked out of a nearby cabin, laughing with an older gentleman who was holding an unrolled diagram in his hands.

"How did you become so rich when you think so small?" said Ryan.

The older man smiled. "All right, stop all the laughing at my expense and tell me what you mean."

Ryan pointed to the diagram. "Just make those conduits a little bit bigger and we could build a mill that could grind grain not only for the southern section of Canada West but for upper New York State as well!"

The man chuckled, rubbing his grey beard. "That's what I like about you, Patrick. You never stop thinking of new ways to spend my hard-earned money."

"Ryan?"

Unable to control himself, Jamie sprinted across the construction site.

"Ryan!"

Ryan staggered backwards at the sound of his name, shocked. "Jamie?"

Jamie charged in and threw his arms around his brother. The man accompanying Ryan stepped back in surprise, and nearby construction workers lowered their tools. The moment seemed to freeze in time as the two young men hugged and slapped each other on the backs with unbridled happiness. Jamie gripped his brother's face.

"You don't know how good it is to see you! I thought you had died at sea!"

Ryan beamed an ecstatic smile and embraced his brother. "It's so good to see you, Jamie!"

Jamie wiped back a tear. "I don't know where to begin.… I can't believe you're alive! What happened? Why are you here? I thought you were dead!"

"Everything is all right, Jamie. I'm right here and I'm very much alive."

"But how? I don't understand."

"Well, there's no mistaking that you two are indeed brothers," said the older man. "I take it that this a reunion of some sort?"

"Yes, sir," agreed Ryan, grinning from ear to ear. "Mr. Montgomery, I'd like you to meet my little brother Jamie. Jamie, this is Mr. Thomas Montgomery. He's the owner of the canal."

"A pleasure," he replied, shaking Jamie's hand. "Well, this isn't the first time I've had the privilege of witnessing a reunion on my worksite. You and Jamie take as much time as you need to get reacquainted. I'll be in my office thinking about your conduit idea."

"Thank you, sir," said Ryan.

Jamie laughed, still in shock, as Mr. Montgomery walked away and the workers turned back to their tasks, looking pleased to have been part of such a happy moment.

"It's so good to see you!" exclaimed Jamie.

"And you! The last thing I expected to see at the canal site was my little brother from Ireland. How did you find me?"

Jamie smiled. "It wasn't easy."

Jamie related the entire adventure to his brother while Ryan listened, awestruck. Ryan looked off past the blue horizon of Lake Ontario, trying to imagine the incredible scenes. Then, he sank to his knees when Jamie described the moment of finding the family text within the burning House of Parliament.

"The book was destroyed in the fire?" Ryan whispered, his face turning ashen.

Jamie grinned and lifted up the leather flap to his satchel.

"Wrong. I rescued it."

"You have it now?"

Ryan wiped his sleeve across his face to remove the tears that streamed freely down his cheek. He took the book from Jamie, holding it against his chest. Jamie waited patiently while his brother recomposed himself.

"I thought our family's book had been lost forever! I'm so sorry, Jamie. This was all my fault! If I hadn't rushed into that skirmish with the British soldiers, none of this would have happened."

Jamie helped him back to his feet. "We can't change the past. But tell me, how did you end up losing the book in the first place?"

"I had been told that it had been washed overboard during a terrible storm. We were approaching the North American coastline. I was helping the crew battle through the gale, and when I returned to my berth, the door was wide open, everything was wet with sea water, the furniture had been thrown about, and my satchel with the book was gone!"

Jamie squeezed Ryan's shoulder. "It's all right. It was stolen from your room by one of the crewmen, and then likely sold to the captain. After that, it ended up in the parliament library. There was nothing you could have done about it."

"But now *you* have the book. Fantastic!"

"*We* have the book. And now *I* have some questions for you. What brought you way out here, Ryan, to work on a canal? Why didn't you come home?"

"It's a long story."

Jamie smiled. "Your boss told you to take as much time as you needed."

Ryan guffawed and nodded. "I started off the crossing in the fourth-class hold, unconscious. When I woke up, I was stunned to find myself surrounded by destitute Irish immigrants on a packed ship. I was told I was on the *Carpathia* and we were just starting a crossing to Canada. Shocked at the situation, I argued with any and every crew member I could find to let me out and allow me to leave the ship. But the British soldiers must have informed them that I was troublemaker. I was beaten every time I complained until we were well out to sea and there was no going back. Then, the sickness started. Jamie, it was the worst living nightmare I could ever imagine! I saw so much suffering, disease, and death that I will be haunted for the rest of my life. I personally carried thirty-seven bodies to the deck railing for burial at sea and I will remember the faces of each and every one of those Irish men, women, and children for the rest of my life.

"I didn't think it could get worse, but then a massive storm hit. Our ship rolled dangerously onto its side, and a sailor fell through a hatch and into our fourth-class hold, landing hard on one of the ship's ribbing. I could tell he was badly hurt. The sailor had both a broken arm and leg. Trying to help, I had narrow strips of wood brought in from a nearby cargo hold. We tore up bits of cloth, and I made splints for both his broken arm and leg. Then, with the help of the crew, we carefully hoisted him back up to deck level."

"Captain Chamberlain heard about my medical talents. He came down and said there were more wounded up on deck and asked, since there was no physician aboard, if I would be willing to tend to them as well. Of course, I volunteered my services, but when he asked me my name, I took the name of a passenger that I'd helped bury at sea, a young lad named Patrick Kell. Many men were lost at sea during the storm, and I decided Ryan Galway was going to be one of them. Once up on deck, it wasn't hard for me to change the name in the deceased manifest when no one was looking. It was kept in the infirmary that I had set up near the officer's quarters. I even attached one of my letters to the manifest as proof that I had died. I thought having a different identity would make it easier for me when I eventually returned to Ireland, in case the British were determined to try and keep me out of my home country."

"So that explains your death certificate and why everyone around here calls you Patrick," commented Jamie. "But how did you end up working at the Welland Canal?"

"One of the patients whom I tended, a gentleman by the name of Martin Bigglesworth, was a British mechanical engineer who had broken his arm at the height of the storm. He stayed in his own bed to recuperate, and it was while I was in his cabin that I spied some notes and diagrams on his desk. I started asking him questions about the drawings, and he explained that he had been hired to help solve a problem with one of the canals being built in Canada West. I made several comments on the written calculations and offered a new solution to the conduit problem he had been working on. Martin was intrigued by my engineering insight. He paid for me to move up to an empty room in first class so that we could continue our discussions.

"Before long, we were mentally tearing down models of the canal system and rebuilding it to see if we could solve the many dilemmas facing the project. You see, they wanted to use the water of the canal to help power the machinery in factories that were to be built along the base of the escarpment. Their original designs were all wrong for what they wanted to do, but after a week of problem solving, we had re-engineered the conduits properly so that they could carry enough water to power the machinery."

Jamie held up his hands. "Okay. I understand you wanting to pass the time with mathematics and engineering, but once in Montreal, why didn't you simply jump on the next ship back to Ireland? Why did you come all the way out here to St. Catharines?"

Ryan's face flushed red with embarrassment. He patted the book in his hand. "This is the reason. I had lost the *Book of Galway*, our ancestors' ancient text. I lost it, and by doing so, I lost the key to our people's treasure. How could I face you or the Brotherhood again after such an act of selfishness and stupidity?

"As we approached the Port of Montreal, Martin informed me that he was too weak to make the next leg of the journey to St. Catharines, so he asked me to go to the construction site in his place. He sent me on with a note of explanation that was addressed to a Mr. Thomas Montgomery … so here I am. For three weeks, I've been helping Thomas re-engineer the conduits to his canal."

Jamie suddenly stared at his brother with a tinge of anger. "Were you going to let me go on thinking that you were dead? I was devastated when I saw your death certificate in Montreal."

Ryan looked down. "I know. And I'm sorry. I would have contacted you, very soon, in fact. I swear. I didn't think you would have found out so soon. I had no idea the Brotherhood would have sent you out after me. After I came to grips with the loss of the book, I was going to write the letter."

Jamie grabbed him by the shoulders. "But now we have the book back! Don't you see? You can return home with me, back to Ireland!"

"Yes, I know," said Ryan defensively. "It's truly a miracle that you were able to rescue the book. But now it's my turn to ask you a question. After recovering the book, however did you track me down? You thought I was dead."

Jamie reached into his pocket, unfolded a sheet of paper, and passed it to Ryan.

"I found this."

"This is one of the sketches of the lock system I made for Martin! Wherever did you find it? I left all those drawings with him when I left the ship."

"It was hidden in the back of the *Book of Galway*. And look at the date."

Ryan smiled. "June 17th, 1847."

"Days after the date written on your death certificate."

"Brilliant! You knew then that I hadn't died!"

"Wrong. I didn't know you were alive for sure, but at least there was a chance you were still alive, and now I had a reason to keep on looking."

"And the drawing led you here?"

Jamie nodded. "Mr. Kessler, a friend I met in Montreal, a bookseller, helped me figure out that it was likely a diagram of the Welland Canal, so I made my way down here as quickly as possible."

Jamie then told him about the adventures on the *Flying Dutchman*, and Ryan hooted with laughter.

"Serves the Western Star Shipping Line right for what they did to us and the book. Well done! So I've lost count of how many people you have saved since leaving Ireland. Are you aiming to beat Moses' record?"

Jamie shook his head. "Forget any record. Forget everything else. All I want, Ryan, is for you to come home with me."

Ryan tried to speak, but turned away.

"What is it?" asked Jamie.

"Jamie, you have to understand, I was tormented by the fact that I had lost the book, lost you, and betrayed the Brotherhood. You have now released me from all of that guilt by finding me and showing me the book. I'll never be able to thank you enough. And I'll never forget this moment of seeing you again. But that doesn't mean I'm about to leave this project or this new country. Jamie, there's a lot more going on here than you realize, something even bigger than the Brotherhood. I've already decided that I want to be a part of it and that I'm going to stay."

* * *

Jonathon Wilkes casually walked down the wharf and up the gangplank to the *Maid of the Rideau*. After stepping through a hatch, he made his way along the plush hallway and let himself into the captain's quarters. Captain Chamberlain and Mr. Reeves were waiting on leather chairs on either side of a large oak coffee table, both nursing a strong drink.

"Ah, Mr. Wilkes," said Reeves, "I'm so glad you've returned. Can I offer you a whiskey as well?"

"No thank you, but you might want to pour yourself a second glass after I share with you the information I've gathered from the St. Catharines locals."

"Is it that bad?" asked Chamberlain, reaching over for the bottle. "Did those delinquents sink my baby?!"

"Say it isn't true!" stammered Reeves, who downed the remaining alcohol from his glass. "I'd be finished!"

"No, I'm fairly confident that the *Carpathia II* is still afloat. It's just docked in a location that you might not like."

"Please," begged Reeves, "no more games. Tell us what you know. Where is the *Carpathia*?"

"It seems that she did make a short stop here three days ago. According to the locals, the ship was crammed full of Irish immigrants."

"What?" gasped Reeves. "How can that be? There were supposed to be only a dozen children on board my ship. Where in blazes did all the Irish come from?"

Wilkes chuckled. "It seems our child captain pulled a fast one on the town of Toronto by rescuing all of the Irish immigrants they had rounded up and penned on Queen's Quay last week. After the rescue, the ship stopped here for a short time, where only a few of the passengers disembarked. The ship was still full with many Irish families when she left port and headed south."

Reeves paled in shock. "South, as in towards the United States of America?"

Wilkes lowered his head in sympathy. "I believe so. I just talked to a seaman on shore leave from a schooner based in Rochester, New York. He claimed he saw a large ship that matches the description of the *Carpathia II* tied to a little-used wharf just on the other side of the Niagara River. If that is indeed her, then your ship is docked on American soil."

Reeves jumped to his feet. "This is awful! If the U.S. government sinks their claws into her, they'll hold her as evidence of human smuggling! This whole travesty could become an unending legal nightmare — which will cost the company a fortune!"

Chamberlain pounded his fist angrily on the table. "My ship is less than an hour's sail away from here. Perhaps there is something we can do to help salvage the situation."

"Yes!" agreed Reeves. "After sunset, we could sail the *Maid of the Rideau* up to the *Carpathia II* and tow her the short distance back into Canadian waters, but we'd have to get to her before the Americans claim her for their own."

"As long as she's still in one piece," exclaimed Chamberlain, "my crew and I will get her back into Canadian waters, that I can guarantee."

"Then we must leave immediately! There's no time to lose! My job depends on it!"

"I believe retrieving your ship at this time is the right course of action," concurred Wilkes, "but I'm afraid you'll have to continue on without me."

"What?" questioned Reeves. "I thought we had an agreement that you would help catch the wretched pirates who took my ship. You're not keeping up your end of the bargain."

Wilkes smiled. "Actually, I *would* like to keep my end of the bargain and that is why I will be leaving you at this time. I heard further reports that several children disembarked with the handful of Irish here in St. Catharines. I have a hunch that these children might be the ringleaders of your whole nasty situation. If I'm wrong, then I will catch up with you in a couple of days' time. Don't worry, Mr. Reeves. One way or another, I'll bring those children to justice."

"Fine," huffed Reeves, dismissing Wilkes with a wave of his hand. "You go and do your investigating. As for you, Chamberlain, I want you to get this ship on its way immediately! Reclaiming the *Carpathia II* is our top priority!"

Chapter 20

The raucous mess hall brimmed with a festive spirit. The workers cheered and raised their drinks when the man they knew as Patrick Kell proudly announced that he had been reunited with a long-lost brother. Beth and Colin were also invited to the celebration. Everyone enjoyed the enormous portions of celebratory food that Mr. Montgomery provided for the event. After dinner, Ryan stood up and gave an emotional toast to family, lost and found. Soaking in the smiles and good tidings, Jamie felt, for the first time since leaving Ireland, truly happy. The cooks served up a special dessert of peach cobbler and by the time the dishes were cleared, everyone felt as if they had been part of something very special.

The sun was setting behind the escarpment as the two Galway boys and the children left the mess hall. Colin tugged on Jamie's satchel. He was staring at their fishing rods leaning up against the frame of the mess hall.

"Jamie, can Beth and I go fishing?"

"How about saying thank you to Ryan for that delicious meal first?"

The little boy scrunched up his face in a big smile. "Thank you, Ryan!"

"You're welcome, Colin. And Beth, it was a pleasure having this chance to meet you."

Beth ran and wrapped her arms around the brothers. "I'm so happy that you two are together again!"

"So are we," agreed Jamie.

"Come on, Beth!" said Colin, grabbing her sleeve and yanking her away from the embrace.

"All right, Colin," said Beth, looking back over her shoulder towards the boys. "Someone told us there is a great creek for brook trout just on the other side of the locks."

"I know the creek," said Ryan, pointing towards the woods. "After you go over that small hill, follow the creek back a little bit until you come to a big boulder. Just sit on that rock and lower the worms. You'll get lots of bites!"

"Good luck!" said Jamie.

"Thank you!" they both shouted as they grabbed their poles and ran off.

"Your children are very sweet; Beth nearly talked my ear off at dinner," said Ryan, cheekily. "You should be very proud of them."

"You make me sound like I'm their dad," said Jamie, giving his brother a shove. "I'm just helping them out. They've both been through a lot, just like us."

"Aye, it does take me back, watching those two supporting each other, and all on their own."

"I'm hoping that they won't be on their own for much longer," replied Jamie. "Colin's aunt and uncle should be here in a few days' time."

"Good. It's important for kids to have a place to call home."

Jamie stopped and stared at his brother. "Just like you have back in Ireland. The Brotherhood is your home. It needs you."

Ryan shook his head. "Let's go for a walk."

Ryan led Jamie across the top of the worksite. The cleared site portrayed a stunning vista of Lake Ontario and the distant shores of Canada West. To the right, a cloud of mist rising up in the cooling air marked the magnificent natural beauty of Niagara Falls. Ryan opened his arms to the surrounding land.

"I already told you, I'm not leaving this place."

"You said that you're not going back because you've joined this rebellious band of Irish immigrants? What was their name again?"

"They're calling themselves an army. Some members are here working with me on the Welland Canal. That's how I found out about the group. They're purchasing arms to fight for Irish freedom wherever the British have interests, including here in Canada."

"But joining an armed militia goes against all of your priesthood vows!"

Ryan eyed him skeptically. "You're one to talk about going against our vows. What about breaking into the House of Parliament and stealing a brand new steamship?"

Jamie sighed. "I only *borrowed* the ship, and there's no longer any House of Parliament, so that incursion no longer counts. Do you realize what this Irish army is planning to do? You're talking about full-blown warfare! Ryan, you will be attacking and killing British soldiers!"

Ryan locked eyes with his brother. "I know."

"How can you do this? How can you go out and *kill* people?"

"Did King David not lead the Israelites into war? Sometimes warfare is necessary."

"King David was protecting his people from invasion."

"And so are we. Can't you see the connection, Jamie? England invaded our land! This is the only way to remove them once and for all! It's no different from what's described in the Bible."

"How is killing going to solve anything?"

"The British government only respects power! How did the American people achieve *their* independence? Did they simply write a nice letter to the King of England, asking 'Please, your highness, can we run our own country?' Of course not! The British responded to their requests for freedom by sending in shiploads of armed redcoats to destroy all those who supported any idea of independence. But unlike us, the American people quietly organized themselves into militias. They gathered weapons. They practised their assaults. When the time was right, the British colonies erupted into a bloody war of independence. It took years and they had to sacrifice much of their own blood, but eventually they gained their freedom for future generations. And I'm saying that the time has come when the people of Ireland must follow the same path."

"War is never the answer," countered Jamie. "There are also peaceful ways of achieving freedom."

Ryan shook his head. "But that is only if you command respect from your adversary. Do you think the British government has any respect for us? They take no interest in millions of our people dying of hunger, right next door to their very own country. We're mere animals to them and to get the respect we need, for us to win back our own country, we must stop rolling over to their every whim and learn how to bite."

"I don't agree," countered Jamie. "If we do what you say and support militias like this, then we're really no better than the British government. And don't forget, there are many people in Britain and around the world who also care about Ireland and its people. Distant world leaders have sent us money and food. And you know how important the church is to our people. We provide the food, clothing, and spiritual guidance our people need to survive this tragedy. Our role is clear. It's non-violent. We cannot take up arms."

"I know there are some out there who care about the Irish," Ryan said, taking the Brotherhood ring off his finger, "but there just aren't enough of them to make a difference. I'm sorry, Jamie. I'm finished with the priesthood, and the Brotherhood. Sometimes there are moments when you just have to fight for what's right."

He handed the ring to Jamie. Jamie rolled the ring around in his palm and shook his head.

"You know, I wouldn't have joined the Brotherhood if it weren't for you."

"And I am so proud of you, little brother. We've been through so much together, but it's time to find our own paths. Yours is in the Brotherhood. Mine is fighting for Irish independence."

A third voice suddenly boomed into the conversation. "And mine is relieving you of the *Book of Galway*."

Ryan and Jamie spun to find a tall, narrow-faced man pointing a double-barrelled handgun at them.

"Do I know you?" demanded Ryan, eyeing the gun.

The stranger chuckled. "No. Not really. But I do know the two of you. You are brothers, correct? Ryan and Jamie Galway. You both belong to the Brotherhood, a collection of Irish monks who protect a long forgotten treasure. I aim to get myself a boatload of that treasure and I'm going to need the book that's sitting in your leather satchel to do it. So, if you don't mind, just pass the satchel to me and I'll be on my way."

Jamie's eyes flared with recognition. "That was you tracking us in Montreal! You threw Beth into the fire at the House of Parliament!"

"She was simply a loose end. All would have gone according to plan if you had simply put the book into the sack that was brought up ahead of you. I have to admit, I didn't think that you'd risk keeping it on your person while surrounded by an inferno."

"I'm going to kill him," growled Jamie. The man aimed the gun at Jamie's chest and pulled back the trigger.

"Whoa there, my pacifist brother," growled Ryan, blocking Jamie with his arm. "If he wanted to kill us, he could have pulled the trigger by now."

"A splendid observation," agreed the stranger. "You see, I'm a changed man since that incident in Montreal. I could have killed the children who are sitting over there by the creek and then you in order to claim the book for myself, but the fact that you escaped the fire unharmed ... well, I would say that moment falls under what I would call the miraculous category. So who am I to argue with God for choosing to save your life? I shall, in turn, respect His decision and do the same. All I want is the book, and then you and the children can go free."

"But the book alone is no good to you," argued Jamie. "Having it in your possession will not get you any closer to the treasure."

The stranger scratched his chin in thought. "Ah yes, you are speaking of the other keys to the treasure. It's true that you need all of the keys in order to find the treasure's location, but I have also discovered that without the book, the other keys will be rendered useless. So that will put the Brotherhood in a rather awkward pickle.... Are they going to share some of the treasure with me to get their book back, or will they allow the treasure to become lost forever? I'm betting that members of the Brotherhood are reasonable folk. They will surely come to see the situation my way. All I'm asking for is enough treasure so that I can live the rest of my life in reasonable comfort. And if the Brotherhood chooses to be stubborn in this matter, then I will at least have in my possession a book that could fetch a very hefty price from a private collector.

"With the sale of the book, I'm afraid that the Brotherhood's secret of an Irish treasure will finally be out in the open. Treasure hunters from all over the world will descend upon your tiny little island. They will tear apart every inch of countryside looking for it, and they are very good at what they do. I can guarantee, the treasure will be found, if not by me, then by one of them. So really, I am offering the much better alternative. All I'm asking for is a cut of the least important pieces of the treasure and then you monks can keep the rest. Its location will remain a secret for as long as you want."

"We're talking about the national treasure of an entire country," hissed Jamie. "You have no right to take any of it for yourself."

The stranger waved his gun. "I think I'll let the other members of the Brotherhood make that decision.

Now, Mr. Galway, hand me the book. Even though I don't want to use force, you may leave me with no alternative."

Sitting on a large rock, Beth and Colin soon came to realize that Ryan had led them to an almost magical fishing location. They barely had to dip their worms into the rippling rapids of the creek before their rod would snap down with a tremendous hit. Squealing with delight, the children pulled up trout after sparkling trout.

Beth couldn't contain her smile. Since being orphaned from her parents two years previously, she had never been happier. She finally felt important and needed. She had saved Jamie's life from a fiery disaster, and now she was witness to a wonderful reunion with his brother. Sitting cross-legged, she silently hoped that these times would never end, that their adventure could continue on forever and ever.

Beth sighed. She also knew that was just silly day-dreaming. Jamie, from the very beginning, had said that he needed to go back home to Ireland. She couldn't bear the thought of not being with him any longer. Besides her family, she had never been closer to anyone in her whole life. Beth made her decision. She would go back to Ireland with Jamie. That seemed like such a crazy thought, but she could think of no alternative. Yes, he was a priest, but she cared so much for him, perhaps she could join a nunnery so that they could still be together in some way. Then, she remembered the ashen faces of her parents, their spirits slipping away from her down in the dark putrid belly of the ship. Her parents had died trying to get her away from that diseased island, and now she was determined to go back. Her heart broke as she contemplated her dilemma. But what else could she do?

Above her on the hill, she had seen Jamie and Ryan walk by as they caught up on all of the activities of the past few weeks. She couldn't imagine their happiness. What would it feel like to be reunited with members of her family, her mom or dad, after she thought that they had passed away? What would be the very first words she would share with them? How different would her future be?

Colin suddenly lifted up his rod and broke her train of thought. A golden brook trout wriggled furiously on the end of his line.

"Beth, can you help me?" he asked.

"Sure, hold it still. Let me grab the line. There we go."

While holding the line steady with one hand, she grasped the slimy fish with the other. Then, she slipped her small fingers into the fish's mouth and carefully worked the hook out of its gasping gills. As she turned to throw the fish into the bucket, a movement caught her eye. She looked up the hill to see a tall, thin man with a long coat walking in the same direction the brothers had just taken. His long hooked nose and cold eyes instantly sent a shiver down her spine. She gasped. She had seen that face before.

Beth quietly lowered her rod to the ground.

"Why aren't you putting a new worm on the hook?" complained Colin.

"Shh!" commanded Beth. "Quietly put down your rod and follow me."

Colin could sense Beth's apprehension and did as he was told. Together, they carefully slid off the rock until they were shielded from view.

"What's wrong, Beth?"

"I think Jamie and his brother are in trouble."

"Trouble?"

"I just saw a bad man follow Jamie and his brother into the woods. They might need our help. Remember how Jamie is helping you find your aunt and uncle?"

He nodded.

"Would you like to help him now?"

Bravely, he nodded again.

"You must promise me two things. You mustn't say another word and you must do exactly as I say. Promise?"

He nodded.

"Good boy. Now let's go find Jamie and Ryan."

Jamie pulled the *Book of Galway* out of the sack and held it against his chest. "I can't give it to you."

Ryan looked to him in shock. "Jamie, what are you doing? Just give him the book!"

"Just as you're prepared to die fighting for Ireland, I'm prepared to die for this book."

"We'll figure something else out!" Ryan argued. "He's going to kill you! What about the kids?"

"They'll be all right. Beth can look after Colin."

"Well, I don't want to lose you! You're my brother! Give him the book!"

"No."

Wilkes sighed. "Well, I suppose I knew it was going

to come down to this." Wilkes raised the gun and pointed it at Jamie's head.

"Jamie! Jamie! Jamie!" a little voice called out. Colin burst into the clearing, ran towards Jamie, and threw himself into his arms.

"Colin," Jamie cried, "what are you doing? You shouldn't be here!"

Distracted, Wilkes lowered the gun slightly. A child in Jamie's arms complicated things and he hesitated, not sure what to do next. He had only two bullets loaded in his gun. Jamie turned sideways to protect the child from the firearm, giving Wilkes another clear target, the back of Jamie's head. He lifted the gun and began to pull the trigger.

Behind Wilkes, Beth crawled out as close as she dared, then burst out of the bushes. Wilkes heard her and turned, swinging his pistol, but it was too late. Beth threw herself into his long, spindly legs, her shoulder hitting him right behind the knees. He screamed in agony as both he and Beth crashed into a heap before the boys. Ryan grabbed hold of Beth's hand and launched her up and out of the tangled mess. Jamie kept his grip on Colin and together they fled from the armed attacker. Wilkes, still with the gun in his hand, cursed and scrambled back to his feet.

"Come on!" yelled Ryan. "This way!"

There was a bang, and a bullet whistled past Jamie's ear. Wilkes was not about to give up. With Ryan in the lead, they splashed through the creek and turned back towards the canal. A second shot rang out and bits of stone exploded from the rock Beth and Colin had been fishing on only moments earlier. Jamie stole a glance behind him. The stranger was limping slightly but still moving towards them with surprising agility. If he didn't have Colin in his arms, and Ryan leading Beth, then the young men could have easily outrun him. Now it was an even race.

They scrambled over the hill that led down to the highest lock. Ryan ran up to the work shed at the top of the canal, tried the door, but it had already been locked for the night. It was getting dark and the work site was deserted. They needed a place to hide. The area was wide open and provided no hiding spots. Ryan looked to the lock itself.

"Follow me!"

When they reached the edge of the finished first lock, Jamie noticed that the canal behind the lock was full of water from the distant Lake Erie. The water was being held back by the set of large wooden doors. They came to a stop at the top of a metal ladder that led down into the bottom of the empty lock.

"Climb down!" he ordered.

"Down there?" Jamie argued. "We'll be sitting ducks! It will be like shooting fish in a puddle! We won't have a chance!"

Ryan gripped his brother's shoulder. "Trust me!"

Jamie took a deep breath and nodded to Beth.

"Go!"

Beth clambered down the ladder with Jamie and Colin close behind. Ryan glanced over to the shed while descending and, just before his head disappeared behind the stone lip of the lock, saw Wilkes running to the shed.

Bursting upon the construction site, Wilkes had scanned the open area for the children and the young men, but they were nowhere to be seen. He knew they hadn't had time to cross the entire barren area before he'd arrived so they must be somewhere close. The shed was the logical place to hide. He limped quickly over to the door, but it was locked. He glanced in the window, checking every nook and corner of the shed. It was empty. He saw the mess hall in the distance but decided that there was no way the group could have made it all the way across before his arrival. He was just about to curse his bad luck when his ear picked up the echo of a kicked pebble. It came from the direction of the locks. Senses alert, he limped over to the edge of the first lock and looked down. Then saw Ryan, the older brother, bending down into a large round pipe at the bottom of the canal. Wilkes aimed his reloaded gun and fired. A spray of blood splattered the side of the lock as Ryan disappeared into the pipe. He'd been hit. Wilkes reloaded his gun once again. Now there was no need to rush. The whole lot of them were trapped inside the pipe. With his gun pointing at the mouth of the pipe, he walked cautiously toward the steel ladder and lowered himself down into the bottom of the lock.

"Stop here," ordered Ryan as they huddled in the pipe. Jamie could hear him gasping for breath.

"Are you all right, Ryan?" asked Jamie, unable to see anything in the pitch darkness of the pipe. "I heard a shot."

"I've been shot in the shoulder," replied Ryan, "but I'm fine,"

"Shot?" Jamie exclaimed. "Let me see!"

"No! Listen! We don't have much time! Wilkes knows where we are, and I can guarantee he'll be right on our tail in just a few seconds. Jamie, I can't move my right arm so you're going to have to do everything. Now listen carefully. Here's the plan." After Ryan had explained his idea, Jamie left the children with his brother, swung open a metal door on the side of the pipe, stepped through the small opening, and entered a second pipe. He then closed the metal door behind him and locked it in place with a metal bolt.

"Ryan, I don't like the dark." whispered Colin.

"I know this pipe like the back of my hand," soothed Ryan. "I know every weld and bolt, and I can walk you through it with my eyes closed."

"But my eyes are open, and I still can't see anything!" complained Colin.

"Shhh," Beth commanded.

"Beth, I'll hold your hand, and you hold Colin's. Whatever you do, don't let go of each other's hand! Now follow me."

They took a few more steps along the pipe until Ryan abruptly stopped in the pitch darkness. He sat down on the floor of the pipe. He reached back and pulled Beth down onto his lap. He then had Colin sit on her lap, as if they were ready to zoom down a snow-covered hill on a long toboggan.

"Why are we sitting like this?" she asked.

"Do you like slides?"

"Oh, yes!" said Colin.

"Well, here's a good one for you. Beth, this has to be a silent ride. Cover his mouth and don't let go."

"Okay."

Ryan put his good hand over Beth's lips and then without warning, pushed them off the edge. Beth and

Colin gave a muffled scream as they all shot straight down the pipe and into the unending darkness.

Jamie had to time his move perfectly. Reaching the base of lock number two, he slowly stuck his head out of the pipe and looked backwards toward lock number one. The huge wooden doors of the lock were shut and everything seemed to be quiet. As silently as he could, Jamie stepped across to the metal ladder and started the climb up, one rung at a time, toward the top edge of the lock.

Upon reaching the ground, Jamie quietly rolled onto his stomach. He stayed low and crawled over to the edge of lock number one. He peered over the stone edge of the lock. There! He could see their attacker. He was just reaching the bottom of the ladder, gun drawn and aimed toward the pipe. Wilkes was moving slowly, cautiously, not taking any chances. Jamie knew he assumed they were trapped in the pipe and had nowhere to go. Finally, Jamie saw him disappear into the pipe.

It was now or never. Jamie got to his feet and burst into a sprint for the head of the lock.

Ryan helped Beth and Colin crawl onto the floor of a huge building. Their wet, dark ride in the pipe had ended just feet away from the paddles of a massive waterwheel. Ryan, Beth, and Colin clambered over the top edge of the sluice channel which would, when full of speeding water, power the waterwheel. Ryan held a finger to his lips, reminding them to be quiet.

Suddenly, from inside the pipe, a faraway voice echoed down to them.

"There's no point hiding any longer. Give yourselves up now, and I'll let the younger two live."

Ryan stumbled over towards a pile of building material left from the construction of the sawmill. Beth grimaced at the sight of Ryan's back as he made his way across the massive building. The back of his shirt was completely soaked in blood. Ryan slung two pieces of wood under his good arm and returned to the children. He passed one piece to Beth and kept the other for himself.

"The piece of wood for you is in case I pass out," Ryan whispered as he leaned heavily against the wall. "I want you to watch that pipe like a hawk, young lady. If anything but water comes out of it, I want you to start whacking it as hard as you can and don't stop whacking it until it stops moving for good. Understand?"

She nodded, gravely, lifting the wood above her head.

"Good girl."

Ryan pulled Colin around until the little boy was behind him, protecting him from what might soon come their way. Together, they stared silently at the opening in the pipe and waited.

Wilkes stepped further into the darkness.

"I know you're in here. Sitting quietly and waiting for me to leave isn't going to work. I'm going to hunt you down, one by one. If I have to come in and find you, I'll have to kill each one of you as I flush you out of this rat hole. The deal to save the children will then be off."

Wilkes paused and listened. Only a thick silence hung in the air. Something was wrong. His intuition was telling him that he should be hearing at least a slight sign of life in these tight confines ... a shuffle, a whimper perhaps, at least something ... but there was nothing. Had they found another way out? His foot came to the edge of a sudden drop downwards in the pipe. He didn't want to risk a suicide plunge into the unknown. Then, a noise did come down the pipe, but it was coming from behind. It was a sound that sent a shiver down his spine. It was the sound of rushing water! Wilkes turned and sprinted as fast as he could for the mouth of the pipe.

Jamie cranked the handles as fast as his arms would turn. The handles were attached to a round gear, which was then connected to a long metal rod. The rod extended down to the bottom of the gate and was attached to a door. The door held back the water from the canal. As Jamie cranked the gear, the door rose and a torrent of water sprayed into the lock. There were four doors in all. After cranking the first one wide open, Jamie ran for the second gear and started turning that handle as well. A second geyser of water erupted into the lock. He watched with satisfaction as the water frothed along the base of the lock and angrily disappeared into the pipe that contained their attacker.

Jamie finished the second gate and was jogging to the third when a movement caught his eye. Much to his disbelief, a hand suddenly appeared from the pipe that was quickly filling with rushing water. It reached out and grabbed on to the ladder next to the opening. A second hand swung around and wrapped its fingers around a different rung, while somehow still holding on to a gun. Wilkes, drenched and exhausted, pulled his body out from the frothing current.

Stunned by the turn of events, Jamie left the gates and ran along the side of the lock, keeping away from its edge so that Wilkes couldn't see him approach. When he was within arm's reach of the ladder, he removed the leather satchel from his shoulder and lifted the flap. Eyes closed in prayer, Jamie took the ring of the Brotherhood off his finger for the first time since receiving it years ago and placed it, along with the book and his brother's ring, in the satchel. He put the satchel on the ground, and then crept to the top of the ladder and waited.

First a hand and then Wilkes's head appeared over the stone lip of the lock. Without a moment's hesitation, Jamie lashed out with his foot and crashed it into Wilkes's wrist. Wilkes screamed in pain as the gun went flying into the flooded lock below.

Before Wilkes could get himself off the ladder, Jamie lashed out again with his foot, catching Wilkes on the shoulder. Wilkes felt his shoulder explode in pain, but this time he was prepared for the attack and on contact, he wrapped his arm around Jamie's leg. Jamie wasn't expecting such a quick move, and he stumbled off balance toward the edge of the lock. Trying to stop himself from being thrown into the water below, Jamie made a desperate grab for the top of the ladder, reaching out with his left hand. He swung off the edge of the lock and caught the ladder, but his momentum carried Jamie out over the water and swung him about in a big arc. He grabbed the far side of the ladder with his other hand and buried his two knees hard into Wilkes's lower back. Wilkes howled in pain as Jamie tried to scramble up his attacker to reach solid ground. Enraged, Wilkes swung a fist up and over his head, which connected squarely with Jamie's jaw. Jamie felt his head explode as the fist smashed his jawbone. Jamie lost his grip on the ladder and in desperation, grabbed on to the only thing he could, Wilkes's coat. Wilkes, hanging on by only one hand, couldn't handle the sudden weight on his back and his remaining hand slipped off the ladder. Together, Wilkes and Jamie fell with a tremendous splash into the bottom of the lock.

Lying on their backs and gasping for air, the two men were swept into the pipe by the raging current. Both were momentarily stunned by their predicament as they were swallowed up by darkness. Their bodies accelerated down the slippery metal tube. Jamie's only advantage over Wilkes was that he knew what was coming. The sudden drop would be upon them in a second. He only had one chance. Catching Wilkes by surprise, Jamie clawed and crawled like a madman over Wilkes's body, pushing him ahead in the water, while Jamie fell in behind. Before Wilkes could respond, they hit the edge. The bottom of the pipe seemed to drop out from under them as the two men were sent into freefall with the gushing water. Like bullets from a gun, the men accelerated down the tube until the pipe suddenly levelled off. Jamie braced himself. He curled himself up into a ball, praying that Ryan's plan would work.

Wilkes screamed in horror. A giant paddlewheel suddenly materialized in the gloom, its blades briskly spinning in the torrent of rushing water. Wilkes's legs were the first to emerge from the pipe and then disappear under the paddles, the bones in his legs snapping like toothpicks. The waterwheel then crushed its way up his body until it reached his chest, grinding to a halt, impeded by the sheer mass of his body. Wilkes managed a final gurgle as water sprayed out in all directions, searching for a way around the human obstruction. Jamie came next, crashing hard into Wilkes's pinned head and shoulders. Jamie, too, was caught in the torrent of water, his body thrown up against the stationary waterwheel and pinned there by the sheer force of the torrent. He thrashed about, trying to find something to grab on to. Suddenly a hand grabbed him under his armpit, pulling him out of the raging torrent and onto the wet wooden floor. In the dim light, he could make out Beth's drenched face looking down at him, alarmed.

"Jamie, are you all right?"

Jamie hacked up a lungful of water.

"Thanks to you...." He coughed. "You saved me again."

"Can you stand? Ryan's badly hurt. He needs to see a doctor."

Jamie looked over to the wall to where Ryan was slouched, unconscious. Colin sat next to him, stroking Ryan's hair. Jamie somehow staggered to his feet and made his way over to his brother. He bent down, gathered Ryan in his arms, and found the strength to pick him up off the floor.

"I'll take him down to base camp with Colin to find a doctor. Beth, I need you to run back up to the highest lock and grab my satchel. It has the book in it."

"And what about him?" she asked, pointing to the jammed waterwheel. A pale arm hung over the side of the pipe below the tremendous spray of water.

Jamie staggered towards the door with his brother. "I don't think we have to worry about him anymore."

Chapter 21

Beth, Colin, Ryan, and Jamie enjoyed their cold lemonades as they watched the Saturday shoppers pass them by from the steps of the St. Catharines post office. It had been four days since the shootout at the locks. Jamie had reported the strange discovery of a body jamming the waterwheel in the brand new sawmill to Mr. Montgomery himself. Both Mr. Montgomery and Jamie agreed that the discovery of a dead body in their new mill would make for a lot of bad publicity and a possible delay to the final phase of construction for the canal. Mr. Montgomery hired several trusted men to quietly clean up the mess. Everyone agreed that it was best if the incident were simply forgotten.

Jamie kept glancing north along the long expanse of St. Paul Street.

"So do you think it will be today?" asked Colin.

"I really don't know," said Jamie. "But we'll keep coming out here to the post office every day at this time to wait until they do show up."

"I'm glad you could join us, Ryan," said Beth.

"I am too," said Ryan, hoisting up his lemonade in salute. "All those foul-tasting liquids the doctor kept pouring down my throat seem to have done the trick."

"Well, take it easy, brother," said Jamie, examining the cloth sling that helped to immobilize Ryan's arm. "Even if the bullet didn't hit anything major, you still lost a lot of blood. You don't want those sutures to pull apart and start the bleeding all over again."

"Hello, there," called out a friendly voice. They looked to the street where a man and a woman waved to them from atop their rolling four-wheeled wagon. It was an older couple. The man sported a wide-brimmed straw hat on top of a head of tight grey curls, his pants held up with a pair of dark blue suspenders. The open face of the wife was lined from constant outdoor work, but her smile was warm and genuine. She shielded herself from the sun with a colourful bonnet and a long, checkered dress. The farmer pulled the old mare to a stop in front of them.

"Are you Aunt Sharon and Uncle Robson?" asked Jamie, standing up.

"Yes, we are," the woman said, warmly. "And you must be Jamie Galway, the young man who wrote us that beautiful letter. Oh … and there is Colin!"

Jamie took Colin's hand and led him to the cart. Beth and Ryan followed close behind. Colin's aunt and uncle climbed down and met them at the sidewalk. She lowered herself onto one knee and wrapped her arms around the little boy as tears flowed down her cheeks.

"Thank you so much, Mr. Galway," she sighed, cuddling the little boy in her arms.

Jamie, choked by the emotion of the moment, could only nod.

"To have Colin here with me means more than I can say. I couldn't believe your letter when I first read it. Erin and her family … all gone."

She gave Colin another kiss on the cheek, then turned to Beth.

"And this must be Beth, the young girl we've heard so much about."

"I heard you've done a great job looking after Colin," added Uncle Rob. "You've travelled all the way from Quebec City with him and kept him safe? That's quite an accomplishment for someone so young."

"I had Jamie helping me," she added, blushing at the compliment.

Jamie chuckled. "It's more likely the other way around. Beth saved my life more than once. She's an amazing young woman. I'm going to miss her lots."

Beth looked at Jamie quizzically. "Miss me? What do you mean?"

"Colin's aunt and uncle have agreed to adopt you as well, Beth."

Beth froze in shock. "What?"

Aunt Sharon walked to Beth and wrapped her up in a loving hug. "Jamie asked if we could use a caring young woman on the farm. Rob and I agreed without hesitation. We would love to have you join us in our home, Beth. My children have all left and we could use the extra help around the house. Plus, I'm sure Colin would love to have an older sister as he grows up."

Beth looked to Jamie, to Aunt Sharon, then back to Jamie. "But … I was going to go back to Ireland with you, Jamie!"

Jamie knelt down and looked her in the eyes. "There will be nothing for you in Ireland, Beth. When I return, I'll be once again taking on my duties as a priest. Your place is here. Colin needs you. Sharon and Rob need you. This is where your parents wanted you to be. Don't get me wrong. I'll miss you and Colin. You're both like family to me now. But this is what your family would have wanted for you. This is where you belong."

Beth sniffed and wiped a tear. "Will I ever see you again?"

Jamie took her hands. "I promise we'll meet again."

Colin's Uncle Rob stepped up. "Beth, it would be an honour to have you join us on our farm and have you become part of our family."

Beth turned to Colin and looked at him in wonder. "I guess I'm going to be your new sister."

"Yes!" shouted Colin. "Beth's my sister!"

Everyone laughed. Soon, Beth and Colin's meagre belongings were safely stowed in the back of the wagon. Colin was sitting on his aunt's lap up on the bench. Beth sat in the back of the wagon, her legs dangling out the back.

"Are you going to be rejoining the Brotherhood?" she asked Jamie as he circled to the back to say goodbye.

Jamie thought for a moment. "I'm not sure."

"Then do you mind if I keep this?"

She held up his ring. It was sitting on her fourth finger.

He eyed her suspiciously. "You took it out of the satchel?"

Beth's freckled cheeks flushed red with embarrassment. "I wasn't going to take it without asking you. If you don't want it any more, I'd love to have it so that I can remember our time together."

He smiled. "How many times did you save my life again?"

"Too many to remember," she teased.

"Then it's yours."

"Really?"

He nodded.

Beth jumped down to give Jamie a final hug. He then lifted her back onto the cart, went around to the front to give Colin a final rustling of his hair, and then stepped back onto the sidewalk beside his brother. Uncle Rob nodded to the boys, then clicked his tongue. The old mare lurched the wagon forward. Ryan and Jamie stood on the steps of the post office as Beth continued to wave until the wagon rolled out of sight.

"So, now what?" asked Ryan.

"Well, you're in need of some rest, and I hear that Niagara Falls is a spectacular site. Let's go explore the Falls, and while we're there, I'll introduce you to some good friends of mine who have just recently moved to the United States of America."

Epilogue

Kilkenny, Ireland, 1887

Jamie Galway waited outside the medieval gates of St. Canice's Cathedral under a glorious blue summer sky. The street was busier than usual. The market across from the cathedral was infused with the aromas of fresh food. Large crowds were taking advantage of the unusually warm day as they shopped among the maze of colourful stalls. Many passing on the sidewalk said good morning to him and Jamie politely returned the salutation. On most Saturdays, he would have joined the crowd in the market to soak in the wonderful sights and smells of harvest time. But today was different. Today was a day he hadn't been sure would ever arrive. Unsure of what to do, he simply watched the happy crowds until a tall, slender woman wearing a fancy brimmed hat and long bustled dress strolled up to him and smiled.

"Excuse me, Cardinal Galway?"

"Yes," said Jamie. "May I help you?"

"I certainly hope so. I was supposed to meet you here in precisely two minutes' time."

Jamie did a double take. Those clear grey eyes suddenly seemed so familiar. He gripped her by the hands as a grin broke across his weathered face.

"Beth, is it really you?"

She laughed. "Yes, underneath all of these wrinkles and greying hair, it's really me."

Cardinal James Galway wrapped his arms around the finely dressed woman, bringing curious stares from passersby. "I'm so happy that you finally made it back to Ireland! How was your trip across the ocean?"

"Much better than the one our families took to Canada." She smiled. "Unlike those old slave ships, today's large steamers are more like floating hotels! You should come and visit Canada sometime and find out for yourself."

"Perhaps I will." Jamie grinned. "I would love to come and visit Canada again."

Beth laughed. "I'll see what I can do about making your next visit more relaxing."

He took her arm in his. "I'm looking forward to hearing all the news, but I'm afraid it will have to wait for a moment. Time is of the essence."

Jamie led Beth around the cathedral's graveyard and into the west wing of the abbey. Inside the massive stone building, Beth was stunned at the elegant beauty of the huge arched ceilings and stained glass windows, but Jamie kept up a quick pace. This was not intended to be a church tour. They went quickly down a short stairway, then out another door, which led into a small stable. A driver waited patiently on the bench of a polished coach. Jamie opened the door for Beth and helped her climb in. He nodded to the driver and as soon as the coach door was closed, the driver shook the reins to the pair of horses. They quickly accelerated down the cobblestone alleyway.

"I apologize for the covered windows," Jamie said as he took his place on the back bench of the darkened coach. Beth sat across from him.

She smiled. "I completely understand all the secrecy. So tell me, how does it feel to be a cardinal with your own cathedral?"

"My new position as cardinal has a great deal of responsibility, but it certainly has its rewards too. Besides doing the Lord's work here in Ireland, I've also been to Rome and the Vatican several times. Rome is such a marvellous city. Perhaps I might get a chance to show you around its ancient streets some day."

She eyed him suspiciously. "You know, Jamie, I could never understand how you became a priest in the first place. You are so handsome and now with your talk of sweeping me off my feet to far away cities … if it weren't for that collar around your neck, I would almost think that you are proposing something far grander than just a lovely vacation with me."

Jamie chuckled. "I'm sorry, but the only ring I can ever offer you is the one that is already on your finger."

She held out her ringed finger and took his hand so that it could be next to his identical ring. "The ring is one of my favourite possessions. Did you get in trouble when you returned without it?"

He shook his head. "No. This is Ryan's ring. Just as yours reminds you of our time together, this ring will always remind me of my brother."

"And how is your brother?"

"Remember, I wrote to you about Ryan leading the three-thousand-strong Irish militia across the Niagara River and into Canada, where they defeated the British Army in the Battle of Ridgeway? Well, during their retreat to Buffalo, New York, he was captured by the U.S. Army. Instead of being charged for his invasion of a neighbouring country, the U.S. Army was quite impressed with his tactical skills and instead promoted him to a U.S. colonel! He's currently based in Fort Jackson, South Carolina."

Beth leaned forward in shock. "Ryan leads an Irish invasion into Canada from U.S. soil and, instead of throwing him in jail, the government made him a colonel?"

Jamie shrugged. "It seems the Americans were still angry at the British for supporting the South during the Civil War. They simply look the other way on Irish rebel activities to teach Britain a lesson."

"And what of Ryan's Irish militia?"

"Well, the movement is still alive and well, but they are now fighting a direct war with British troops here in Ireland. Many Irish Americans are sympathetic to the rebels and support them with large amounts of money and weapons."

"I'm not surprised about the lingering anger in the United States. Do you think the rebels will help make Ireland a free nation?" asked Beth.

"I don't agree with their tactics. Killing and violence will only perpetuate hate in the younger generations. But there are others here in Ireland, such as our politician Daniel O'Connell, who are fighting for our cause within the halls of the British Parliament. I think there is hope that someday we'll have a political solution and finally see a free Ireland.

"So tell me, what has happened since you last wrote?"

Beth removed her hat and placed it on the seat beside her. "Well, let me see. Colin is now a Member of Parliament for Simcoe County and is doing quite well in the world of politics. He has a beautiful wife and two young daughters. He and his family send their love to you."

"Colin, a politician.... I would never have guessed. I'm so glad that he's happy."

"And all three of my beautiful children have now left home. Francis and Jamie are now working in Toronto, and my youngest, Johanna, married a lawyer, and she is now living in New York City."

"Ah, New York City," Jamie said wistfully. "I remember all too well Shane rowing me across the Niagara River and then the journey along the Erie Canal to New York City for the journey home. But how are you doing? It must be difficult for you, being on your own now."

Beth nodded, taking a deep breath. "It's been a year since my Richard passed away. It became simply too quiet for me in our large Dundas home. I sold the house and his lumber business last month. Then I told my family that I was going to take some of the money from the sale to visit an old friend in Ireland."

He took her hand. "I am so sorry about your loss. Richard sounded like a good man."

"He was, Jamie. Thank you."

There was a moment of reflection before Beth changed the subject. "I still can't believe that the Brotherhood has allowed me to join you here on this journey."

"I'm not surprised," he laughed. "It's their way of thanking you for your heroics in Canada."

Beth smiled. "I've dreamt about this moment my entire life. Does this mean that the treasure will soon be revealed to the world?"

Jamie shook his head. "It's the same situation as it's always been. When our entire island is under self-rule, the Brotherhood will reveal the treasure."

"So the world still has to wait."

"At least we still have a map to the treasure. You saved my life more than once, and in doing so, you saved the treasure."

"You know I saved you only for the sake of the treasure," she teased.

Jamie laughed. Beth was like a breath of fresh air into his usual stodgy existence as a cardinal. "I'm so glad you came to visit."

The coach suddenly came to a jarring stop.

"Do you trust me?" he asked.

"Do I trust you?" she repeated. "Of course, I trust you! I've only ridden in a window-covered coach alone with you for just over an hour. Why do you ask?"

"Because of this."

He pulled a silk scarf from his pocket and covered her eyes. "I'm sorry about the blindfold. It's for everyone's protection."

"It's all right," she said. "I completely understand. Just don't you get any un-cardinal-like ideas while I'm blindfolded, young man."

Jamie laughed. "I know this will be difficult for you, but there's to be no more talking until I take the blindfold off."

Beth laughed. "No promises!"

He took her hand. Beth couldn't see a thing. Upon leaving the carriage, she could hear forest noises and the wind whistling through the trees. She could smell decaying wood and the slight nose-tickling smell of wood smoke. They walked for almost ten minutes before he brought her to a stop. The sound of brushing followed by the scraping noise of a stone made her think that some sort of passageway was being revealed. She then felt his hand take hers once again as he led her down a flight of steep stairs. She could hear a match being struck and then another. Suddenly, there were fingers behind her head, lightly touching her hair. The blindfold loosened and fell to her shoulders. She gasped at the underground vault sparkling with gold, jewels, and exquisite works of religious art. And the books! Hundreds upon hundreds of books were lined up along shelves that extended well into the distant gloom of the underground vault. Her eyes were immediately drawn to the ancient text they had rescued from the fires in Montreal. It stood prominently on a ruby-encrusted stand made of pure gold. She had never seen any collection like it before. She reached out and touched a bell that rested on a stack of books next to the entranceway.

"So what do you think?" he asked.

"Jamie!" she breathed. "It's incredible!"

"It's not very often you get a chance to explore your nation's soul." He took her arm in his and, with his free hand, lifted up a burning oil lamp. "Come on, let me show you around."

Author's Notes

The characters in *The Emerald Key* experience many real moments in Canadian history. The Grosse Isle (or Grosse Île as it is seen today on most Canadian maps) quarantine station did, in fact, exist, and it was located just north of Quebec City in the St. Lawrence River. As in the story, the huge influx of sick and dying Irish trying to escape the devastating famine of their homeland disembarked at Grosse Isle and often overwhelmed the doctors and nurses at the station. Grosse Isle is now a National Historic Site and can be visited by ferry in the summer months. A large east-facing Irish cross has been raised on the island to commemorate the thousands of Irish graves on Grosse Isle.

On April 25, 1849, the parliament building of Canada was nearly burned to the ground by rioters protesting the compensation of those who participated in the rebellions against British rule in 1837 and 1838. The rioters refused to let firefighters battle the blaze and as a result, the building, which included the parliament's two libraries, was completely devastated. Out of the 23,000 volumes of irreplaceable books stored in the libraries, only two hundred were saved from the flames by the brave action of James Curran. The exact location of the parliament building was unknown until 2011, when new construction in downtown Montreal happened to come across its original foundation.

Construction on the Welland Canal first started November 20, 1824, and the first version of the canal opened five years later, in 1829. It soon became evident that the canal needed widening and the building of the second canal, the one mentioned in this story, was completed in 1848. Two more improved versions of the canal were built in following years, including the one still being used today, which was opened in 1932. The Welland Canal continues to be an important link in the St. Lawrence Seaway.

There is plenty of recorded evidence illustrating how poorly the Irish were treated in Toronto, the largest town in Canada West at the time. The recently arrived Irish were described by local media as lazy, ignorant, bellicose, and unthankful paupers. Many of the new immigrants were simply sick, and in one year alone, 1,100 Irish were buried in Toronto graves, a huge number for the time. The surviving sick were rounded up and kept in guarded fever sheds and overwhelmed hospitals. Local politicians, spurred on by an angry public, gathered petitions for higher levels of government that stated Canada West was not to be considered by the British to be Ireland's graveyard.

Although the famine years were devastating to the Irish Canadian population, it is said that those years also helped bond the survivors into a close-knit, supportive community. Since then, many Irish cultural values and traditions have flourished not only within those of Irish ancestry but also among Canadians in general. On the other hand, the anger felt by the Irish toward the British occupation of their homeland manifested itself in many ways. Some Irish

Canadians and Irish Americans supported the formation of militant forces dedicated to freeing Ireland, a cause that first found its roots in the 1860s during the Fenian Raids into Canada, including the Battle of Ridgeway. Other concerned Irish approached the issue of Irish independence through more peaceful and political means.

For three hundred years, from circa 400 to 700 A.D., Ireland was the shining beacon of education in Europe. With the fall of the Roman Empire came the fall of the Roman educational system. Reading, writing, and math became lost arts and the Dark Ages in Europe began. The only large bastion of education still remaining in all of Europe was in Ireland. Early Christian monks first brought higher education to Ireland in the fourth century, but the island nation itself was never under Roman rule. When Rome fell, Ireland's educational systems remained intact while the rest of Europe regressed into the dark depths of illiteracy. Kings and wealthy noblemen heard of Ireland's universities and soon sent their sons to Ireland in order to learn. The Irish, in turn, became very wealthy themselves as they used their higher knowledge to craft the finest books, art, and jewellery in all of Europe.

The little island flourished, but their growing wealth did not go unnoticed. To the north, tales of riches on a far western island reached the most feared raiders of the time, the Vikings. Starting in the late eighth century, waves of Viking raids washed over the once thriving communities of Ireland. Villages were ransacked. Irish families were slaughtered or captured and enslaved. Universities were plundered and buildings were burned.

Fortunately for the rest of Europe, Irish education had been exported continuously for two centuries, and the educational monasteries founded by Irish monks in both Scotland and mainland Europe were able to continue their teachings.

Although Ireland's golden age came to an end with the Viking raids, those ancient Irish can be proud that their work helped bring the rest of Europe out of the Dark Ages and into the Renaissance.

Acknowledgements

I would first and foremost like to thank my amazing wife and front line editor Amanda for her unending patience when I frequently tucked myself away to write during the summer holidays.

To my wonderful daughters, Sarah, Johanna, and Stephanie for their constant encouragement and their willingness to slog through my rough drafts in order to give me early feedback on the developing storyline. It was much appreciated!

To Sylvia McConnell and Allister Thompson of Dundurn Press who believed in *The Emerald Key*. I would not be a published author if it were not for their encouragement. A huge thanks to you both and the rest of the Dundurn team.

There were many excellent sources of historical information while I wrote *The Emerald Key*. The Newmarket and Aurora Public Libraries in York Region are always my starting points for researching a new novel. The McCord and Pointe-à-Callière Museums in Montreal, the Huron-Wendat Museum, Parks Canada, the National Library of Ireland, and the St. Lawrence Seaway Corporation also provided crucial information so that the story could remain as historically accurate as possible.

To the students, staff, and schools of the York Region District School Board, the Elementary Teachers Federation of Ontario, and the Ontario Library

Association, who were a constant, encouraging presence while I was writing. After each book, I always feel as if it might be my last, but their enthusiasm for my stories is a great reason to persevere.

I would especially like to thank my mom, whose unwavering love and support has been crucial in allowing me to pursue my goal of becoming a published writer.

More Adventure from Christopher Dinsdale

Stolen Away
978-1894917209
$10.95

Keira, kidnapped from Ireland by Vikings, is a slave living in legendary Vinland. Two Native bands, the Beothuck and the Thule, are also fighting over the land, thrusting the Norsemen into war. While the Vikings search for a new home, an accident at sea leaves Keira miraculously saved by a Beothuck warrior. Keira settles into the Beothuck way of life, learning their customs and coming to care for them. But she dreams of risking everything in order to find a way home. Ultimately, she is torn between the cultures in which she has lived — her homeland, the Viking world in which she was welcomed, and her new Beothuck family. This is a thrilling adventure and an exciting introduction to the history of Canada.

Shortlisted for the Red Maple Award

Betrayed: The Legend of Oak Island
978-1894917919
$10.95

Connor MacDonald and his mother have encountered Henry Sinclair, Norwegian prince and Earl of Orkney, who rescues them from highwaymen. Prince Henry is an adventurer who has sailed to the farthest reaches of the known world. On a dark Egyptian beach, he was given a treasure so precious that kings would sacrifice everything in order to acquire it. But unlike the warmongering monarchs of Europe, Prince Henry intends it to become an everlasting beacon of peace and devises a plan so bold that only the exiled Order of the Knights Templar could even dare conceive of it. Events soon lead Connor, now a squire, his friend Angus, and Prince Henry to the shores of Vinland and to Oak Island. The fate of the Templar Knights rests in the hands of two Scottish teenagers and their Mi'kmaq friend, Na'gu'set, as they desperately try to identify the dark forces that threaten not only to destroy them but the entire Templar Order.

Available at your favourite bookseller.